DANGER IN THE DA

Even in the pitch dark, Daphne had no doubt who was in her bedroom. *Him.* And she said as much.

His response was as angry as hers. "Miss Templeton, you are the most irritating female I have ever met. How the deuce can you know who I am?"

"Who else would be mad enough to crawl in my window in the middle of the night?" Daphne said. "I have half a mind to scream."

"We should be thoroughly compromised if you utter one tiny moan. Scream, and let us see who regrets it," he replied.

Fury washed over her. She wanted to beat her fists against his arrogant chest, kick his shins, scratch his eyes out. But the thought of reaching up to accomplish such a thing stirred far different emotions in her . . . as she realized that the real danger came not from him but from her own wildly beating heart. . . .

PATRICIA RICE was born in Newburgh, New York, and attended the University of Kentucky. She now lives in Mayfield, Kentucky, with her husband and her two children, Corinna and Derek, in a rambling Tudor house. Ms. Rice has a degree in accounting and her hobbies include history, travel, and antique collecting.

MAD
MARIA'S
DAUGHTER

Patricia Rice

A SIGNET BOOK

SIGNET
Published by the Penguin Group
Penguin Books USA Inc., 375 Hudson Street,
New York, New York, 10014, U.S.A.
Penguin Books Ltd, 27 Wrights Lane, London W8 5TZ, England
Penguin Books Australia Ltd, Ringwood, Victoria, Australia
Penguin Books Canada Ltd, 10 Alcorn Avenue, Toronto, Ontario, Canada M4V 3B2
Penguin Books (N.Z.) Ltd, 182-190 Wairau Road,
Auckland 10, New Zealand

Penguin Books Ltd, Registered Offices:
Harmondsworth, Middlesex, England

First published by Signet, an imprint of New American Library,
a division of Penguin Books USA Inc.

First Printing, April, 1992

10 9 8 7 6 5 4 3 2 1

ONE

"You want to what?" Daphne's voice broke on a high note with the last word as she stared incredulously at the gentleman holding her hand. Only her awareness of the crowd behind him kept her nervous question from reaching a shriek.

"Marry you." Albert's cheeks reddened behind his military whiskers, but then, his normally ruddy color prevented anyone but a close observer from noticing.

"Marry me?" She sounded like a shrieking parrot despite herself, and heads turned in the ballroom behind them. This alcove certainly did not lend itself to an intimate setting.

Daphne read the uneasiness in his eyes easily as they shifted from her face to the velvet draperies and then to the floor. He was thanking his stars he'd had the sense to propose in a crowded room, and at that thought, Daphne took a deep breath and tried to control her soaring temper. She wouldn't let her temper fly. She wouldn't.

"Don't be absurd," she answered sharply, lowering her voice an octave.

His ruddy cheeks grew redder, but a stubborn line marred his mouth. "Absurd? What other offer have you?"

Control. One. Two. Three. Daphne squeezed her eyes shut to eliminate the staring crowd. Why did they always stare? She wasn't her mother. She wasn't. She chanted the familiar refrain to cool her ire. She was perfectly normal, and this absurd little man wouldn't prove her wrong.

"We don't even know each other," she offered reasonably, although her legs felt as if they were shaking beneath her. She needed to sit down. It had been four years, but sometimes . . . She shut out that thought along with the crowd.

"We've known each other forever," he remonstrated.

"We've danced one dance at each occasion we've met since you came home from the Continent." She couldn't believe this was happening. Just as she had made up her mind to leave London and set herself on the shelf, this abysmal little man had to come along and shake her newly won confidence. Why did he have to do this to her?

He stared at her as she stood there with her eyes closed, her hands clenched in fists at her side, and he glanced cautiously to the people behind him. They were staring. He coughed slightly to gather his courage and tried again. "Surely that is sufficient to judge we suit?"

Daphne heard the meaning behind the words. That was "sufficient" to know she wouldn't have hysterics in public as her mother had been apt to do. That was sufficient to know she wouldn't cause any public scene as had been rumored she might. He'd been in Spain when she first came to London. He hadn't seen her stumble awkwardly across the dance floor, or fall attempting to enter a carriage. Most of all, he hadn't seen one of her uncontrollable rages when these things happened. But he'd heard, as he had heard about her mother. Instability ran in the family, it was whispered. One had only to remember her grandmother Pierce, who proclaimed pigs were superior to men in every way. And there was her Aunt Agatha, who lived the life of a recluse in the backwaters of Devon. And of course, there was always her mother, her dashing, lovely, charming, and very dead mother.

No. It wouldn't do. She had been right to decide to leave London, where her mother had left such an indelible impression upon society. Daphne had tried to eradicate that impression, but she had her own flaws to cope with; she couldn't hope to cover her mother's as well. The memories of her mother's dramatic departure from this world and its effect on her daughter's life hadn't faded from the petty minds of society, would never fade as long as Daphne was available to remember them. She had been young and foolish when she had come to town. She no longer had that excuse. They would never forget, and they would never let her forget.

Daphne opened her eyes and commanded her suitor's

attention. He shifted nervously from foot to foot. "No. I will not marry you," she stated calmly but without the requisite murmurs of honor and flattery. His proposal had just barely been honorable and certainly not flattering.

Albert looked vaguely startled. "Of course you will. What other choice have you?" he repeated.

It was really quite the last straw. She had forgotten that the hand he didn't hold was also occupied. Until now. Lifting the crystal cup of punch, Daphne poured it gently and carefully over his elegantly combed gray hairs. Sweetly, she replied, "This," then handed him the empty cup and strode off.

Clutching her reticule in her lap, Daphne stared out at the growing darkness beyond the carriage window. It had been kind of Lord and Lady Lansbury to loan the use of their carraige to take her to her aunt's. But then, everyone had been so kind and sympathetic—once she had announced she was leaving. And relieved. She shouldn't forget how relieved they were at her departure.

Daphne bit her lip and tried to retrieve her straying thoughts from the debacle that had capped her stay in London. She was almost at Aunt Agatha's. There seemed no purpose in stopping for the night despite the driver's protests. He could travel on to the Lansbury estate in the morning. The carriage had to come this way anyway. The Lansburys had merely been offering a minor kindness, after all.

Clutching her gloved fingers in the lap of her wool traveling gown, Daphne wrestled with the twin devils of ingratitude and cynicism. She could have taken a post chaise like anyone else. She was not helpless. She was not even incompetent. She was actually quite intelligent. Not that anyone cared. Biting her lip, she watched the road to her voluntary exile go by.

In a society that demanded perfection, she lacked the essential requirement, though she was not to blame. She supposed she looked well enough. Friends and family had assured her that her brunette curls were just as they ought to be, that her features were quite well-formed, even to the point of prettiness and past. They even claimed that her eyes were a most extraordinary green, and if they seemed a trifle hazy and mysterious at times, that was more to her account than not. The fact that they were her mother's eyes created the problem. Part of the problem, she had to admit. The rest of the problem she created herself.

Biting her lip and clenching her fingers, Daphne fought back the tears and forced her chin up. She had been green enough at first not to realize why the young gentlemen passed her by for flighty, less presentable girls. Oh, there was always someone's kind relative to bow politely and ask if they might fetch her some punch or to exchange meaningless gossip through a dance set or two. She was never left to feel alone and neglected, but she was seldom asked for more than one dance, either. Once was daring enough. Twice would have been foolish. After all, what if she took leave of her senses in the middle of the dance floor? Not that her mother had ever committed such a social solecism. She had been very polite about her madness. If her effervescence sometimes reached the heights of hysteria, or her dismals became black whorls of discontent, no one paid them any mind. That was just Maria. Charming, ever-maddening Maria. Even her suicide had been committed with exquisite care to make it look an accident. It was only by pure, horrible chance that she had been discovered.

Daphne closed her eyes against that long-ago pain. She could remember her mother as sweet and smiling and ever gentle. Why could society not remember her that way, instead of as the lady who had suddenly driven her carriage off a cliff one dark night, in full view of her only daughter? The period of mourning for her mother had long passed, but the *ton* continued to look at Daphne askance, waiting for her to show signs of her mother's instabilities, finding them all too frequently in the sharp lash of Daphne's temper, her cool withdrawal when anyone approached the subject dominating their minds, and in her inability to be one of the crowd. They would nod their heads sagely and give each other knowing glances, then treat her to saccharine smiles and insipid pleasantries until they could make their escape. After all, who wouldn't be unstable after such an experience?

At times, Daphne felt as if the *ton* resented being reminded by her presence that the world outside their hallowed halls was not a perfect one. Perhaps if they knew how imperfect she was, they would turn their backs on her completely. As it was, Daphne had persisted, refusing to believe all of society could be so shallow and thoughtless as to disregard her because of her mother's tragedy. Besides, she had no where else to go, naught else to do unless she wished to play the part of sheltered invalid in her father's house. And then she truly would go mad. For four long years she had determinedly beat her head against society's thick walls. Now, she had given up. She would not go back.

Gazing blankly out the uncovered carriage window, Daphne tried not to imagine what her future would bring. Like any other young girl, she had set out in society with the dream of finding a young man who would understand and care, someone she could share her thoughts and her life with. She certainly hadn't set any higher goals than that. Considering her imperfection, it mattered little to her if the man of her dreams were handsome. She had a secure competence from her mother's estate, not a wealthy one, but sufficient for a comfortable life, so she didn't require great wealth. She didn't even need a title. Her father was only the younger son of a relatively obscure north country title. Titles meant nothing. But she had expected to be found pleasing by someone, somewhere. It was not as if she were a complete antidote, after all.

But, as it turned out, apparently she was. After four years on the Marriage Mart, despite the kindness of all her relations, she had received only that one proposal of marriage, and it had been an insult. She had scarcely known the man. Albert wasn't the sort her very protective relations would normally allow near. Bankrupt and twice her age, his offer had been made out of desperation. If that was the best she could do, she was better off remaining unmarried. Society could pity her little more for her unmarried state than it already did for her mother's death.

Her maid snored slightly, jolting Daphne back to the present. Aunt Agatha's house couldn't be far. They had just come through the village a little while ago. It had been a long time since she had come through here. She had forgotten how steep this road was as it wound down to the riverbank. Or perhaps she had never known. She had probably been just as soundly asleep as her maid the summer she traveled here with her father.

The world outside seemed darker. Daphne looked up, trying to tell if clouds were covering the moon that had just risen. From the varying shades of darkness, she surmised the bank down to the river was overgrown with trees. The road appeared to travel along the river a little way before the bridge, and there must be trees all around. She would have to ride here one day and investigate. It ought to be a lovely place on a sunny day.

If Aunt Agatha would allow her to ride. Throwing herself back against the seat in disappointment, Daphne had to consider that possibility. With her brother's reluctant assistance, she had escaped her father's home because he had insisted on watching her every minute, forbidding her the stables, insisting that she be accompanied every time she ventured out of the house, all but ordering her to remain inside for fear she would be lost to him as her mother had been. She had been unable to tolerate the restrictions. If he had written Aunt Agatha with those same orders, would she obey?

Her mother's relations in London had been more understanding, but that had been London. She had been accompanied everywhere by her cousins and footmen and maids. The size and sounds and smells of the city had intimidated her and she had accepted the fact that a lady could not travel alone, so she had not protested the limitations there. But the country was different. She used to love solitary walks with nature, and she had learned to ride as soon as she could walk. She did not wish to abandon those pleasures altogether to please her grief-stricken, anxious father.

For all that mattered, Daphne thought petulantly, she didn't see why she couldn't learn to navigate the streets of London just as well as a garden path, if only people would leave her alone. There had been so many exciting things around her, places she would have liked to linger, people she would like to know, but she was limited to those her family chose to visit. Now that she was older and more sure of herself, she resented their interference. She was not likely to go berserk or collapse in the middle of a busy street in broad daylight.

But she would never have the opportunity to explore London now. If she and Aunt Agatha rubbed along well, she would in all likelihood spend the rest of her life in splendid isolation in the rugged wilds of Devon. Relatively speaking, of course. She had heard of the mountains in Scotland and Wales, and learned of the magnificent scenery of Europe and America from her tutors, but unaccompanied, she wasn't destined to see them. So she really ought to make the most of this rough bit of coast and moor. She and Aunt Agatha would just have to come to an understanding.

A shout outside the carriage shocked Daphne from her reverie. What on earth was the driver doing? She grabbed the strap as the carriage swayed and pitched forward wildly. The horses' neighing protests as the carriage rocked to an abrupt halt drove a sharp spike of fear through her. Had the bridge gone out? Had a wheel broken? What was wrong?

The instant the carriage came to a full halt, Daphne shoved open the door. Behind her, her awakened maid wailed a protest, but she wasn't going to calmly sit here and wait for someone to inform her that they were about to fall off a precipice or something. Memory sent a *frisson* of fear through her, but she refused to retreat in the face of her cowardice. The shouts outside sounded like several men. Had there been an accident?

A dark shadow veered close to the Lansburys' elegant landau. Daphne recognized the sound of horse's hooves and before she knew it, the shadow of a horseman loomed before her. Cast in darkness outside the carriage lamps, he presented an otherworldly appearance. The specter made a gentlemanly bow and doffed his hat.

"What is happening? Has there been a mishap?"

The interior lamps she had insisted on lighting when it grew dark illuminated the warm ivory of a delicate face etched in worry. The horseman smiled against the darkness. "I have only come to relieve you of a few baubles, my lady, and any coins you might have in your reticule. Consider it a contribution to charity, if you will, and you will soon be on your way."

Thieves! That was impossible in this day and age. High-waymen had been long banished to . . . The wilds away from London where there was little or no law, Daphne finished the thought belatedly. Still, she could not just give up her entire quarter's income at his request. She leaned out to pull the door shut again.

At that moment, a shot rang out farther down the road, and a scream of warning vibrated through the cool night air. From a distance, someone shouted, "Soldiers!" and closer to hand, the mounted highwayman muttered, "Damnation, a trap!" Before Daphne could jerk back out of reach, he leaned over, hooked his arm around her waist, and hauled her over his knees.

She screamed a terrified protest. Her maid wailed in a soprano crescendo that pierced the ears. The highwayman merely kicked his horse and sprinted off into the darkness, one hand holding his prisoner safely in place.

"Cease the caterwauling and you'll be safe," he ordered as the horse leapt a small hedge and dashed through a clearing between the trees. "Continue, and you'll live to regret it. I mean only to keep you hostage until the soldiers are gone."

Daphne was silent, more from lack of breath than obedience. The horse's rough gait jarred knees against ribs, and to her utter humiliation, she found herself clinging to a very masculine leg from a very intimate position. Still, she felt as if she would slide off at any moment.

She strained to detect any sound of pursuit, but her blood was throbbing in her ears and panic clouded her senses. Never in all her years had she been subjected to this kind of ill treatment, and to think, she had thought he sounded a gentleman!

They splashed across a river, soaking her woolen traveling gown at the hem and spraying water up the back of her heaving pelisse. She shivered as the icy water soaked through, and the horseman adjusted her more comfortably.

"Not far now. You'll be fine."

Daphne scarcely considered his promise reassuring. What did the highwayman consider to be fine? She was already soaked, cold, and humiliated to the marrow of her bones. She couldn't wait until she had breath to release the outrage choking in her throat.

The smell of his boot leather filled her nostrils, and she became gradually aware of other scents besides that of damp vegetation. The faint scent of bay rum mingling with masculine perspiration confused her. Did highwaymen wear bay rum? It was an odor that choked the ballrooms of London, but out here in the desolate countryside it had an almost pleasant scent. Perhaps it just reminded her of civilization.

The horse reared abruptly, and the thief chuckled as Daphne's fingers dug into his leg and creased his trousers. A hard arm lifted her with casual ease and slid her to the ground as a shrill whistle in the distance cut the air in a vague resemblance to a bugle's all-clear. He released her in obvious response to the signal. "My men should be safely away by now. You'll find a short walk down this path will lead you to a cottage where a very kindly widow and her servants live. If you'll hand over your trinkets, I shall leave you alone."

Now that her feet were back on solid ground and the breath was returning to her lungs, Daphne stared up at the immensity of the man and beast and the old, familiar anger struck again. She had promised to learn to control her temper, and she had honestly tried, but this was more than any one person should have to bear. Anger was better than fear, in any case, and she unleashed it without thought upon this masked stranger.

"You can't do this! This is an outrage! How dare you desert me like this! You must take me back to my maid and carriage at once. You cannot leave me out here miles from civilization. What kind of gentleman do you purport to be to thus treat a lady?"

The highwayman leaned over slightly in the saddle to study

the angry face beneath the disheveled bonnet. He had been quite prepared for her to faint and weep and plead for mercy. This mixture of rage and haughtiness from one so delicate caught him by surprise, but the fury underlying her words held something else. If she were afraid of him, wouldn't she use her anger to run? What kind of woman would demand that a thief linger to return her to her maid?

"The carriage is further than the cottage, miss. Did you enjoy our ride so that you wish to repeat it?"

The taunting mockery of his words drew blood into her cheeks, and Daphne had to clench her fingers to restore the proper decorum she had almost lost. "I am not familiar with these woods, sir. I could be lost for days. If you will not return me to the carriage, you must take me to the cottage." She said it as firmly as she could manage through chattering teeth. The icy river water was responsible for only a small part of the chill, she feared.

Beginning to lose his patience, the highwayman leaned over to wrap his fingers around the gold locket at her throat. "Are you so rich you have forgotten how to walk? Then you won't mind if I relieve you of this feeble trinket. I daresay Lansbury was too smart to bait a trap with real jewels."

Daphne smacked at his gloved hand and stepped backward. Her foot slipped on the damp moss and her weak leg betrayed her. The aching cold of the river water had done its damage, and she would have fallen had he not dropped to the ground and grabbed her. She righted herself hastily and attempted to elude his grasp, but the thief's fingers kept their grip on her shoulder.

"I don't know what you're talking about. Let me go." Daphne tried to disguise her fear. Now that he stood before her, she knew her abductor to be very tall, and the broad shadow of his shoulders conveyed his strength, even if his grip had not already warned her. Gentlemen were supposed to be languid and incapable of such violent swiftness of action. He could not be the gentleman her other senses said he must be. Yet she could not run from him if he showed himself to be scoundrel.

Her air of fear and defiance puzzled him, and instincts ever alert, the thief pursued his curiosity further. If she truly were Lansbury's bait, then perhaps she did not know what he was talking about, but surely even Lansbury wouldn't send a lady out to trap a highwayman without warning her! That meant she had to be some common trollop off the streets eager to earn a few coins in any way she could. That thought lasted no longer than it took to breathe in the scent of his captive's expensive French bath salts and to hear the aristocratic accents of authority in her bell-like voice. The quality of the fine woven wool beneath his fingers and the delicacy of the bones beneath his grip put the lie to commonness. She had to know of the trap. His fingers tightened.

"Lady, I'm willing to be fair with you. Lansbury won't miss these few baubles, and I'm certain he didn't intend for you to risk yourself in this attempt. We weren't pursued, so you cannot hope to be rescued at any moment. Had you paid any attention at all, you would have noticed the soldiers were on foot. They don't send cavalry after thieves."

"I know we're not being pursued or I would have told you to be on your way." Retreating behind the mask of dignity she donned when she betrayed her weakness, Daphne took the offensive. She dusted down her gown and pelisse and took another step away from his overpowering presence. "I cannot imagine why a gentleman should resort to terrifying ladies, or what Lord Lansbury has to do with any of this since he is exceedingly occupied in the government right now and not inclined to worry about wayward gentlemen . . ." She stopped, trying to remember where this thought was supposed to lead. She was chattering like a nervous magpie, but this man's presence had unnerved her as no other had. She gathered her scattered wits and tried again. "I have no wish to do anything but reach Aunt Agatha's safely, and I cannot do so if you desert me in the middle of the woods. And you can't have the locket. It belonged to my mother and is worthless to anyone but me. I have a few coins in my pocket, you may have those. And this silly ring that Cousin Sally insisted I must wear." She pulled off the despised object and joined it with the coins she carried so that her footman and driver could enjoy the occasional draft of ale, thankful that the reticule with her allowance was still in the carriage. "Now, take me to the cottage, please, and you may be on your way."

This was most extraordinary. He generally didn't stop unaccompanied young ladies, but her pensive face in the window had lit a wicked bit of mischief in him. He hadn't meant to do more than relieve her of a few coins and compliment her beauty. Lansbury was wealthy enough that he could afford to replace a few stolen coins. But in the few months since he had taken up this life of crime, he had never met so self-possessed a victim, even if she were as barmy as a Bedlamite. He almost felt inclined to obey her commands. Almost.

He pocketed the trinkets and reached for his horse. "The cottage is straight ahead. You cannot miss it. Good night."

Fury overcame dignity at this certain desertion. She had been scarcely left alone for a moment these last five years, and certainly never in a strange place. Her knee throbbed with pain and threatened to give out under her. Refusing to admit to anything so telling as terror, Daphne stamped her foot and grabbed the thief's coat sleeve. "I'll not be left alone like this, without even a lantern to light my way. I will not, do you hear? Show me to this cottage if it is so close by."

Astonished at her behavior, the highwayman took his boot from the stirrup and turned to stare at her. No one had ever spoken to him in such a manner. Obviously, she was badly spoiled. Or was she? Did he detect a trace of something else behind the fury of her soft voice? She did not strike him as the shrewish type. The memory of her lovely face in the window worried at him. He caught her chin in his fingers and raised her face to study it.

"And if I don't?"

She had been leading a sheltered life much too long. She had faced down other fears; it was time to conquer still one more. Closing her eyes to control her temper, Daphne summoned her flagging courage to reply with the arrogant flippancy of her cousins. "Were I still in London, I would have my groom flog you. Since I must now adapt myself to country ways, I suppose I shall have to hunt you down myself and shoot you.''

A hint of amusement laced his voice. ''You are quite mad, you know.''

Daphne heard none of the amusement or admiration in his voice. She heard only the word "mad" and her temper soared beyond the boundaries of reason again. Ignoring her aching knee, she swung from the thief's grip and struck off blindly in the direction he had indicated earlier.

No one had ever spoken to her as had this wretched thief, confronting her with her worst fears. They had whispered about her mother and voiced their suspicions behind her back, but never had she been forced to face their accusations directly. ''Look at the eyes,'' they'd say. ''Just like her mother's.'' That epithet was the one that terrified her the most. Perhaps she was mad. Perhaps her mother's madness had started this way, with fears she could not control. Daphne tried not to think it, but the stranger's words cut through all pretense. She would rather risk falling on her face than plead with him again.

Watching her limp as she proudly walked away, the thief cursed. He was as mad as she, but he could not leave a lady in distress. Stepping forward, he caught her hand and placed it on his arm. ''I am sorry. I had not realized I injured you in my haste.''

Daphne grasped this support with a shudder of relief. The pain had been sufficient to cool her temper. In a little while, it would go away, but she was too terrified of disgracing herself by falling to turn away a helping hand. At the concern in his voice, she answered honestly, '' 'Twas not your fault but the water's. And the cold. Just call it an old war wound, if you will.''

At the pain in his victim's voice, the highwayman let her comment go by unquestioned. Old war wound? His gaze surveyed her slender figure consideringly, wondering what to make of that. ''You are come to stay in these parts?'' he questioned randomly, leading her a little farther down the path, watching carefully as she fell into step beside him.

"With my aunt, Lady Agatha Templeton. I can only be thankful she will not worry when I do not arrive tonight. She does not expect me until tomorrow."

It was very probable that the carriage had gone on to Lady Agatha's by now, and the entire household would be in an uproar, but he did not tell her of that. He was beginning to feel very ashamed of himself for frightening a mere woman and a harmless old lady for the sake of a coin and a pretty face. A hell of a highwayman he made.

"I will take you to the widow's light. I dare not go too close to the cottage, for the widow's sake as well as my own. If the soldiers are still about, they may think her an accomplice."

Daphne grasped the warmth of his arm haughtily. "It is absurd to thank you after the harm you have done, but I do know you could have left me. I am something of a coward when left alone." That was an understatement, but she didn't enlarge upon it. "I will thank you for this small kindness."

He could have done a great deal more than leave her there, but such topics did not come easily to a lady's mind, and he certainly wasn't one to introduce them. It had been a few months since he had escorted a delicate female about, and he was rather enjoying the moment. She smelled delightful, although anything clean would smell delightful after months of living with unbathed villains. Now that she had his arm, she moved gracefully and with some assurance at his side. He could not discover any sign of limp or injury now. Actually, he could almost believe he was calmly walking down Bond Street with a beautiful companion for all she showed any fear of the situation now that he had accepted her company.

"Shouldn't you be afraid of me?" he asked out of curiosity.

She tilted her head to look up at him. "Utterly terrified," she assured him.

"You're roasting me."

His reply was so decisive and so much the gallant chatter of London that Daphne smiled. "My word, sir, how you do go on. Do you doubt my sincerity?"

He chuckled at the mimicry. She sounded just like one of the lovely Toasts of the Season he had briefly flirted with many years ago. Things hadn't changed in London then.

"I shall try not to in the future. I fear I would lose any battle of wits with you. Can you see the light now?"

The welcoming gleam glittered not too far off. Daphne gave a sigh of relief and released his arm. Any light at all was welcome in this darkness. She preferred company against the night terrors, but even she wasn't mad enough to believe this man was safer than the light ahead. Still, the light was a long way off. "There are no surprises between here and there?"

"Just lawn. I wish I dared lead you closer. . . ."

Daphne waved a hand in dismissal. "I shall be fine. This is all very adventurous. I think I shall enjoy the country more than I suspected." She offered her best imitation of courage. "Shall we say good night, then?"

It was utterly preposterous, but he bent over her hand as if he had just escorted her to her townhouse and delivered her safely into the hands of her servants. He felt a light squeeze, then she stepped out onto the lawn, tentatively testing the uneven expanse of ground before proceeding haltingly toward the cottage.

The highwayman stepped back into the shadows, wishing he could at least have had her name.

TWO

"I regret that you had to meet with such an inhospitable welcome to our neighborhood, Miss Templeton." The tall gentleman settled into the seat across from Daphne as her aunt handed him a cup of tea.

He smelled of fresh air and faintly of horses, not of bay rum, yet his voice . . . Daphne held back her frown as she accepted the cup given her. "Actually, it was the most adventurous night of my life, though I know I shouldn't say that." She was twenty-three years old and about to embark on an independent life of her own. People would have to begin accepting her as she was, she vowed. No more would she keep her tongue still for fear every word would be held against her. The man across from her was in all likelihood considered very eligible, he spoke with that kind of confidence, but she had no intention of trying to impress him.

"Adventurous? Surely not. Your poor aunt can only be relieved that you came to no harm in such an adventure. It was a reckless, heedless thing to do, and I am quite grateful no more came of it than this. Until now, the man and his band of thieves have harmed no one, but if he continues, I fear we will find the village and its environs overrun with soldiers."

Daphne sipped her tea and tried to puzzle her way through the variety of clues the man's words seemed to leave unsaid. His voice still bothered her. He had been introduced as Gordon, Lord Griffin, and his cultured accents evidenced his claim to aristocracy. The squareness of his strong face and the burnished gleam of his golden-brown hair gave her no clue, however. She had never met the man before—not to recognize, leastways.

But his voice revealed a strong similarity to the highwayman's. There were differences. Lord Griffin's voice was quieter, his accents a little more refined. Of course, he spoke in a lady's drawing room. A gentleman would more likely speak with gentleness there. Yet, the thief's voice had the ring of command to it that this man's did not. And she remembered a hint of amusement behind many of the thief's words, while this gentleman seemed all that was proper and concerned.

His words, too, were odd. Who was reckless? She, or the highwayman? She didn't think highwaymen were supposed to be anything but reckless. Did this area breed cautious thieves, then? The idea made her lips turn up in a smile, and lost in her own thoughts, Daphne didn't notice the suddenly smitten look on the young man's face as she turned that smile and her brilliant eyes in his direction.

"I should think the government would find better uses for its men than combing the countryside for a gentleman thief. Is there some reason for your concern over a sudden inundation of handsome soldiers? I should think the ladies in the area would be delighted."

The viscount lowered his cup and his usually serious mien offered a tentative smile. "You are quizzing me, Miss Templeton. I do not fear the competition of a company of soldiers. In fact, it might be a great relief to my social obligations. No, I fear the havoc such men can wreak in our peaceful village. I have no liking for guns in an area that previously knew only contented sheep and cows. As you saw last night, the presence of the military resulted in near catastrophe. I am convinced the highwayman would never have harmed you had those soldiers not appeared."

How very extremely odd. He seemed to be defending the highwayman. Most men would have blustered and declared all thieves should be hung or transported. Was he laughing at her as people so often did behind her back? Could this be the highwayman sitting right here in her aunt's drawing room, laughing at her? She didn't like to think so.

"You are exceedingly considerate of your resident thief, Lord Griffin. Wouldn't it be more proper to be out hunting him down?" There, let him see that she doubted his sincerity.

It was her aunt who answered. "Oh no, you don't under-stand, at all, my dear." Lady Templeton wasn't much taller than Daphne, but her regal carriage gave the impression of height. Exceedingly slender to the point of thinness, she dressed in the full skirts and whalebone of an earlier age, and her petticoats rustled as she moved. "Our highwayman apparently pictures himself as something of a Robin Hood. He only robs those wealthy enough to afford the loss. He is always exceedingly polite. And the next day, some poor unfortunate in the area is blessed with those things he needs most. If there is illness in the house, a physician is paid to visit. If the children are without shoes, several pair miraculously appear on the doorstep. He seems always to know who is in the most need. It is tremendously exciting to the villagers, of course, although a few passing nobles may have a different view on the sport."

Daphne was beginning to like her Aunt Agatha better and better, despite the whispers of London gossip about her. Her aunt possessed a sharp mind and a blunt tongue. She could well picture the dismay of certain drunken gentlemen galloping through the countryside being brought up short by the reckless highwayman or Robin Hood. But still it was wrong.

"It would be much more sensible did he find decent employment and share his earnings for charitable purposes," Daphne announced determinedly. "Frightening people in the dead of night is not the work of a gentleman."

Lord Griffin spoke firmly in agreement. "You are quite correct, Miss Templeton. He must be stopped." He set the incongruously small teacup aside and rose to his towering full height as he bowed politely over her hand. "I regret that I cannot linger. I only wished to see for myself that you escaped unscathed. You are a very brave lady. I hope I can expect your company at a small entertainment I will be holding on Friday?"

Daphne smiled acceptance, and he departed.

Agatha watched her niece's dazed stare follow the viscount out, and she smiled. "He is a handsome, polite young man, is he not? How very fortunate that he chose to live here this summer instead of returning to his grandfather's estate. His father only died last year, you know.''

"Did he? How very sad. Were they close?'' Daphne picked up her teacup again and feigned disinterest. There was a mystery here, she was sure of it. Two voices could not be so similar, and the viscount seemed almost the exact same height and size as the masked highwayman.

"I do not know if they were close. They seldom resided here except when the boys were younger, for a summer or two. They seemed happy enough, as lads do. Poor man, hard on the heels of his father's death, he lost his brother, too. Very tragic. It is strange he is not still in full mourning. He has been very brave about all this.''

"Brother?'' Daphne forgot to show disinterest as she turned to her aunt. "Older brother?''

"No, younger. He was quite distraught. I cannot believe they've been close these past years since Evan has been overseas in the military, but as boys, I believe they were. It is a pity. He is such a nice young man. And he seemed quite struck with you, too. I cannot imagine why you have not married before this. In my day, the gentlemen would have been at your door on bended knee in your first Season.''

"Perhaps, dear aunt,'' Daphne replied, smiling sympathetically, "Lord Griffin was so kind because you have not yet informed him of my history. That was thoughtful of you, but someone is certain to tell him sooner or later.''

"Fustian! What your mother did is no reflection on you. You are quite as sensible as I am. And you don't appear at all the invalid. My brother was simply much too protective of you. I can understand, you are his only daughter, and he wanted what was best for you, but men are so extremely foolish sometimes. I will rely on your own good sense to decide what you wish to do and how much you wish to tell to whom. I'm just too happy to have your company to complain.''

Since her aunt had never married and had happily lived here the better part of her life without any sort of a companion, Daphne felt there might be a modicum of insincerity in this last, but she appreciated the thought. Leaning over, she kissed her aunt's cheek and rose to leave.

"You must tell me when I become an awful nuisance. I am grateful for your invitation, but I do not wish to be a burden."

"Off with you, then. I can see you are spilling over with energy and the need to be about. Oh, to be young again," she sighed, and casually dismissed her niece.

Daphne hurriedly departed for the gardens. She had missed having her own garden in London. Perhaps her aunt wouldn't mind if she dabbled a little in this one.

A few days later, feeling bolder, Daphne borrowed one of Lady Agatha's placid carriage horses to begin exploring the lines of the property. A groom offered to accompany her, but as she had no intention of going any distance, Daphne politely declined. She wanted to try being alone again, to learn living with herself without critical eyes following her every action.

The horse made an excellent guide. He willingly responded when she noticed the line of trees along the riverbank and turned toward them. She hadn't realized this area was so close to her aunt's house, and curious, she wished to explore.

Not familiar with the terrain, Daphne found an old tree stump to use for dismounting, and trailing the reins in her hands, she methodically began to find her way into the grove. To her, it seemed a vast, lonely forest of towering limbs and trunks, but she suspected it was merely a rough piece of land unsuitable for farming. She heard the rush of water and felt the downward slope and knew the river was near, but judging from the distance she had been carried from the place the highwayman left her until she reached her aunt's, this was a different part of the river than she had seen that night.

The day was warm and the shade felt deliciously cool. She hated the restriction of her heavy riding habit, but she was not yet brave enough to discard appropriate attire in public. Alone here, she unfastened the jacket and threw it over her saddle. A breeze whispered through the linen of her shirt and ruffled the jabot, and she smiled in delight at this small freedom. It was good to be herself again.

The horse whickered nervously, and Daphne hesitated, looking cautiously around. She could see the tree trunks sloping gradually downhill. There did not seem to be any dangerous precipice. All was quiet around her except for the crunch of her feet in the dried leaves. That was when she realized it was too quiet.

In the field she had crossed, birds had been singing. It was spring, after all, and the trees should be full of bird song. Perhaps her presence had intruded, but it had been quiet even before she entered the grove. She stood still, waiting to hear the sounds of scampering feet or rushing wings that she remembered hearing when she stood quietly in the woods of her home.

Nothing. Not a sound. A ripple of fear coursed down her spine, but Daphne proceeded onward, more determined than ever not to be frightened. It was broad daylight. There was nothing to fear of the day.

A moment later, she had the distinct impression of being watched. The hair on the back of her neck prickled, and she frowned in concentration, trying to find the source of the sensation. She could see nothing but trees and shrubs. No movement caught her eye, yet the feeling was all around her.

Annoyed at herself, refusing to admit her fears were becoming irrational, Daphne looked up, trying to scan the density of the branches overhead. A patch of blue appeared where she didn't think there ought to be sky, and her heart gave a nervous lurch.

Determined to conquer her fears, she announced firmly, "Whoever is there, come down at once. I do not like being spied upon. It is impolite and cowardly."

A chuckle and a rustle followed her words, and before she could jump back, a tall, lithe form fell from the branches to land at her feet. The scent of bay rum was stronger this morning, and she scowled ferociously.

"You! I should have known. I carry no jewels or money today. What is your purpose in frightening me this time?"

Pulling his hat farther down over his face, and relying on

the obscurity of the dense shade, the intruder caught her elbow and began to turn her back the way she had come. "I don't think anyone or anything is capable of frightening you, Miss Templeton. I think it is all a hum. Where is your groom if you fear walking on uncertain ground? You shouldn't be wandering about alone."

Daphne shook her arm free and halted their progress. "Do you tell all the ladies to stay at home where they belong? Fie on you, sir. And how do you know my name?"

She could see his broad shoulders in the fitted blue coat lift in a shrug, but she could not see his face. "This is a small village, Miss Templeton. Everyone knows everything. And any young lady of good breeding should be accompanied. There are brigands living along this river whom you wouldn't like to meet."

"Obviously," she replied, her voice tinged with irony. She feared to look too closely at his features, and the broad-brimmed slouch hat he wore pulled low hid him well.

"I have answered your questions, Miss Pert. Now tell me what you are doing here and how you recognize me. It is not at all healthy for either of us for you to know me."

Daphne gave a supercilious sniff. "I am merely exploring my aunt's property. And I cannot think that many thieves wear bay rum. It is hard come by outside of London and not generally worn by any but gentlemen familiar with the clubs of London."

His grin was one of wry mockery at himself. "I see that I shall have to grow a beard and cease bathing to better blend in with my surroundings. You are too sharp by far, Miss Templeton. I would advise you not to let anyone know that you can recognize me. It would cause both of us some difficulty."

"I can imagine it would cause you a few sleepless nights," she agreed with alacrity. "But I do not think anyone would believe me if I told them. You overestimate the general populace. Now tell me how it is that the Hanks girl received only sufficient fare for a coach ride to visit her ailing mother when that ring you stole was worth enough to pay her fare by post chaise all the way?"

The highwayman leaned one arm across the horse's saddle and stared down into her intrepid expression with amusement. Her face was all frail bones and delicate angles, dominated by the largest, most vibrant green eyes he had ever had the misfortune to encounter. Long, dark lashes swept upward as she stared back at him angrily, and he had the sudden urge to kiss that rosy flush on her cheek to see if those lashes would close in pleasure. It was an insane urge and he resisted it.

"Thieves have to live, too, Miss Templeton. Did you think those men I had with me that night robbed carriages for fun? What I do with my share is my business, not theirs. They have naught else to live on but what we steal. It is a sad state of affairs that the men who fought so bravely to save our country from Napoleon's maw must be reduced to thievery to eat, but you need not understand that."

"No, I need not." Furious, but more because of the unsettling effect his proximity had on her than by his words, Daphne took the offensive. "They could work like honest men. You do them no favors by encouraging them to an occupation that only can lead to the most violent of deaths." She did not know where she got the assumption that he was their leader, but he had a commanding air about him that could not cause her to think otherwise.

His laugh was short and bitter. "What kind of occupation do you think they had in the army? They are hardened to the inevitability of death, and a violent one is preferable to slow starvation. Look around you, Miss Templeton, and try to imagine who would employ crippled men whose only skills are to shoot other people? It is a wonder England is not overrun with cutthroats and thieves now that this war is over. I, at least, keep them from violence."

Daphne knew first hand the prejudice society held against the unfit. It didn't justify wrong, but she certainly was not one to hand out advice on how to combat it. She wrapped the reins more tightly around her gloved hand and began to search for a fallen tree that might serve as mounting block.

"I am sure you are to be commended, sir," she replied haughtily. "Just know it is on your head if anyone comes to harm. Lord Griffin seems most upset by your escapades, and he has vowed to see them halted.''

"Has he now?" Amusement laced his voice as he lifted her forgotten jacket from the saddle and handed it to her, then calmly caught her by the waist and threw her up on the horse before her faltering attempts at mounting could become an embarrassment. "Well, I shall certainly take that into serious consideration. Does he come calling often, Miss Templeton? A viscount makes quite a handsome catch.''

"You are insulting, sir." Whipping the reins from his protective grip, Daphne spurred her horse into motion. She did not have to endure the insinuations of a thief, gentleman or no.

"Don't come back here, Miss Templeton!" he called after her as she rode off toward the beckoning sunlight. For his own peace of mind, don't come back here, he thought as he watched her proud back ride away.

It had been a long time since he had held and been with a lady. Too long, if he was beginning to look fondly on a brittle termagant like that. He must have jelly for brains to even consider it.

THREE

That Friday evening, garbed in what she considered a modest costume of green sprigged batiste with the new flounced hem, a wide green satin sash, and long sleeves ending in a small ruffle, Daphne entered Lord Griffin's home accompanied by her aunt. The mounting whispers as she entered the salon caused her to stiffen. Assuming they were the usual rumors and speculation about her mother's death and her own involvement, Daphne held her chin high and barely touched Lord Griffin's arm as he led her to a chair.

Before she could be seated, a young lady all in white with the puffed sleeves of several seasons ago hurried to join them. "Lord Griffin, please, introduce me before Mama comes back in the room. I have never met someone who's talked to a highwayman before, and I have so many questions to ask."

Daphne heard the warm amusement in the viscount's voice as he made the introduction. Judging by Miss Jane Dalrymple's breathless forwardness, she was considered the town beauty. It seemed that only attractive people could get away with such behavior.

"Please, Miss Templeton, do not think me encroaching. I have so wished to meet you. You are the only lady hereabouts even close to my age, and you have such a dashing reputation, I just thought I would die should we not be introduced."

Dashing reputation? Daphne's brows rose and she heard Lord Griffin's chuckle, but she managed a polite smile. "Then we must get to know one another, Miss Dalrymple. It will be good to have someone of my own age to converse with." She was quite certain she was at least five years the girl's senior, but she would not quibble over age differences.

If the girl wished to consider her reputation dashing because her mother had comitted suicide, standards were considerably different between town and country. Or did her conversation with the highwayman truly rate that ranking?

"Oh, I knew you would be all that is proper. Mama would keep me hidden under a stone if she could. Imagine, thinking you fast simply because you have talked with a highwayman! I think it ever so exciting, don't you?"

Dashing, now fast—what kind of reputation had she developed in these rural circles? Daphne sent her host an inquiring look, but he merely squeezed her arm gently and released her.

"I shall leave you safely in the company of Miss Dalrymple, shall I? I must see to my other guests." Lord Griffin strode off, leaving Daphne momentarily stranded in a strange room with only this frippery female for company. Lady Agatha had already wandered off to gossip with her own cronies.

Cautiously, she took a chair. Miss Dalrymple eagerly took the next one. Daphne was about to begin on the polite series of questions she had learned to fulfill her social obligations when Miss Dalrymple made an expression of annoyance.

"Dash it all! Here comes Mama. She will drag me away, I know. Please say you will come riding with us Monday. Mama cannot complain if I say you are of Lord Griffin's party."

Having been an object of pity and suspicion, and a nuisance to be politely invited along with her cousins for the last years, Daphne found it extremely irregular to suddenly be considered a fast woman not to be met in polite company. She made a wry smile and a murmur that could be considered assent before the protective matron arrived to snatch her daughter away.

"Come along then, Jane. You must not be occupying all of Miss Templeton's time. There is Mr. Riggs just come in. Let us greet him and thank him for the lovely seeds his gardener sent over last week."

Daphne thought herself suddenly abandoned only to have a voice intrude upon her from behind. The familiarity of the accents sent a chill down her spine until she realized it was Lord Griffin. She mentally shook her head over the lapse in her perception and turned to give him her attention.

"You must forgive Mrs. Dalrymple, Miss Templeton. She has lived all her life in the country and abides by the rules of another age. She will come around soon enough, but you must expect to be a stranger here for a while. London ladies seldom visit these environs, particularly not ones as lovely as you." He took the chair that Jane had just recently vacated.

Such flattery did not often come her way, and usually then only in the most perfunctory of manners. Lord Griffin's charm had an immediate effect, and Daphne relaxed in his company.

"I shall be quite overwhelmed momentarily, my lord, if you continue so. How is it that London ladies do not visit here but you seem very much at home? I cannot believe that London has not been your life for some while."

"For a number of years it was, but I grew bored of it early. I have spent most of my life learning my grandfather's estate. One rural neighborhood can be very much like another, I suspect."

The call came for dinner then, and they were interrupted. Daphne found herself led to the table by the local squire while Lord Griffin escorted her aunt. It seemed very strange to be considered part of the social hierarchy after years of playing the part of everyone's dependent, invalid cousin, but she was not certain she enjoyed her new status any more than the old. She was assigned a place and expected to stay there without anyone's consulting her wishes, as if knowing where she belonged was the same as knowing who she was. Being Lady Agatha's dashing London niece was no more her style than being her mother's family's peculiar relative. What would it take to make these people see her as herself?

After dinner, when the gentlemen rejoined the ladies, the company formed foursomes for whist. Not appreciating the niceties of this social accomplishment, Daphne politely bowed out. To her surprise, Lord Griffin also declined. His tall form loomed beside her a moment later, and he extended his hand.

"I have a flower in the garden that seems only to bloom at night. Would you care to help identify it for me? Lady Agatha tells me you enjoy gardening."

She was twenty-three years of age and not some schoolroom miss. Daphne saw no reason why she should not accompany a gentleman alone into the garden. If her reputation was already fast, she might as well enhance it. Besides, she much preferred the cool night air to the stuffy confines of a salon of cardplayers.

She accepted without hesitation, taking his offered arm and following him through the French doors to the terrace beyond. It did not take many steps into the garden to recognize his night-blooming plant just from the scent, but Daphne refrained from announcing it immediately. She rather enjoyed the opportunity to stroll privately on the arm of a handsome viscount. Such opportunities never occurred in London.

"I understand your aunt allows you to ride alone, Miss Templeton." He spoke with a certain hesitation, as if fearful of giving offense.

Not knowing if he objected in general or because he recognized her slight lameness, Daphne replied calmly. "My aunt's properties are not so large or dangerous as to give me reason to do otherwise, my lord. After London, the privacy is most welcome."

He shook his head and sent her a puzzled look. "Surely by now you must know your loveliness can attract more than flattering attention. Even the plainest of ladies would do well to ride accompanied now that our woods seem to be filled with unsavory characters. I should recommend a small army to keep you protected from unwelcome attentions."

Daphne laughed at the seriousness of his words. "You do that very well, my lord. I was not even expecting it. An army! Well done, I congratulate you. I am most flattered. Although, as I understand it, it is a piece of the army who lives in those woods. I should think my own company better than theirs. Is this the plant you brought me to see?" She touched the round white blossom in the darkness. A sweet scent exhaled upward, perfuming the air around them.

"Not the most attractive of blooms, perhaps, but it is rather magnificent in the dark, is it not?" He pinched a branch to give to her. "And I was not offering gallant flattery, Miss Templeton. These are dangerous times. You almost came to harm your first night here. I would not have it happen again."

Daphne touched the blooms in her hand. Magnificent in the dark, how well he said that. Had she finally found someone sensitive to her pain, who understood that she was herself and not her mother? She desperately wanted it to be so.

"It is a night-blooming nicotiana, my lord, a tobacco plant. How extraordinary to find it here. Did your father travel a lot to bring this home?"

She was diverting the subject without giving him the reassurances he desired, but Gordon made no objection. She did not wear her hair in a fashionable frill of curls, but small wisps of light brown had escaped her coiffure, and his fingers ached to smooth them back from her face. There was something frail and vulnerable about her that he longed to protect, but he could only do that by keeping his hands to himself.

"Yes, he traveled almost constantly after my mother died. There are times when I think he never intended to live long enough to take his title and place in society. It feels very odd to be the Viscount Griffin now, when that is how I thought of him all those years."

Responding to the sadness in his voice, Daphne touched his sleeve with gentle fingers. "My aunt told me he died only a year or so ago, and that you lost your brother not long after. I am so sorry, my lord. I cannot even begin to imagine two such losses. It must be very difficult for you."

Something seemed to snap shut between them at these words. Without replying to them, Gordon formally placed her hand in the crook of his elbow and turned toward the house. "You will be missed inside, Miss Templeton. It was rude of me to keep you from the company for so long."

She didn't know what she had said to cause this reaction. Was it wrong to offer sympathy? Had she somehow overstepped the bounds of propriety? She hurried along at his side, abysmally defeated by his rejection so reminiscent of her days in London society.

"I apologize if I have offended you, my lord," she offered, feeling all the old hurts flooding back at the potential loss of this new friend. "I do not usually gossip, but in the country, everyone just seems to know everything. I will mention the subject no more."

He halted on the terrace and gazed down into her bewildered, pained expression. He had not meant to be so abrupt as to cause her consternation. Damn Evan into eternity, but he did make things difficult.

"I am not offended, Miss Templeton. It is a subject I still find difficult to discuss. Perhaps, one day . . ." Gordon's voice trailed off as he stared down into the lovely mist of her eyes. A man could lose himself easily in those eyes, and his thought halted, only half-formed.

Slightly giddy from the intensity she sensed in his voice and gaze and from the flood of relief that he did not reject her, Daphne touched his arm. "You will find I am quite easy to speak to. Come, let us go in, my lord. Your guests will wonder at your neglect."

She had much to think about when she went home that night. Lady Agatha's chatter about Lord Griffin's flattering attention verified what she had felt herself—he did seem to single her out above the other ladies present. After all these years she was unwilling to allow herself to believe someone would be interested in her as herself. She thought there very well might be a different explanation, and that the local Robin Hood might somehow be involved.

That was a dismaying thought, for she found the viscount to be a charming and attractive man, much more so than any of the other gentlemen of her acquaintance. Why was it that she could not be allowed a small flirtation like other ladies had with regularity? Just a flirtation, something to soothe her confidence before she made him aware of her background. He would lose all interest then, she knew, but it would be pleasant to have a beau just for a little while.

Only it was too difficult to believe that he would seek her out just for herself. She had too much experience at being ignored to believe she had the kind of beauty or charm to attract wealthy, titled gentlemen. And there was something decidedly odd going on around here. She sensed it. She just could not put her finger on it.

Why would Lord Griffin not talk about his brother? He had talked willingly enough of his father, but he had closed up abruptly when she mentioned his brother. How was it that Lady Agatha had said Evan Griffin had died? She hadn't. She hadn't mentioned how his father died, either. She really could place no consequence on that. Yet the coincidence of their voices . . .

The viscount had warned her away from riding alone. The man in the woods had warned her away from his hiding place. What were they trying to keep from her? It would be much wiser to puzzle that out than to think of the viscount's haunting sadness and the way he held her hand.

Next morning, Daphne set about to discover a few facts. It couldn't be too difficult. Judging by her conversation with the highwayman, everyone knew everyone else's business around here. She had only to ask the right people, and they would tell her.

She found Lady Agatha taking tea on the terrace. The day promised to be another warm one, but the sun had not quite reached this part of the house yet, and it was pleasantly cool. Garbed in a white muslin morning dress with short puffed sleeves and eyelet at the hem, Daphne considered fetching her shawl but settled for moving her chair toward the sun. It seemed a shame to wrap in wool on a day like this.

"Good morning, my dear. Lovely day, isn't it? I take it you are not riding today." Lady Agatha set aside the letter she was writing to look up expectantly at her niece. In that flimsy gown with only a bit of ribbon to frame her face, Daphne really was quite fetching, and Agatha nodded approval. This business about her mother's death and fears for her state of mind and health was a lot of faradiddle. The

girl had good sense, good looks, and a plump pocket; no
gentleman in his right mind could ignore that combination.
Her mother's relatives had to be all about in their heads to
discourage her. Agatha wagered the cousins looked like
mudhens and the aunts had mush for brains. She really should
have stepped in sooner, but the young so seldom appreciated
the isolation of the country. It was much better that she had
waited until the young viscount was in residence.

Daphne poured a cup of tea and added a piece of sugar.
"I thought I would try walking into the village today if you
would spare a maid to accompany me. Tillie is unfamiliar
with the roads, and I am not yet ready to attempt strange
places alone."

"Of course, take Marie. You must think of her as your
own. She is useless to me. I have too little hair anymore to
bother over and can arrange it just as easily, if not better,
than she can. But she does very well for you, I see. You
are quite in looks this morning. If you intend going into the
village looking like that, it might serve you better if I sent
a groom and a footman with you."

Daphne looked down at her outmoded gown in bewilderment. "But what is wrong with how I look? I realize the
simpler styles are not out of favor in London, but I thought
surely here . . ."

Agatha laughed, her proud gray head tilting backward to
regard her niece with fondness. "Child, there is not an ounce
of conceit in you. Your new French fashions have not reached
this rural outpost, if the whispers when you entered the room
last night did not tell you. No one here will know the gown
is outmoded. They will see only your bare throat and short
hem and how very dashing you look and every female tongue
will flap and every male one will pant. Do you not have a
suitable walking gown that trails in the dust and covers you
all over?"

Daphne drew her brows down in a pucker. "But that would
be so very warm and it is such a lovely day. I shall carry
a shawl and a parasol and gloves and surely look all that is
proper. I did not think I must be on display every minute."

"Oh, but you are more so here than in town, my dear,"
her aunt laughed. "But if you do not mind the biddies
clacking, I do not. Wear what is comfortable to you. Do you
have some errand in the village?"

"I hoped I might see Miss Dalrymple. She mentioned a
riding party but I never had time to learn the details."

"I should avoid her mother, then, were I you. She is a
monster of propriety, though it is said dear Jane was born
but eight months after the wedding."

It was Daphne's turn to laugh at the thought of the plump
and toplofty lady dallying before the wedding. The wry twist
to her aunt's noble lips encouraged further confidences. If
she went to a bad place for gossiping, it might as well be
for gossip worth having.

"You mentioned the other day that Lord Griffin had a
brother who died not long ago. He seemed reluctant to speak
of it last night. Did I do wrong to mention it? Shall I hold
my tongue in the future?"

Lady Agatha looked thoughtful as she refilled her cup.
"There is nothing for him to be ashamed of. It was an
accident, pure and simple. The boy had bought out of the
cavalry after his father's death and was returning home as
I heard it. He apparently rode too hard for too long in his
haste to be home. As best as anyone could tell, his horse
stumbled on a bad plank at the bridge and he fell in the river
and drowned. They recovered the horse, but they never found
Evan, just his coat and such where he must have tried to
swim. The river is quite high in the spring, and I understand
the current is strong. It was a great tragedy. Lord Griffin
was so grief-stricken that he refused to have more than a
private funeral. It was said he did not leave his room for
days. Perhaps he still has not learned to bury his grief. I
would leave it up to him to mention the subject the next
time."

Oh, yes, she most certainly would, Daphne vowed grimly
as she contemplated the impact of this story. Perhaps she
was jumping to hasty conclusions. She really had no right
to be so suspicious. Lord Griffin had never done anything

to her to excite such cruel thoughts. But their local Robin Hood had.

Casually, she probed for further facts. "You said he was a younger brother, but he could not have been too young to be in the cavalry. Were they much alike, then?"

Lady Agatha finally sent her niece a sharp glance. "What is all this interest in a dead man? Evan Griffin was only a few minutes younger than Gordon, and yes, they were much alike. They were identical twins."

Daphne set her cup down and stared blankly at the rolling front lawn. Twins. Of course. How very stupid of her.

FOUR

The maid Marie was a silly widgeon, but as Aunt Agatha had said, she had a decided talent for arranging hair. Pity that she had no talent for intelligent discourse. The walk into the village was long and dusty and even the marvelous scenery could not distract from the prattle of the maid. The slight ache in Daphne's knee was a minor inconvenience in comparison.

Perhaps she ought to learn to drive a curricle. How difficult would it be to guide a pair of horses down this open country lane? It was not as if it were crowded with vehicles. Large ruts like the one she skirted now might be a problem, but if she drove slowly, she could not do much damage even if she hit it. She must learn to go about on her own. She forced the memory of her mother's wildly careening vehicle out of her mind with determination. She had to go on with her life.

The thought of driving her own vehicle buoyed Daphne up for the last leg of their journey. She would have to buy it with her own funds. She felt quite certain Aunt Agatha did not have so frivolous a means of transportation as a curricle. Where did one go about purchasing carriages out here? Perhaps she should write to London, but the image of the horror on her relative's faces at the mention of her driving instantly quelled that notion. Perhaps Lord Griffin might help her.

The walk was much longer than she had thought, and they arrived hot and dusty in the little stone village. The foxglove and campion in the hedgerows had been lovely to look on, but these old stone buildings built on the road with only a fringe of flowers for yard fascinated Daphne. She wondered how many generations of families had lived behind those

ageless walls. Such stability amazed her after the frantic pace
of London. A lazy cat sunned itself on a spotless doorstep.
A sturdy matron stepped from the greengrocer's with her
shopping basket and strode briskly toward the butcher's. Two
children rolled and giggled in the dust, their homespun
breeches coated with the thick dirt. The tranquility soothed
the mind.

To the right a two-story inn sat slightly apart from the connected houses of the village. Paned windows of a century
ago glistened in the sunlight, and a picket fence concealed
a riot of color beyond the gate. Daphne lifted her skirt from
the dusty street and hurried to investigate the garden in the
inn's side yard.

The alley on one side of the inn led back to a stable, but
on this side some industrious person had mixed a kitchen
garden with a love of flowers. Admiring the lovely colors,
Daphne looked around and seeing no one to object, she
slipped the latch from the gate, and strolled onto the stone
path, leaving her maid on the street flirting with some stable
lad. Perhaps this pleasant garden might only be for patrons,
but surely the owner could not mind an admirer when there
was obviously no crowd of patrons to fill it, and she badly
needed to sit down and rest her leg.

June was always her favorite month. Finding a stone
bench, Daphne perched upon it and gazed around admiringly.
Rambling roses spilled up the stone side of the inn and across
the stable in back. Larkspur bounced and danced in the wind,
and the last of the rhododendrons filled a far corner by the
fence. Daisies and poppies brightened the rows of vegetables,
and the effect was so cheerful, Daphne just sat among the
dancing heads and admired.

It was a minute or two before she noticed the voices coming
from an open window at the back of the inn. She really would
never have noticed them at all had there not been a familiar
cadence to one that caught her ear. She hesitated, wondering
if she ought to just slip out of the garden and be on her way,
but the idea of a known criminal's taking his ease in such
a pleasant village, endangering the inhabitants, roused angry
instincts and dispelled any need to rest.

He had no right to be here, none at all. She had stayed away from his turf, now he must learn his place. Perhaps she ought to find a constable or soldier or someone, but not knowing of a certainty the connection between viscount and Robin Hood, she hesitated at going thus far. Perhaps if she accused him of her suspicions he would see the error of his ways and depart. Then Lord Griffin could relax and be happy again.

Summoning up her small courage, Daphne lifted a gloved hand to her face and made a small moan. She had seen enough vaporish ladies in London to mock their actions now.

Marie instantly came scurrying to her side, and Daphne rose and rested her hand on the maid's shoulder. "I feel frightfully warm. Is there a place inside I might sit a spell?"

"Oh, yes, mum. It is a most respectable place. My mum once worked here. Let me see you inside."

Daphne allowed herself to be guided through the small side entrance nearest at hand. The shadowed coolness of the white-washed interior was refreshing, but she wouldn't let the maid know that. She settled on a rough wooden bench just inside the door and closed her eyes and leaned her head back against the wall. "Some water, Marie, please. I feel quite faint."

She ought really to despise herself for such dramatics, but she could not let the poor maid come face-to-face with the notorious criminal. She had done it herself twice now and come away unscathed, but she was certainly trying her luck with a third time. It made no matter. Now that she was here, he would have to change his vagrant ways. It was unfair to the kind Lord Griffin to be saddled with this Robin Hood's treacherous antics.

As soon as the maid disappeared around the corner, Daphne leapt to her feet and allowed the low murmur of voices to guide her. The room she wanted was right beside the door they had entered. She need only find the door to the room . . .

Her hand hit upon it almost before she recognized the rectangular irregularity in the wall. Without a second thought to what she might find behind it, she shoved open the door.

She had enough sense of self-preservation to know the
gentleman thief would not harm a lady. She needed no other
weapon but her womanhood.

The two men inside jumped to their feet as she barged in.
The taller, broad-shouldered one in shirt sleeves and slouch
hat immediately relaxed his stance at recognizing the
intruder. The slim young man in livery remained at stiff
attention, however, as Daphne's gaze swept consideringly
over him. She did not need to recognize the servant's face.
The discreet gray and black of the viscount's household told
all.

Her scathing glance brought a shrug from the thief but he
dismissed the footman before the diatribe that would undoubtedly follow. "Fetch the lady a lemonade, Michael."

The servant sent a nervous glance to Daphne but hurriedly
did as instructed. As the door shut quietly behind him,
Daphne bent her lips in a straight line that did not quite suit
her femininely frail lace-edged attire. The highwayman
surveyed her slim figure admiringly even as the storm broke
from her lips.

"How dare you treat your brother this way?" she
demanded. "What can he have done to you to deserve this
treatment? Would you have him hanged for your misdeeds?"

That wiped the admiration from his face quickly enough.
He straightened his long, lean figure to gaze piercingly at
her. "How does a coward dare repeat such slanders, Miss
Templeton?" he threw out defensively, searching for some
means of stemming this attack.

"Coward I may be, but stupid I am not. The similarity
in the voices is telling enough, but you cannot believe there
are two men of the same height and breadth with the same
cultured accents in this remote area, can you? Take off your
hat and tell me I am wrong. Do you mean to embarrass your
brother, sir, or is your scheme more nefarious than that?"

He swept off his hat and made a courtly bow. The
resemblance was startling to a high degree. Golden-brown
hair fell over a high, intelligent brow, accenting the lively
snap of thick-lashed brown eyes and the aristocratic lines of

a long nose and angular cheekbones. When he spoke, his voice was suddenly softer and more refined. "You have caught me out, Miss Templeton. Please do not speak of this to anyone. I am attempting to find my brother Evan's murderer, and I cannot do it in the role of viscount. No one must know of my charade. You will help me to keep my secret, will you not?"

She faltered uncertainly. She had been so certain that they were two different men. Could Lord Griffin truly be playing the part of coarse ruffian? It seemed highly improbable, yet the accents had changed from military to refined, and she was not yet familiar enough with his features to discern any physical differences. The golden hair glittering in the sun seemed the same as the man's who had walked her through the garden in moonlight.

A breeze from the open window brought a faint whiff of bay rum, and Daphne's back straightened angrily. "Do not give me that flummery, Evan Griffin. Perhaps others are fooled by your physical resemblances, but I know how to rely on my other senses, and they tell me you lie. You are a rogue and a thief, and I would have one reason why I should not turn you over to the law."

"Because it is none of your damned business?" He stalked toward her, his hands on his hips, his expression threatening. "Why don't you go back to London where you belong, Miss Templeton? This isn't a game and you can't play in it."

She refused to retreat before his fury. "I don't intend to play, Mr. Griffin. I wish only to see justice done. You may hang for all I care, but consider the effect on your brother, unless you are beyond all conscience."

Staring into her lovely, outraged face, Evan Griffin growled something irascible and stifled his temper. In that white gown with the frilly parasol, she appeared some avenging angel, and he certainly looked the part of devil. Thoroughly ashamed of his disreputable appearance, he rubbed a hand over his unshaven cheek and glared at her for her interference.

"You are almighty considerate in his defense, Miss

Templeton," he said mockingly. "Have you decided you
would make the ideal viscountess for poor, harmless Gordon?
Why don't you go turn your sharp tongue on him?"

Red rage overwhelmed her. She had spent years perfecting
an image of grateful courtesy as suited her dependent
position, but that shield evaporated under his harsh attack.
Never had anyone spoken to her like that. She would not
have it. Without even thinking, Daphne reached for the
pewter mug of ale on the table. It only took a little extra effort
to reach high enough to dump the contents over his swelled
head. She had been expelled from London for just such
behavior, but it seemed satisfyingly justified this time.

Evan Griffin spluttered, opened his mouth to bellow with
rage, and closed it swiftly with the sound of a light tap and
a voice at the door.

"Miss Templeton?" The maid's voice hid a nervous
quaver. "Are you in there? I have your lemonade."

Streams of strong-smelling liquid slid from the thief's hat
to drip on his shirt sleeves and smudge the dirt on his face.
Daphne sent his frozen stance a quick glance and shivered.
He was not only furious, but trapped. She sensed the danger
as swiftly as he. The last time this had happened, she had
been the one to suffer. Not this time. Wordlessly, she pointed
at an ancient wooden cabinet teetering against the wall. She
didn't care if he had to fold himself like a piece of linen to
fit on the shelves. She didn't intend to be caught in his
presence.

As Evan pried open the warped cabinet doors and disappeared from view, Daphne settled onto what appeared to be
a comfortable chair and answered vaguely, "Yes, Marie,
do come in."

The door swung open and not only did the little maid stand
there, but a soldier in a red coat with gold trim about the
shoulders and sleeves. Daphne gave a silent shudder, then
lifted her head and held out her hand to her maid.

"You have found some lemonade? How thoughtful you
are." Then frowning as if only just discovering the stranger,
she inquired, "What is this? Marie, you cannot keep
company—"

Her words were cut off by the soldier's polite bow. "My apologies, Miss Templeton. Your maid was concerned by your disappearance from the hallway, and when she thought she heard your voice," he glanced carefully around the room to reassure himself she was alone, "and that of a stranger, she was worried. I was nearby, and knowing me to be an acquaintance of your aunt's, she naturally summoned my services."

She had not expected such perspicacity from the silly maid. Daphne smiled in genuine fatigue as she tried to imagine how to rid herself of this very proper servant of His Majesty while concealing a thief in a closet. It was all very distracting, to be sure. She took the lemonade offered and sipped gratefully.

"An acquaintance of my aunt's? I am sorry we have not been introduced . . ." Her voice trailed off. How did one address a soldier? Officer? Sir?

"Captain Rollings, ma'am. Are you quite all right? The countryside has been beset with brigands of late. I would not see you harmed." His gaze roved to the large cabinet.

Daphne didn't need to open her eyes to know where his attention had wandered. Smiling cheerfully, she rose, and twitching her short skirt hem to draw his attention back to her, she patted her hat in place and twirled her parasol. "How very kind of you, Captain. I have foolishly caused myself some fatigue in this heat, but I can assure you that no harm comes from a little overexertion. Do you by any chance know the way to the Dalrymples'? I was on my way to visit Jane, and I would be glad of an escort."

It would be exceedingly ungentlemanly to shove a lady out of the way to inspect what was in all probability a linen cabinet, and the soldier bowed his acceptance. "I know the house, but I have not had the pleasure of being introduced. I have only been in the area a short time."

Daphne lay her gloved hand against his sleeve and determinedly started for the door. "I am certain Jane would be delighted with the introduction. I shall presume on your acquaintance with my aunt, if I might, and insist that you accompany me."

She thought she heard a muffled noise from the cabinet,

but ignoring the dratted thief's discomfort, Daphne proceeded out. Let Evan Griffin stew in his own ale for a while. With any luck at all, the cabinet did not open from the inside. See if he could find his way out of that one.

Some time after the soldier was well out of sight, the terrified footman crept back into the parlor and darted nervous glances all about. A muffled curse drew his attention to the cupboard, and he jumped back, startled, as a knife protruded through the crack between the doors and began to saw at the latch. Hastily, he closed the parlor door and twisted the latch to open the cabinet.

Evan tumbled unceremoniously to the floor. His hat reeked of ale, and the disgruntled expression on his handsome features clearly revealed his state of mind. The footman hurriedly reached to help him to his feet. Being new to his exalted position and uniform, the servant did not dare crack a smile as the gentleman began a series of curses on the perversity of the female sex as he straightened his decidedly rumpled and odoriferous clothing.

Finally recovering some of his self-possession, Evan cast a glance to the closed door and then back to the nervous footman. He muttered a pithy curse and ran strong brown hands through already rumpled golden-brown locks. "Deuce take it, Michael, have the ladies changed so much while I was away? They never used to be so damned clever."

"No, sir." Michael shifted from foot to foot, uncertain of the proper reply.

"Well, you'd better inform his lordship that we have been caught out. He'll not be happy. Mayhap if he wore cologne like any civilized man, we'd not be in this now. Persuade his valet to douse him in bay rum in the next time Miss Templeton calls. That ought to muddy the waters a while longer."

Not having the least idea of what the gentleman was talking about, Michael merely nodded and tried desperately to memorize the message.

Evan wrung out his hat, sniffed it disagreeably, then shoved it back on his head. Producing a large coin, he handed it to the servant. "Give this to Beckworth for the use of his room. I'd best slip out the side way. Give me a warning if there are any strangers about."

Evan grimaced wearily as the footman left. Subterfuge wasn't his strong point. Miss Templeton had made that savagely clear. Remembering those furious green eyes in that delicate face, he stalked for the exit and the safety of the woods. Lud, but Gordon had all the luck. It didn't seem quite fair that his brother got to sleep between clean sheets and enjoy the company of lovely damsels while he had only the hard forest floor to comfort him.

But it had been his own suggestion that had put him there. He had no one to blame but himself. At the time, it had seemed the smartest thing to do. His brother had no knowledge of how to survive in the wild. But he certainly did have an ability to tame the ladies. Cursing, Evan searched the inn yard and slipped out the back door to the riverbank beyond.

He would like the pleasure of spending an evening or two in the company of one Miss Daphne Templeton. He owed the lady either a sharp setdown or a thank you, and he wasn't at all certain which he would administer.

Why had she hidden him from the soldier?

FIVE

Evan Griffin spread his long legs across the entrance to the cave overlooking the riverbank and watched as the man outside whittled away at a thick branch of pine. The whittler sat sprawled against a slender sapling, his good leg tucked under the bad one, whistling a tuneless song, and tapping the wooden stump where his foot should be in time to his own music. His thick dark locks fell across a craggy face dark with exposure and the heritage of his Welsh parents. Evan grimaced as he noted his comrade's disreputable rags of clothing and glanced down to his own.

He had tried to rinse the stench of ale from hat and shirt, but he greatly suspected the lady would be able to identify him henceforth from that odor instead of bay rum. He grimaced at the mass of wrinkles his shirt had become. It was no worse than the grass- and mud-stained wreck of his trousers.

It was time he sent for a change of clothing, but Rhys down there had no such source to call upon, nor did the others. They all knew bits and pieces of Evan's story, knew he was a pretender, but he had difficulty accepting the fact as easily as they did. To offer to send for new clothes for all of them when the servants brought his would humiliate them, but donning a new wardrobe when they wore rags was worse. He should have considered a few more of these prosaic factors when he made this choice.

Chewing a piece of the unpalatable leather that passed for their evening meal, Evan stared up at the darkening sky. He had lived like this in Spain for years. It wasn't anything new. Odd, though, he had thought when he came home it would be to the life of luxury in which he had grown up. He had envisioned crowded ballrooms filled with lovely dancing beauties, their diaphanous gowns tempting him, their soft perfumes and moist lips and laughing eyes giving him a choice of ecstasies. He had dreamed of soft beds, soft bodies, weeks of sleep, and hours of wine and food, not necessarily in that order.

But first there had been the army of occupation, and at the request of his superiors, he had agreed to stay a while longer. That life hadn't been unpleasant, but it hadn't been home. He had begun dreaming of green trees and fog and rocky shores. Then Napoleon had escaped and it had been back to the camps again, training new recruits who would undoubtedly be mown down the first day of battle. By the time Waterloo had ended, he was heartily sick of the glorious career he had envisioned. Still, it had only been word of his father's death that had brought him home, and that, months after the fact.

Evan swallowed the unpleasant bite of meat and grimaced. There really had been no excuse for the message to be delayed that long, just a string of bad luck as it kept arriving at places he had just left. By the time it reached him, he had recovered from his injuries but there were dozens of his men who had not. He'd managed to get as many as possible onto the hospital boat, but there were some who were well enough to travel with nowhere to go. He had left them his direction and fled in response to the message, never dreaming what he would be leading them into.

As he threw away the bone he had been gnawing on, Rhys looked up and gave him a grin. "Did the pheasant not please you, milord?"

"Oh, shut up." Growling, Evan didn't disdain to give his loyal friend a glare. Rhys had been with him long enough to be called brother. There were no secrets between them.

"You don't stop thinking about that woman, you won't be worth a ha'penny tonight. What's she got that the others ain't, I ask you?"

Before Rhys could begin a graphic catalog of womanly assets, Evan interrupted impatiently. "The damned female has nothing to do with it. We've run out of time, and you know it. I'd have thought he would have acted by now."

"Maybe it's all in your head, after all. That plank could have been loose, you said so yourself."

Evan closed his eyes and leaned back against the hard rock behind him. He remembered that night all too clearly. The plank might have been loose, but it wasn't the plank snapping that had sent his horse rearing into the air and into the river at its most dangerous point. He'd been at war far too long to mistake that sound.

He transferred his thoughts to the interfering female Rhys had accused him of daydreaming about. Why in hell he had stopped that carriage that night was beyond his capability to imagine. He never stopped females. They were more trouble than they were worth. Even under civilized circumstances he tended to avoid the respectable kind. They expected him to make elegant comments and come when they giggled and fluttered their fans. That wasn't his style and never had been. He'd always left the wooing to Gordon, who was the heir after all and was expected to make a proper match. He'd spent his time with the Fashionable Impures who might sulk if he didn't compliment them, but smiled happily enough when he presented them with baubles. That was the kind of transaction he understood.

The only reason he thought of Daphne Templeton at all was that she was the only person who could reveal his identity. He couldn't trust such knowledge in the hands of a female. Gritting his teeth, Evan swung around and contemplated the campfire Rhys was starting.

"I'm damned sorry I started this. I've solved nothing."

Rhys shrugged with his usual fatalistic nonchalance. "You didn't have much choice. You intending to rise from the dead now? That should be a show to be seen."

Restlessly, Evan skittered a pebble across the dry leaves. "I can't rely on Gordon to convince her we're one and the same. She has him wrapped about her finger already."

His former sergeant raised a skeptical eyebrow. "What makes you think that?"

"He's read me the riot act twice now, and his choice of adjectives is revealing. Miss Templeton is by turn a 'delicate' lady, 'too sensitive' for my crude behavior, and 'too kind and gentle' to be treated rudely. I wonder that he thinks he's wooing some saint instead of the fire-breathing termagant she is.''

Rhys snickered. ''You're the one sitting in trees watching for a glimpse of her. Are you afraid she will catch you unawares again?''

Remembering how the female in question had looked when she shed her jacket with a gleeful smile and threw her head back to allow the sun to bathe her face, Evan warranted he had good excuse to spy. He couldn't decide whether he liked the sight of her better in tailored linen with her breasts pushing at the fine fabric and her hair caught in tight pins waiting to be plucked, or in lacy batiste with wisps of curls and feminine frills to tease his eyes. She was a torment and a temptation, and he would be wise to keep an eye on her.

''She's too sharp by far,'' Evan admitted irritably. ''Coward, she calls herself, but she identified me faster than my own brother.''

The sergeant's grin grew more wicked. ''Doesn't that tell you anything, Captain? It's coward you are yourself, if it don't.''

Evan scowled. ''It tells me she has a nose for trouble. Why else would she follow me into a common inn where no respectable lady goes?''

Rhys chuckled and gave his friend an almost affectionate glance. As an officer, Evan Griffin was a hard man and a demanding one, but as a friend, he was generous and loyal beyond the bounds of friendship. Unlike those of the other officers, Evan's hands bore the calluses of hard work, and his noble features wore the evidence of harsh weather as much as those of his men, though much had faded with the passing of time and circumstance. He was the kind of leader who demanded loyalty by his actions, not his words. He had personally saved the lives of several of the men here, risking his own in the process. Rough lot that they were, there wasn't a man among them who wouldn't lay down his life for Captain Evan Griffin. And that bold and brave officer sat there like a besotted fool, not knowing what had hit him. Rhys chuckled again.

"Why else, indeed?" his friend repeated cheerfully, adding a bit of kindling to the fire. "Why does any young lady follow a gentleman except to get him into trouble? You have her pegged, indeed, Cap'n."

"You're a mincing fool if you believe that, Welshman. She was protecting my brother. Females do the strangest things in the name of love."

"Aye, and they do that. That's why she dumped the ale over you, ain't it? In the name of love?"

Evan threw a stick at the fire and stood up. "In the name of loathing, I should say."

Before his friend could stride away, Rhys threw in the last word. "Aye, and in the name of loathing, she hid your hide from the soldiers, didn't she?"

Not deigning to reply, Evan stalked off into the protection of the trees. Who was he to know the mind of females? All he knew were their bodies, and damned if Miss Daphne Templeton didn't have just the body he had dreamed of all these long and lonely nights.

Coward, indeed, he snorted as he made his way to the roadside. Had she full courage, she would be a lethal weapon. All he could see in his mind were those flashing green eyes, the impertinent dimple at the corner of those luscious lips, and those delicate, fully feminine curves that beckoned a man's hand. He didn't even want to go into what his other senses told him. He was already in well over his head.

Jane Dalrymple seemed to prance as excitedly as her horse as she rode up next to Daphne. The swooping feather of her hat bounced pertly and her blue eyes danced with laughter as she whispered, "Have you ever seen such handsome gentlemen as Captain Rollings and Lord Griffin? I cannot decide between them. The captain is so dashing in his uniform, but there is something about a title . . ."

Daphne laughed at this nonsense. It was very easy to see that Jane was a mischievous minx, but there was no harm in her. Freedom from her mother's overprotective presence had only released her high spirits. She glanced at the two men riding ahead and smiled. To her, from this distance, they were merely a scarlet coat and a blue one. Both rode exceedingly well, with the aristocratic grace of hours in the saddle. Lord Griffin was noticeably taller, but Captain Rollings appeared broader in the shoulder. Perhaps that was just the uniform.

"Why don't you choose on the basis of color? Lord Griffin, I have noticed, favors blue that looks well with his light-colored hair. The captain, of course, wears scarlet and looks quite dashing since his hair is so dark. I should think you would favor the captain since he provides such a striking contrast with your own light coloring," Daphne announced judiciously.

Jane's peal of laughter brought both men to a halt. Allowing the rest of their party to ride ahead, they waited for the two slower horses to catch up. No one questioned Daphne's cautious pace. The party had alternately slowed and spread out so that she was not always alone or in anyone's particular company. Their graciousness endeared them to her, but she was still wary of it. Had the rumors yet circulated about her? Aunt Agatha swore they hadn't.

Lord Griffin gave Jane a mocking grin of familiarity. "Are you saying shocking things to Miss Templeton, Jane? I'll not have her thinking badly of us already."

Jane wrinkled her pert nose at him and turned to the more serious mien of the soldier. "Do I look the sort to say shocking things, Captain?"

Having only just met the lady a few days before, the captain was extremely reluctant to put his foot forward. He took only the most cautious of steps where the blonde handful was concerned, but his dark eyes shone with admiration as he replied. "You could never be anything but what is proper, Miss Dalrymple."

Daphne grinned. "Then saying shocking things must be proper, and we must all indulge in it from now on. Am I correct, my lord?" She threw Lord Griffin a laughing look that brought a twinkle to his eye as he drew closer.

"Undoubtedly, Miss Templeton. Shall I begin by calling you Daphne? It is a most enchanting name and one I have been eager to use."

He was swift on the uptake; there was no doubting that. Before Daphne could reply, the remainder of the party swarmed down the hill, shouting with excitement, and she was saved the need of response.

Despite Jane's protestations to the contrary, the neighborhood did boast a number of young people. Some were not old enough to be out yet, and some were already married and looking for diversion on a sunny day, but they made a group of nearly a dozen. Captain Rollings was the only officer in the area, and his introduction to the group had resulted in a number of spontaneous invitations to impromptu routs and entertainments. At the moment, the boisterous riders inundated the laggards, demanding a race across a nearby field to the clapper bridge in the field beyond.

Daphne froze at the thought of racing an unfamiliar path on a strange horse or of straggling cautiously along behind. As daring as she might be on some occasions in her attempt to return to normal, even she knew the dangers of racing when she did not know the terrain. But to refuse to join in would be humiliating. She was not yet certain enough of her mount or her ability to control him with her weak knee to know which choice to make.

The decision was easily taken from her by Lord Griffin. "Line up on the hill there, and Miss Templeton and I will give you the signal to start. We should be able to judge the winner from that height."

There were protests that they did not join them, but only half-hearted ones. The Griffin stables sported some of the finest horseflesh in the shire, and the outcome would be a given should Gordon join in. If the race had been a malicious design by some prankster to draw the London lady into a pratfall, no one stepped forward to complain of the ruin of their plans.

Under Gordon's direction, they lined up and dashed off at the drop of his crop. Daphne couldn't help but feel superfluous. Lord Griffin didn't give her time to feel that way for long. When the others had set off, he moved his restless mount next to hers and took her reins.

"I daresay we can judge the winner while resting in the shade of that hedge, don't you agree?"

Daphne suddenly felt nervous that Lord Griffin had singled her out to this degree, and her mind worked feverishly to discover the reason, but she acquiesced when he dismounted and lifted her off to stand by his side. A sapling sprouting from the hedge gave adequate shade, and they could easily see the entire field spread out below them. Daphne wasn't certain she could discern the narrow wooden clapper bridge, but she could see the riders galloping wildly toward it.

"There is room for only one horse to cross the bridge at a time. It will be easy enough to judge the winner without our help."

His warm voice murmured startlingly close to her ear, drawing Daphne from her daze with a jolt. The accents were so much those of the highwayman that she had difficulty separating the two, and for the first time, she caught a faint scent of bay rum. Her mind froze, and she stared up at him with the frightened eyes of a trapped rabbit.

Gordon had the urge to apologize for his similarity to his brother. She had the fairest skin, with just a touch of color from the sun despite her fanciful hat. Beneath the curled beaver brim, a pair of terrified green eyes stared back at him, and he had to wonder at the depth of their terror. Gently, he brushed back a wisp of curl on her cheek.

"I did not mean to startle you, Miss Templeton, or may I call you Daphne? It would give me much pleasure to hear you address me as Gordon. I still think of 'Lord Griffin' as my father."

Said that way, she could scarcely refuse his request. His proximity was beginning to unnerve Daphne as much as his brother's, if the Robin Hood of the woods were his brother. Now was the opportunity to find out, and she sent him a hesitant look before staring resolutely back to the riders in the distance. It appeared the scarlet coat was in the lead.

"I'm not at all certain that is proper, my lord. Our acquaintance has been very short. I daresay you will be returning to your grandfather's estates before long and would find it dismaying to be on terms of such familiarity with a country miss such as I intend to be.'' That wasn't at all what she had wanted to say. Daphne bit her lip and cursed herself mentally. She never used to be so backward. London life had diminished her more than she had thought.

A firm hand gently touched her shoulder, causing her to look up to him in startlement. He was not so very tall that she could not see the mobile curve of his mouth as he gazed down on her.

''I am not planning on leaving Devonshire any time soon, and even if I should, I would be honored to call you friend. Perhaps our acquaintance has been short, but I think we are both mature enough to recognize a friend when we see one.''

A friend. Yes, that would be right and proper. One did not have this easy companionship with a suitor. Daphne had seen that from observation of her cousins, not from any experience of her own. Courtship was a stiff formality with one intent in mind. Friendship was a freer flowing feeling, an easiness and a familiarity that she felt in the company of Jane Dalrymple, or Lord Griffin. Relaxing, she smiled up at him.

''You are very persuasive . . . Gordon.'' She tried the name cautiously, waiting for some sign of repulse from the charming man beside her.

''I can be when I know what I want . . . Daphne.'' He paused before her name for emphasis, smiling as he lifted her gloved hand and bowed over it.

Now. She should act now. Ask if he knew his brother were alive and well and stealing from the rich and giving to the poor. Or perhaps that wasn't Evan Griffin in the woods, but this man. The scent of bay rum confused her. How could she insult him by asking such questions? How could they be friends without knowing the answers?

There was no time to find out. The shouts and yells from below declared a winner, and with a gentle squeeze of her hand, Gordon assisted her back into the saddle.

The thought came to her then that she could be riding beside a thief, an imposter, and once again, fear and confusion froze her into silence.

SIX

This way lay madness, Daphne declared to herself as she urged the young pony down the lane.

Her aunt had remembered a long neglected pony cart buried in the stables and the grooms had dragged it out, repaired it, and given it a fresh new coat of green paint. It wasn't fashionable, but Daphne had little use for fashion. Going to the village in the pony cart was much more comfortable than walking, and the road was less fearsome from its lower height than from a carriage. She had already made the journey once without mishap, so she was feeling fairly confident.

It wasn't her trip into the village that was madness, but her tumultuous thoughts about the viscount and his wayward brother, or the two of them as one, whatever the case might be. She had gone so far as to return to the woods and river in hopes of discovering the elusive Robin Hood, and now she was making spurious trips to the village in hopes of finding him there again. She had to get to the bottom of this mystery, although why, she couldn't say.

The thief had struck again last night. This time, Squire Dalrymple had been the target, and this morning the countryside was in an uproar. Captain Rollings had already been out to the house inquiring if anyone had heard or seen anything unusual during the night. The blasted thief had set his trap practically at their front door.

How dare he! Daphne gritted her teeth and lashed the reins to speed the pony's progress. He had to have escaped through their side lawn, practically under their windows. If she could only lay her hands on that man . . .

Madness. What could she do with a man twice her size? Curse him? She should have let Captain Rollings have him that first time. For all the world she could not imagine why she had not. That would have solved the mystery and she would have been able to live in peace. As it was, she kept waiting for the devil to show up every time she turned her back.

As they clattered onto the cobbled road of the village, Daphne slowed the pony. The maid beside her let out a sigh of relief and released her death grip on the side of the cart, but Daphne gave her little notice. She concentrated on avoiding the unusual number of strollers in the road this morning.

"Out! Away with ye! We don't take to beggars in these parts!" The woman's harsh voice caught Daphne's attention. Halting the cart in front of the millinery, she glanced about, trying to locate the source of the commotion.

"I'm not begging. I'm just looking for a bit of work. Do ye not need your garden spaded or your steps scrubbed? I'll do aught for a coin or two."

It took Daphne a moment to realize this plea came from a young boy a few yards away. A young man, she amended as she recognized the tattered remnants of his uniform.

"Aye, and how ye expect to do that?" The woman's voice asked scornfully. "Be gone with ye now. This is a poor place. We have naught for the likes of ye."

The thin young man turned away, and it was then Daphne realized one sleeve of his jacket blew in the breeze. Anger raged hot and cold through her. Perhaps she ought to feel pity or sorrow for the lad's plight, but she only felt escalating fury at the villager's treatment of someone who honestly wished to work despite his infirmity. Evan Griffin's words came back to mock her, but she refused to let him have the right of it.

Before she could climb down from the cart, she noticed another man stepping from the tavern door. She tried to see the reason for his uneven gait, fearing to become embroiled with a drunkard this early in the day. But the sound of his wooden leg on the cobbles dispelled that notion. She gathered her narrow skirt in one hand and stepped out.

"I told ye, lad, there's none to be had in these parts. Come with me, and I'll see you fed, leastways." The peg-legged man raised his hand to the young boy's shoulder, but his words came to a sudden halt at the sight bearing down on him.

Wearing a fetching green spencer and straw hat with matching ribbons streaming behind, the delicate eyelet overskirt of her walking gown catching and blowing in the wind to reveal a frail muslin gown and kid shoes, the lady hurrying toward them did not appear the fire-breathing dragon that she obviously thought herself. The two men gaped at this vision of loveliness, hastily reached to doff their hats, and stared in open-mouthed astonishment when she stopped before them.

"You are looking for work, sir?" Daphne snapped crisply, addressing the younger man while holding on to her straw hat in the brisk breeze.

"Yes, mum, milady," the lad answered nervously.

"Then come with me. We will find you work." She started down the street, but the older man's polite cough caused her to halt and raise a delicate eyebrow. "Yes?"

"Perhaps you ain't noticed, milady, but he ain't got but one arm. You might want to . . ."

Daphne's stare froze him into silence. "And you have but one foot and you still walk, do you not? I do not believe it is necessary to state the obvious. The gentleman wishes to work. It is up to him to devise a means of doing it." She turned to the lad who could not be older than herself, perhaps even younger. "If you are asked to do something that you do not feel capable of doing, you must speak out. It is very hard to do, I know from experience, but you surely must have more courage than I. You have been a soldier. If you can face cannonballs, you can face a blustery squire. Do you wish to come with me or go live with those other layabouts in the woods?" She sent a disdainful glare to the unbathed scoundrel with the wooden leg.

Rhys pursed a silent whistle. Beyond any shadow of a doubt, this was the termagant who had turned his captain into a haunted ghost of himself. No other lady in town would have knowledge of the handful of miscreants living off the land, nor would they have spoken of having experience in facing their limitations if Evan's speculations about her lameness were true. Besides, only a lady as lovely as this could have turned the captain's head so easily, and he hadn't seen another like her, ever. By the devil, he could easily understand Evan's problem, but the solution wasn't so easily discovered.

"If you're handing out jobs, miss," Rhys hurriedly replied, "I'm as willing as any man to work. There's just not many as takes to my looks."

Daphne could see why. Coming out of the tavern in those disgraceful clothes with a week's unshaven beard, he appeared no better than a rum-soaked old reprobate, but she should not judge by appearances, she reminded herself. Unfortunately, if he looked that disgraceful to her, what could he possibly look like to someone else? The thought did not bear dwelling on.

"Very well." She frowned. The squire had needed someone to help with the clearing of old shrubs and debris in an unused section of his park. Perhaps he could hire two men to do it, but that would leave both men with half the expected wages. It would be better could she find two jobs, particularly since she found it highly improbable that Squire Dalrymple would wish to have anyone as disreputable as this near his family. Her frown cleared and she pointed at her pony cart. "Stay here while I take . . ." She turned to the young soldier. "Your name?"

"David, mum, David Stone." He twisted his battered hat nervously between the fingers of his one hand.

"All right, Mr. Stone, we will go to Squire Dalrymple." She turned to the peg-legged man. "Your name?"

"Rhys, milady." He hesitated before offering his whole name, but in for a penny, in for a pound. He shrugged. "Rhys Llewellyn, milady."

The name as he said it had a noble ring to it and Daphne looked momentarily startled, but occupied with other thoughts, she merely nodded. "Very well, Mr. Llewellyn, if you wish to work, wait for me by the pony cart." She threw the sturdy vehicle a nervous look, but her maid had already wandered off on her errands. That was why she had brought Marie; the little maid always left her alone.

Having arranged everything to her satisfaction, Daphne set out for the modest Dalrymple house at the edge of the town. It boasted a small fenced park with an overabundance of trees and very little landscaping since none of the squire's family had any interest in gardening.

As she had feared, it took some persuasion to convince the squire that a one-armed young soldier might take on the arduous task of cleaning out one of the long-neglected corners of the park. The innocent mention that the young man might otherwise fall in with the band of thieves in the woods brought him around with reluctance.

"You won't regret it, sir," Daphne assured him. "After all these poor boys have done for us, keeping Napoleon from our doors, we can only do our best to see them taken care of when they return home. I am certain Lord Griffin will commend you for your patriotism."

That was a compelling argument, and the squire finally nodded doubtfully and glanced at the young man. " 'Tis a pity we cannot replace the uniform and give him a gun. With thieves swarming about, a bodyguard is what we need."

David straightened his shoulders and met the squire's eyes. "I can still shoot straight, sir. If you have a weapon, I can ride behind your carriage."

To Daphne, that was an alarming thought, but the squire brightened perceptibly, and she dared raise no objection. With a few parting words, Daphne left them discussing the war and hastened back toward her pony.

The wooden-legged man was leaning against the cart as she approached. He straightened at the sight of the faint frown on her pale brow, but politely he did not speak until spoken to.

Coming up against her next project, Daphne regarded his revolting clothes with a shudder and glanced around for some sign of Marie. She found the maid huddled nervously in the doorway of the notions shop, staring at the vagrant whose unkempt form had usurped their vehicle. Daphne gave a sigh of exasperation and turned back to the odoriferous Mr. Llewellyn.

"You will have to bathe before I can take you with me," she announced severely, refusing to acknowledge her creeping embarrassment at speaking so to a stranger. "Ask the innkeeper the cost of a bath and I will advance you the funds."

Rhys glared at her in astonishment, then growing amusement. She was red about the ears, and he had to acknowledge the justice of her decision. "The boy, milady?" He persisted in using the title even though he knew she didn't possess one. "Did he find a place?"

Daphne looked even more uncomfortable. She worried about the idea of placing an eager young soldier with a gun on a private carriage. It didn't seem at all wise. She wondered if there were any way of warning the thief; then she wondered why she should care.

Her concern came out in her sharp reply. "He has a place, and if the squire has any say in the matter, he'll be riding as an armed bodyguard as well as working in the yard."

Rhys hid his alarm. "I've had enough shooting, ma'am. If that's what you have in mind for me, I'll be going now."

Daphne sent him an exasperated look. "That's not what I had in mind for anybody, but Mr. Stone is no longer our concern. Will you follow my suggestion or shall I let you wander back to your pig sty?"

Rhys had half a mind to stalk off and leave Miss-High-and-Mighty to her busybody ways, but the blow to his pride wasn't as strong as his sudden desire for a real bath or his curiosity as to what she had in mind for him. He made a slight bow. "I'll make inquiries, milady, but the clothes will have to bathe with me."

Her flush at that remark served to bolster his sagging pride to some small degree.

She really had bitten off more than she could chew this time. This wasn't any grateful or subservient creature eager to obey her every word. He was a grown man, probably a career soldier who had seen a good deal more of this world than she. Whatever on earth had given her the notion that she might redirect his wayward habits? And he was undoubtedly right. He would have to have clean clothes before a bath would benefit him. She wished heartily that she were anywhere else but here.

Sublimely unaware of the other splashes of color passing her by or idling in doorways watching this scene, Daphne didn't recognize the horse and rider coming down the street until she heard the excited whispers of a couple of the housewives behind her.

"It's his lordship!"

"Ain't he grand? Look at them boots. Wager some poor bloke had to spit and polish for a week to make them shine like that."

"Do you think he'll . . ." The whisper trailed lower to a voice Daphne couldn't hear, but she had heard enough. She lifted her head to the sound of hoofbeats and found the navy coat and immaculate breeches that identified Lord Griffin. She sighed in profound relief.

Rhys followed her gaze and frowned as the viscount approached. Insolently, he leaned back against the cart again and waited for the handsome lord to discover this little tableau. It didn't take long. The street was short and narrow, and Miss Templeton stood out like a rose on a mud flat against the backdrop of dreary stone.

"Miss Templeton." Lord Griffin dismounted and came forward, shooting the shabby vagrant at her side a quick glance which turned to one of astonishment and then vanished as he bowed and returned his gaze to Daphne. "Well met. I thought to take some tea and persuade Mrs. White out of some of her delicious tarts. Would you care to join me?"

Not catching the swift exchange of glances between the two men, Daphne smiled welcomingly. "That would be lovely, but first you must rescue me. I have promised Mr. Llewellyn that I could find him employment so he need not live in the woods any longer. We have not had time to discuss his skills, but surely there must be some that can be put to some use in an estate as large as yours."

Amusement curled the viscount's lips as he turned to the

insolent ex-soldier leaning against the cart, glaring at him. "To be sure, Miss Templeton. If you vouch for the man, I'll be certain to find him a place. Mr. Llewellyn, is it?" He removed a gold piece from his pocket. "Take this coin and tell Beckworth at the inn to provide you a bath and change of clothes. We'll discuss employment after Miss Templeton is on her way."

The filthy vagrant made a sardonic obeisance and caught the coin flipped to him. "Certainly, milord."

As he walked off, Lord Griffin offered Daphne his arm. "I'm surprised at you. How do you come to be speaking to creatures such as that?"

Still irritated and flustered by the incident, Daphne answered curtly. "We are all God's creatures, my lord. Who am I to judge between them?"

The laughter in his voice hid the look of concern in his eyes as he glanced at her proudly held head. "Well said, but whatever happened to calling me Gordon? I shall have to remind you until you realize I mean it. We must be friends, my dear Daphne, if you are to go about rescuing the country-side. Do you have plans for our resident Robin Hood as yet?"

There it was again, that hint of amusement that said he knew more than he revealed. Daphne clenched her fingers and bit her tongue. How was she ever to persuade him to tell what he knew?

With a crisp smile that said everything and nothing, she replied, "Of course, my lord, Gordon, I mean to bring him around the same as you. The two of you are very much alike, you know."

To his credit, the viscount only made a startled jerk before reaching to open the door to the tea shop. His thoughtful gaze fell on the smiling uplifted face of the daring Miss Templeton as they entered the shop, and he experienced the sinking feeling that he had met his Waterloo as she stepped inside in a swirl of skirts.

How could one slender, interfering female wreak such havoc in so short a time? Thank God she wasn't working for the enemy.

Even as he thought it, he watched the scarlet coat of Captain Rollings rise up from the table inside and bow in greeting.

By all that was holy, they were in for it sooner or later.

SEVEN

"Have you taken leave of your few remaining senses? Of all the caper-witted, maggot-brained . . ."

Rhys dusted an invisible mote off his new broadcloth coat. It was a servant's plain brown sack coat without an ounce of fashion to it, but it was blessedly clean and whole. He was rather proud of it for the moment, and he gazed at his friend with more amusement than concern.

"She's a rare dragon, that, you know. A golden dragon with wings of gossamer. While the two of you battle over her, I think I'll steal her away."

Evan swung around and aimed a furious punch at the Welshman's nose. Rhys ducked, and the fire died out of Evan just as swiftly as it had flared up. He shrugged his own filthy coat back on and stared out over the sloping riverbank. "She's not for the like of either of us. Gordon's welcome to her. She'll beat the countryside into shape in no time. And when she's done here, she'll be a grand countess with an entire earldom to reform. We need to put our minds to ensuring that will come about."

Rhys gave a disdainful snort. "That means keeping both of you hale and hearty. Now what's the chance of that? And if the lady becomes involved with either of you . . ." He gave another shrug. "She'd be better off with me."

Evan gave an explicit curse as to the origin of his friend's birth, then grimaced in recognition of the truth of his words. "How in hell are we going to get her out of here? Damn Gordon for encouraging her! Had he not thrown his cap over the windmill, she might have grown bored with the countryside and left."

Rhys threw another branch on the fire and crouched warily on a log. His new trousers were a trifle tight, and he didn't wish to ruin them. "Had you not stopped her coach, she might never have met either of you, and Rollings would be the lady's only concern. Looking back is to no advantage. How are you going to get rid of her? Scare her off?"

Evan clenched his fists and glared at the dying light of the sun behind the trees. He was being an imbecile. This was no time to be arguing over women. Damn, but he was out of his mind to even be thinking of a woman he had only met three times, and then under the worst circumstances. Rhys was right. They had to get her out of here. Maybe later, long in the future, he could contemplate wooing and winning her.

"Give me time, I'll think of something," he muttered, and stalked away.

Rhys stared after him, wondering if it wouldn't just be wiser to go to the lady and tell her the truth. She was the first female he had encountered who hadn't looked at his mutilated foot in pity or horror. She might be sensible enough to handle the truth. But it wasn't his story to tell. Kicking at the fire, he settled more comfortably on the log. Lord Griffin knew better than to expect him to sleep in the stables.

Evan stared up at the darkened windows of the house. He had watched as candles flickered out until only one burned behind the heavy draperies, then went out a brief while later. What was someone as lovely as she doing in an isolated village like this? Why had she never married? What was the story behind her real or imagined cowardice? Or lameness? What was there about her that drew him like a moth to a flame? There were so many questions he would like to ask, but he had no right to speak of any of them.

How did one go about scaring off a lady as intrepid as Miss Daphne Templeton? Imagine finding employment for a villainous looking character like Llewellyn! She was beyond the bounds of reason, on a plane all her own, evidently. Perhaps she compensated for her fancied cowardice by being fearless in all she did.

Frowning, Evan glared upward. He could try reason, but he daren't endanger her with the facts. Well, then, he would have to make it clear that she was in danger without giving explanations. He stroked his jaw thoughtfully, wishing he hadn't just shaved. He ought to look the part of ruthless mercenary, at least. Remembering her treatment of the disreputable Rhys, Evan grinned. Looking the part wouldn't aid his cause. In all probability, she wouldn't even see him in the dark. He needed to smell the part.

He had just bathed in the river, but at least he had refrained from dousing himself with his favorite scent. Drawing a silver flask from his pocket, he took a quick gulp, then sprinkled the contents liberally over his already ruined clothes. The ale had faded out after several washings. He would see how well brandy worked.

The next task was tricky, but not difficult. Mounting his horse, Evan rode quietly to the shrubbery beneath the portico. It was a moment's work to grasp the arch between the Corinthian columns and swing his long legs to the flat roof. He then need only find a foothold in the vines and stones beneath the open casement . . .

Evan swung onto the window ledge, one leg in, one leg out as he halted to survey his position. Through a partial opening he created between the draperies he could see only the shadows of an armoire and one post of a curtained bed in the heavy darkness. Miss Templeton would undoubtedly be lying in that bed, and he tried not to allow his imagination to roam over what might be revealed had he a lamp to light his way. His intent was to terrify, not admire.

He hadn't completely thought this through. Should he make this a verbal attack? A physical assault to her belongings? Both? Perhaps he should have just brought a written message warning her away. Too late for that now. He was here and he'd have to make what he could of it.

Evan swung his other leg into the room and was met with a solid blow to his stomach just as he straightened. With an "oomph," he staggered slightly backward, catching himself on the window sash. A second blow lashed out, and he found himself grabbing at billows of silk and bits of whalebone in the darkness. Caught by surprise, he let it go, and the weapon made a third and equally silent strike. Finding himself in great

danger of falling backward out an upper story window, Evan
wielded his forces a little better this time, and his hand filled
with the silken stuff and didn't let go.

A muffled cry of frustration followed this ruse, and Evan
felt a chuckle rise in his throat. He stifled it, and tried to
sound gruff as he jerked the flimsy parasol from her hands.
"It ain't particularly smart to go after them that's bigger than
you are." He thought the false accent a particularly fine
touch. He flung the parasol into the bushes below and stood
to his full height, looming over the delicate maiden in her
long nightrail and braid.

Instead of giving a cry of fear and trying to escape, Miss
Daphne Templeton merely gave a sound of disgust and
stalked away, muttering, "You! I should have known."

Evan stared after her in astonishment. She couldn't
possibly recognize him. It was dark. He had disguised his
voice and his accent. How the devil could she know it was
him? It had to be a bluff.

"You expectin' someone else?" he asked in his most
churlish tones, moving threateningly after her.

Daphne removed a robe from the armoire and tugged it
on, struggling with the bits of ribbon that tied it beneath her
breasts as the ungallant Robin Hood advanced into her room.
Perhaps she ought to be terrified. He smelled to high heaven
of brandy and was most probably drunk, but she didn't think
real miscreants went to the trouble of disguising their voices.
She finally managed to knot the ribbon and took up a stance
on the far side of the secretary, using it as a barrier to his
progress.

"You could certainly have found a better way to talk to
me than this. It is most improper. Have you come to say
you're taking your criminal services to other parts of the
country? Or are you going to offer some ridiculous explanation of this masquerade?"

Her prim, knowing tones infuriated him. Frustrated, Evan
stood with hands on hips and glared down at his daring
antagonist, wishing he could shake her. He didn't overlook
the fact that she had a silver letter opener and a solid brass

inkwell within inches of her fingers. Couldn't she at least act vaporish at this intrusion?

"Miss Templeton, you are the most irritating female I have ever had the misfortune to encounter. How the deuce can you know who I am?"

She hadn't realized how thoroughly frightened she had been until his familiar accents rang in her ear and the muscles in her back and shoulders seemed to melt with relief. She caught the edge of the desk and glared at him.

"Who else would be mad enough to crawl in my window in the middle of the night? Honestly, will you never grow up? I have half a mind to scream for the servants and put an end to your foolishness forever."

Never grow up? Here he was trying to save her bloody life, and she accused him of a child's game! He ought to wring her pretty neck, but instead, Evan grinned and leaned his hip against the secretary, crossing his arms across his chest as he looked down on her thick, silken tresses. She was severely out of charity with him, and he ought to be berating her soundly for a half dozen causes, but all he could think of was how sweet she smelled now that he was this close. He could have her in his arms in a minute, but he rather imagined she would scream the roof down should he try. That thought led to even more interesting images, and his grin grew broader.

"We should be thoroughly compromised if you utter so much as one tiny moan, Miss Templeton, but I'll not object to that. Scream, and let us see who regrets it later."

Fury washed over her. She wanted to scream and shout and beat her fists against his arrogant chest and kick his shins and make him regret his insufferable attitude. At the very least, she ought to scratch his eyes out, but the thought of reaching up to accomplish such a thing stirred far different emotions, and she managed only a "Conceited oaf" before retreating further into the corner.

At Daphne's retreat, Evan advanced, keeping only a few feet between them. He had meant to terrify her, but instead, he was having more fun than he'd had in a long time. What a dance she could lead him if they were only in different circumstances. He had never paid much attention to ladies before, but beneath that frail exterior, she was as much a soldier as he. Conceited oaf, indeed. He smiled. "I'm only here to warn you, Miss Templeton. Anything else is on your head."

"You could have found a more decorous means of sending a message, Mr. Griffin. This is highly improper, and that was my best parasol you flung in the bushes. How will I ever explain that?"

"Tell them you were experimenting with flying. I should think more modern witches might try parasols rather than brooms. I don't care what you tell them, Miss Templeton, just heed what I have to say."

She wished she had taken the parasol to his head. He was too close, and she could not retreat farther. He filled her senses, his broad shoulders blocking out all view of the room, his masculine frame overpowering her slight one just by standing there. The brandy fumes helped keep her perspective, but only slightly. "Then speak and be gone," she declared boldly.

Momentarily stunned by the proximity of all this dainty femininity challenging him with more than words, Evan did not immediately reply. It had been so long since he had held a woman, heard the rustle of silk, felt the velvet smoothness of a woman's hands, that he ached with the need now. Just a step closer . . .

He resisted. Forcing his mind to overrule his body, he replied dryly, "You have a remarkable propensity for getting yourself in and out of trouble that I can only applaud, Miss Templeton, but you have no idea of the immensity of the danger you are placing yourself in by interfering where you should not. I would recommend an immediate return to London if you value your life."

He was much too close, and the room was so dark . . . Daphne had the insane thought that her most immediate danger was this man filling her field of vision. The desire to be taken into his arms and be held against him fogged her senses, and she could only grasp the wall and pray for rationality. What was there about this commanding Robin Hood that impelled her to him rather than away, as all good logic would demand? She forced herself to remain aloof.

"Are you threatening me, Mr. Griffin?"

Her quiet question nearly broke his control. Evan lifted his hand to bring her closer, then dropped it as if burned. "Forces beyond my control are threatening you, Miss Templeton. For your own safety, you must go away. Not forever, perhaps. Just a little while, just long enough for matters to be settled."

He sounded almost unhappy at the thought of sending her away, and Daphne regained a little more of her confidence. She straightened and drifted an inch closer, wishing she had a candle. There had to be some way of differentiating him from his brother. Instead of questioning his words, she impulsively drew her fingers across his cheek, seeking their differences. She found the same rugged cheekbones, traced them downward to a strong jaw, almost square in its breadth, with a rounded dent in the chin. Her fingers moved upward, exploring the chiseled, mobile lines of his mouth that remained tense and expectant beneath her touch. She found the harsh blade of his nose and reached to stroke the golden thickness of his brows and outline the high plane of his forehead, wrinkled now in a frown of concentration. Her fingers briefly entangled in the warm strands of his hair before quickly retreating.

Somewhat taken aback by her forwardness, Evan struggled to remain still throughout her examination, but when she was done, he expelled a soft sigh. "Can you tell I am not Gordon? Will you believe me now?" He didn't dare put any other construction on her actions, or her proximity. She was close enough to enfold in his embrace, and he struggled inwardly to keep from doing so.

"It does not matter," Daphne answered simply, retreating another step. Her hand tingled from touching him. She had been dying to explore the viscount's handsome features but had been unable to summon the courage to admit her need to do so. How was it that she could be so bold with this man? "I cannot return to London. This is my home now."

Evan gave a hiss of surrender and grabbed her shoulders. "What do I have to do to convince you?" His fingers kneaded the soft flesh beneath her thin robe and without thought, he drew her closer until her hair brushed his chin. "Leave, Daphne, before you distract me from my purpose."

She raised her hands to his chest as she had wished to do earlier. She could feel his heartbeat, sense his tension, and knew a strange desire as she braced herself against him. This wasn't a lover's embrace, she knew, but a contest of wills. She struggled to maintain her superiority.

"Let me help," she implored, not knowing what she asked.

He muttered a curse, and she thought he brushed his lips against her hair, but then he shoved away and strode to the safety of the far end of the room. "Why can you simply not accept the fact that there is danger here and that you are jeopardizing your own life as well as others' by staying? I am not asking it to be forever, just long enough for me to straighten out a few matters."

"And I am supposed to take the word of a common criminal, a thief who must sneak in windows and molest ladies in the middle of the night? Why should I believe you? Why should I not suspect you are after your own advantage in this? What proof can you offer me?" Daphne demanded, recovering her senses now that he was not so dangerously close.

"Do you need to be shot at and thrown in the river to believe me?" Angrily, Evan stalked back to the window. She had neatly set him in his place, and he could not help but feel resentful. Let Gordon deal with her. He was the one who knew how to deal with ladies. For himself, he preferred a horse and rifle any time.

"You are being absurd! The only ones with tendencies toward violence around here are you and your merry band of thieves!" Daphne followed him to the window so she need not speak her accusations in more than a whisper.

Half in and half out the window, Evan turned back and said, "Go talk to my esteemed brother if you believe that!

Good evening, Miss Templeton.'' He dropped out of the window and out of sight.

Daphne ran in terror to see where he had gone, only to find him landing on the portico roof below. "So you admit you have a brother, Evan Griffin?" she threw after him.

Evan glanced up to her white-draped figure in the window above, her long braid hanging past her waist, and he cursed vividly to himself. "Tell that to the world and see how long he lives!" he threw back at her before determinedly striding out of hearing.

Daphne waited in the window as he disappeared from her sight. In minutes, she heard the sound of hoofbeats and knew he was gone. Slowly, she retreated from the casement and into the safety of her room. What had possessed him to come here like that? Could he truly mean she was in danger? She could not see how—except from him. He was definitely a danger—to her sanity, if nothing else.

Remembering his fierce touch, the brush of his lips against her hair, Daphne retreated further, staring at the empty window where he had sat a few short minutes ago. He could not have meant any of those things she had thought she heard and felt. They must be at cross-purposes. She was unaccustomed to dealing with men. Men said things that could be interpreted too many different ways. He was a complete stranger. He could not be concerned enough about her to risk his neck by coming here like this to warn her. He must have meant to rob her but she caught him by surprise.

That made sense. Relaxing a little, she returned to her bed and sat down upon the turned-down sheets. He had thought she would be asleep. Perhaps he hadn't even known this was her room. His hastily invented lies were meant to frighten, that was all. And then she had foolishly encouraged him by touching him. Shame swept through her as she realized how her curiosity could be misinterpreted. Lud, but she was glad she would never have to meet with him face to face again. How could she have been so brazen?

Still, as she leaned into her pillows and sought the elusive clouds of sleep, she could not help but remember the strong force of his fingers pulling her close, the steady heartbeat beneath her palms as he bent over her, and the aching dreams such a touch elicited.

She had denied herself London and the world. Must she deny herself any chance of love as well?

EIGHT

Nervously, Daphne watched Lord Griffin speak to Jane Dalrymple and lead her out into the small, cleared area in the main salon that had been transformed into a dance floor. It was just a small informal gathering of friends, with Mrs. Dalrymple playing the pianoforte and an elderly neighbor wielding a lovely violin. She had no reason to be nervous, no reason for her palms beneath her light gloves to grow moist.

When Captain Rollings came to bow before her and request this dance, Daphne nearly fell from her seat in startlement. Men seldom asked her to dance, but of course, the captain knew nothing of her defects. She was quite certain she could manage that small dance floor, but it had been years since she had actually waltzed around a schoolroom with her dance instructor. She was not at all certain she was prepared to make a cake of herself yet.

Politely declining, she asked if she might have another small glass of sherry. When the captain returned, he remained at her side while several more couples maneuvered around the room's center. "Have you been enjoying your stay in Devonshire, Miss Templeton? It is somewhat remote from London, wouldn't you agree?"

"No more remote than where I grew up," she replied easily. Captain Rollings was one of the reasons she was nervous, although she knew she had no reason to be so. He was polite and respectful and a good deal more civilized than the Robin Hood he sought. She just couldn't help feeling guilty whenever he was around. She was harboring knowledge of a known criminal. Could he have her arrested for that? She felt quite certain he could.

She tried to keep the subject light. "London is exciting,

and there are many things I enjoy doing there, but the country has always been my home. I enjoy small groups over large crowds, and I have a long-standing interest in gardening. I'm quite comfortable here, Captain. And you?''

His gaze followed the blond, lithe figure of Miss Dalrymple as she swung about the floor in the viscount's arms, her laughter keeping time with the music. "I have learned to be comfortable wherever I go. I cannot think that there is any place in England that isn't an improvement over the Continent, however.''

"You were with Wellington?'' she inquired politely. Daphne had gleaned what information she could of the war by eavesdropping on the conversation of gentlemen and scanning the newssheets daily. The awe in which they held the great general had impressed her, and his name came easily to mind.

"Nothing so brave, I fear. My father has seen to it that I am employed only in minor diplomatic posts and domestic situations. Being the eldest son has its drawbacks.''

"So has being an only daughter,'' Daphne said wryly. "Now that the war is over, have you considered resigning your commission?''

He gave her a perceptive look. His dark hair gleamed in the brilliant candlelight, and there was a glint of determination in his dark eyes as he gazed down at her. "I have considered it, but I should like to leave with something to show for my efforts. That was why I volunteered my services to answer the complaints of your local Robin Hood.''

Daphne prayed her courteous smile didn't falter. "I cannot find it in me to judge him harshly. He has harmed no one and helped many. Catching a harmless eccentric cannot be much of a feather in your cap.''

"A harmless eccentric does not rob gentlemen at pistol point nor abduct young ladies from their carriages. It is only a matter of time until someone is hurt.'' His voice was harsh. "Surely you cannot sympathize with a man who must have caused you a great deal of terror.''

Daphne shrugged blithely. "I saw no pistol, and a horse ride at twilight after a tedious day's journey was rather adventurous. He allowed me to keep my mother's locket and only took what I offered him. I repeat, he seems harmless enough.''

She didn't know why in the world she was defending him. She must be quite out of her mind. She ought to tell Captain Rollings everything she knew and be done with it. But first, she needed to speak with Lord Griffin. She turned her gaze in the viscount's direction, but his back was turned to her. She wished she could see his expression. Was he looking at Jane with delight and admiration? Remembering her fantasy of several nights ago with the irritating thief, Daphne quenched a wave of embarrassment. A person was allowed to make a fool of herself once or twice in life. It was good for the soul. She just didn't wish to make it public.

The music came to an end then, and the laughing, chattering couples left the floor. Lord Griffin led Jane to the corner where the captain and Daphne waited. A brief hint of suspicion darkened, then disappeared from the viscount's eyes as he watched them together. His smile was its usual affable curve by the time they reached the corner.

''That was so enjoyable, I would like to do it again. We shall have to switch partners, though. Daphne, would you care to join me?''

Oh, yes, she would, but Daphne refrained from blurting out such eagerness. Besides, she had more important things to do than dance with the viscount and make a cake of herself. She needed to speak with him, and if she did not do it now, she might never have the courage.

''If you do not mind, my lord, it is a trifle warm in here. I would be happy to step outside just a minute and return you to Jane and the other ladies when the music begins again.'' She sensed rather than saw his tension as he placed her hand on his arm and made a dignified bow to their companions.

''Of course, Miss Templeton. Jane, you are not to speak any wickedness to Captain Rollings while we are gone. It can only be done when we are all together,'' he admonished her, laughter concealing any of his concern.

They made the circle of the room, politely chatting with

neighbors and friends, declaring their intention of walking out briefly so none would remark their disappearance and put other connotations to it. Daphne was both grateful and chagrined at this attention. Did he think she would deliberately compromise him should they be alone together too long? It was a dampening thought and just one of many she seemed to be having lately. Perhaps she ought to just come out and tell everyone that she was not marriage material and they had no need to worry. In London, she had not been considered eligible enough to worry over such complications.

Once having run the gamut of their neighbors, they stepped out the open terrace doors with only a minimum of whisper and speculation stirring the air behind them. Gordon still seemed stiff and uneasy as he led her toward the wall separating the large, circular terrace from the gardens. Dark did not come early this time of year, and Daphne could still see the rigid set of his shoulders when she looked up at him. What was it he expected her to say that had him as nervous as she?

"You are looking particularly charming tonight, Daphne. That shade of rose becomes you."

"While your compliment is very flattering, my lord, your dissembling is not. Do I appear the sort to need compliments to still my tongue?"

Gordon laughed softly and turned her to face him. "No, not at all, and whatever happened to calling me Gordon? Am I sunk so far in your esteem that you must scorn me with politeness? I hope we know each other better than that, Daphne. You are very easy to know. I have not felt so with any other woman of my acquaintance."

And he spoke the truth, he realized. There was something so vulnerable about her that he longed to envelop her in his protection. At the same time, she was more forthright and honest than any woman he had ever known. Somehow, she also managed to be loyal and brave, but he was afraid he was about to become a victim of those attributes. Taking the initiative, he offered the opening she sought.

"Did you simply wish a turn about the garden or was there something else behind this request? You realize I do not flatter myself into thinking it is my company you seek.''

Daphne managed a small smile at his kindly face. He really was a very nice man. She just wished she didn't have to be the one to open the unfortunate subject. ''Perhaps, after all, it is, my lord. Your company is very pleasant and I do not wish to be denied it, which is why I hesitate to speak.''

''Call me Gordon and I shall forgive you anything you say,'' he offered magnanimously.

Daphne laughed. ''Now you are opening yourself to Jane's wickedness. I could name you every sort of villain and you would be forced to forgive me . . . Gordon.''

He caught her arms and forced her to continue looking at him. ''Tell me what's on your mind. I cannot stand the suspense any longer. Is it so bad that you cannot say it?''

She looked very worried and his heart froze in his chest, but he refused to give in to his fears. He would have this in the open and pray that she would still speak to him when it was done.

''I cannot say if it is very bad or very good. I cannot know how you feel about your brother. You never speak of him. Surely you must know he is still alive?'' Daphne allowed the words to spill from her lips without thinking. She had to talk to someone. She couldn't contain it any longer. Gordon seemed he only logical person to speak to, but she couldn't help feeling a twinge of disloyalty at this small breach of confidence. Why did she feel it necessary to protect a thief?

Gordon took a deep breath as the secret spilled out and filled the void between them. Just the same, he could not speak the truth, even should he endanger the slight harmony that was building between them. The urge was there, but he could not give in to it.

With a wry twist of his lips, he asked, ''Can you not believe it even yet? I have tried to make it clear so you would stay away from danger. Evan is quite dead. I am the one you must scorn.''

A shiver coursed down her spine at the impact of his words. This wasn't the rogue in the woods lying to her, but Lord Griffin. Could she really be so wrong? Was he truly so superb an actor as to make her believe he was two different people?

"Why are you doing this to me?" she whispered, not at all certain what "this" was. He couldn't be the highwayman. She wouldn't believe it.

"I am trying to protect you, Daphne," he murmured near her ear, his lips brushing against her hair. "Do not ask me to explain just yet. Give me time and all will be known, my word on it."

No, it wasn't. It couldn't be. Before she could utter any of those protests, Gordon lowered his mouth to hers.

His kiss was very soft. And warm. His lips caressed hers with respect, but were quick to take advantage when given no opposition. They plied her mouth slowly, delicately, telling her with action and not words that she wasn't to worry. His hands on her arms slid lower, caressing, reassuring, until Daphne raised her hands to his chest and turned her head to gasp for breath.

He held her there briefly before saying, "We had best go in." He cupped her elbow, giving her time to recover. "I will not apologize, Daphne. I have been waiting to do that for days. But I hope you will be more patient than I and wait until I can give you explanations before condemning me."

Daphne was too stunned to do more than follow Gordon's lead. She had never been kissed before. Really kissed. There had been a few young gentlemen who had attempted to steal more than she was willing to give and had hastily retreated when she made it clear she did not take their attentions lightly. This wasn't the same at all. She didn't know what she had expected, but it hadn't been this.

She felt the kiss all the way down to her toes. Obediently, she followed him. She didn't have any answers, only more questions. She couldn't afford to ask more questions just yet.

In the shadows of the shrubbery, a figure watched them go with a curse on his tongue and pain in his heart. This wasn't how it was supposed to be. He didn't want to fight, but it didn't look like he had much choice.

With resolution, he crept back through the shrubbery toward the side of the house.

* * *

Violin music filled the air as the guests indulged in a late supper. Daphne brought her aunt a fresh glass of sherry and exchanged comments on the delightfulness of the evening with several of her aunt's companions. Before one of the young bachelors could push their way from the buffet to rescue her niece, Agatha requested still another errand.

"Lord Griffin says he left a volume of *Emma* on the library table for me. Will you fetch it so I will not forget it before we go?"

"Of course." Daphne gave her empty plate to a servant and slipped out a side door to make her way to the viscount's male-oriented library. She could not imagine why he should have a copy of Austen's *Emma* other than out of curiosity, since the Regent had requested it be dedicated to him, but she didn't mind the diversion from the crowd in the other rooms. Ever since that stroll on the terrace she had desperately wished for a moment alone, time to think and make sense of what had happened, but she had been kept busy smiling politely and chatting to neighbors and friends as if nothing momentous had happened. She took a deep breath of cool air in the deserted hall and pushed open the library door.

She sincerely hoped Lord Griffin had left the volume in a noticeable place. No candles had been lit in here since the sun went down, and she doubted that she could linger long in this overwhelming blackness without succumbing to the urge to dash for the well-lit hall. It would be exceedingly embarrassing to come out with a volume of world history or Latin essays.

Before she could reach the library table, a figure stepped out of the shadows at the rear of the long room. "Daphne," a familiar voice entreated.

She looked up in surprise at the familiar blue frock coat and white embroidered waistcoat of Lord Griffin. Had he known her aunt would send her here? She took a step backward as he approached, then stood firm. She had nothing to fear but herself. "Gordon?"

Evan Griffin hesitated, regarding her slight figure with

trepidation now that he had her here. He had wanted to stand before her on the same grounds as his brother, scrubbed and decent and looking like a gentleman. Out of habit and in the interest of concealing his identity, he had donned a coat from his wardrobe that matched his brother's. It had not occurred to him that the one time he wished her to recognize him, she would not. That presented interesting, if ungentlemanly, possibilities.

"I didn't think I'd have a chance to speak to you before you left," he murmured in his best imitation of Gordon's low, serious tones.

Daphne wrestled with a sense of unease, a sense of something not right, but his proximity was obliterating her usual perception. His golden head was bent with concern over her, the stiff folds of his cravat were just within reach of her fingertips should she raise her hand, and the clean scent of his shaving soap enveloped her. When his gloved hand caught hers and his other hand went to her waist, she did not even open her mouth to protest. The violin music seemed to swell in proportion to his nearness, and to her amazement, she floated off on waves of music.

They danced in silence, the dim lights of the sconces in the hall casting shadows across their faces as their feet glided along the wooden floor. Daphne forgot how to breathe as a strong hand guided her with easy grace around the obstacles a library presented, but she remembered how to waltz. She remembered how she loved waltzing, and she closed her eyes and let the music and the man carry her off to their own private heaven.

It was only then, with her eyes closed and the blue coat out of sight that she realized her error. A quiver ran through her, but she didn't stop dancing. Perhaps she was losing her mind. If so, she intended to enjoy every step of the way.

A blissful smile turned up the corner of her lips, devastating the man staring down into her face. He pulled her closer, felt the free sway of her body beneath his hands, and almost groaned at the surge of desire crippling him. How could he rage at her interference, curse at her stubbornness, and despise her feminine treachery, while his body cried out to take her, possess her, and never let her go?

When the music stopped, so did their feet, but they didn't separate. Daphne stared up in confusion at his square jaw and continued to cling to his hand. The hand at her back had become a permanent part of her, and she was suddenly, totally aware of the lean length of his body not inches from hers.

"Why?" she asked quietly.

"You wouldn't believe me if I told you." They could be talking about two entirely different topics, but the answer would still be the same. Did she realize who he was now? Or had Gordon succeeded in convincing her they were one and the same?

"Probably not, but you could at least give me the opportunity to try." Daphne backed away then, but he did not release his hold on her fingers.

"So you can turn me over to Captain Rollings? He has been at your side the better part of the evening, has he not?"

Only Gordon would have known that. Evan couldn't possibly have been the genial host in that salon. But this had to be Evan. She couldn't put her finger on the difference, but it was there. The confusion welled up and grew greater and she turned her head away in frustration.

"Do you enjoy tormenting women? Or is it only helpless women that you prefer to pick on?"

"Helpless? You're about as helpless as a she-wolf. If you had a care for my neck, you'd go back to London where you belong. When you grow impatient with the wheels of justice, will you oil them with your knowledge?"

This was Evan. She didn't know how he did it or why, but she could not mistake the harsh irony that was no part of his brother's nature. They were destined to ever be at odds. She wondered briefly at the relationship between these two, but there was little time for more. She shook free of his hand and turned to locate the library table again.

"Believe whatever you wish. It is no matter to me." Angrily, she turned her back to him. She had been sent here civil tongue in your head, you may leave the room. And my business is not yours and never will be. Rhys Llewellyn asked for a job and I found him one. You could do the same for the rest of the men in the woods if you put your mind to it. It is one thing to take up the plight of the maimed with words and quite another to do so with actions. And if you will find me the volume of *Emma* that is supposed to be here, I will leave and you need not endure my opinions any longer.''

Evan easily located the book and clasped it in his hand. ''Are you planning on spending the remainder of the evening reading, Miss Templeton?'' he asked smoothly.

''Of course not! I mean to spend the evening on the dance floor and end it with a jig. Aunt Agatha is waiting. May I have the book, please?''

This wasn't turning out at all as he had hoped. He had only meant to show her that he could play the gallant gentleman as well as Gordon. It was becoming increasingly obvious that he couldn't. All he had done was insult her and raise her ire. Perhaps Gordon was the better man when it came to women, but he'd be damned if he would surrender the fight yet.

''And you would have me find jobs for my men when I cannot set foot out of the woods without being hunted down like a fox? I did not choose this life, Miss Templeton, believe me. Not any more than you chose yours.''

She didn't want to be reasonable. She wanted to remain angry at this provoking man who confused her so thoroughly whenever she was in his presence. It had never been necessary to do more than make polite small talk to any of the gentlemen of her acquaintance before. Why was it this one who led her down such circuitous pathways that what she thought was right became wrong with just a twisting of words?

''Then, someday, Mr. Griffin, perhaps you will explain to me just how you came to be a criminal. Until then . . .'' Daphne walked the length of the table, knowing the door was just beyond that open space at the end.

A confusion of noise in the foyer caused her to hesitate. Had she been gone so long that the gathering was already breaking up? Aware that Evan lingered not too far behind, she hastened toward the door.

As she reached it, the sonorous tones of the butler announced to the company in the salon, ''The Honorable Melanie Griffin.''

At the heartrending groan behind her, Daphne turned a startled glance over her shoulder.

Slumped against the table, Evan gave her a bleak expression. ''My sister.''

NINE

"I'm so glad to have finally met you, Miss Templeton. I know all about you from Gordon's letter. I could not wait to meet such a paragon of virtue and courage."

Miss Melanie Griffin swung her lavender parasol over the tips of her lavender half-boots revealed by the highly stylish walking dress of sprigged muslin with three rows of flounces that stopped just at her ankles. Daphne had no need to judge this breathtaking ensemble to know her visitor was daringly lovely. The sudden silence of the two men at her side told her that much. Melanie's arrival in the company of Jane Dalrymple had effectively ended their wary and rather one-sided interview.

"I did not know Lord Griffin was given to exaggeration," Daphne replied dryly.

Jane Dalrymple giggled and continued the introduction. "Melanie, I don't believe you had a chance to meet Captain Rollings last night. He is here to save us from the dreadful Robin Hood." Jane hesitated as she turned to the second man standing in the drive beside Daphne. He had apparently brought a mount from Lord Griffin's stable for Daphne to use. She recognized the horse but not the man. His stance and mien were not that of the usual line of servant.

Daphne supplied the answer to Jane's questioning look. "Mr. Llewellyn was kind enough to note the mare Lord Griffin loaned me needed a shoe." She did not need to explain he was an ex-soldier currently working in his lordship's stable. The wooden leg and his horsy smell provided that information even to the uninitiated.

To Daphne's surprise, the lovely lady only made polite noises over the handsome captain but turned a melting smile on the groom. "Mr. Llewellyn! It is you! I thought it must be . . ."

Before the lady had a chance to say more, the unsavory groom gathered up the reins of the horse he was returning to the Templeton stable and started down the drive. "If you'll excuse me, ladies, gentleman," he tugged his forelock, "I'd best be getting on."

"But I have not yet . . ." The Honorable Melanie looked dismayed as the groom turned his back and limped down the drive. "Well, I never. I know I have met him somewhere. Is he one of your men, Captain?"

Rollings nearly choked before he could reply to that ingenuous question. "No, Miss Griffin, he is not. Much as I hate to leave three such charming ladies, I must beg my excuses. Duty calls, you know. Good-day, ladies." He bowed and took his mount with a graceful swing of his long legs.

The ladies watched him go before Jane broke the silence. "Isn't he just the most handsome man you ever saw?"

"I am currently not interested in men," Miss Griffin announced. "I am quite out of charity with the whole gender. Why, even your Robin Hood could not be bothered to stop my carriage, and I had a pistol all loaded and ready for him."

This time it was Daphne's turn to choke. Laughter welled up in her throat and kept bubbling outward despite her best efforts. She thought it could very well be hysteria. Imagine Evan Griffin throwing open the carriage door in his best Robin Hood manner to find his own sister pointing a deadly weapon at him! Oh, what a tangled web . . . !

"Miss Templeton, are you all right? Have I brought back terrible memories? Gordon was so certain that you came to no harm . . . . Please, let us take you back to the house."

Daphne waved off any offer of assistance but turned to lead the way back to the house. "I am quite fine. The thief does not normally stop carriages, only inebriated young men. Do not feel yourself slighted."

"Then why did he rob you? I so wanted to be as brave as you and show Gordon I am no longer a child."

Why her? That was an excellent question, one Daphne had

not resolved yet. She lifted her shoulders lightly. "It must have had something to do with Lansbury's crest on the door. Perhaps he had some grudge against Lord Lansbury. I did not think to inquire at the time." As they reached the front entrance, Daphne realized what had been bothering her since her first introduction to the lady, and she turned to inquire bluntly, "How is it that you and Lord Griffin do not wear mourning for your brother, Miss Griffin? Do not mistake me; I am not criticizing, only curious."

A shadow passed across the lady's face, but she replied honestly enough. "We had only gone into half mourning from our father's death when Evan was killed. Gordon convinced us that Evan would not want us to return to black on his behalf. As his twin, he knew best, so we all followed his advice, for Gordon's sake, if no other. I doubt that I saw Evan above twice since I left the schoolroom, but he and Gordon were very close. I remember Evan as a jolly fellow, always eager for a lark. I do not think heavy mourning would have impressed him."

"I'm certain you're right. Forgive me for prying. I am growing much too used to country ways, I fear. Will you be staying long? We really must arrange some entertainment for you, if so." Daphne led the way into the small parlor.

Melanie gave a deep sigh. "Gordon is very angry with me for appearing unannounced. He said it was a shatter-brained notion and he had half a mind to send me back to grandfather, post haste. Gordon has ever been a high stickler, so I assume it's only my shocking impropriety that has him in the boughs. I cannot imagine that I have interrupted anything improper on *his* part."

"That will not do at all," Jane exclaimed. "We shall have to speak to Lord Griffin and persuade him you are needed. I am certain he is glad of your company. He just feels obliged to act as a head of the household should."

As Lady Agatha joined them and the ladies all made plans for picnics and musicales and how they would persuade Lord Griffin to come around, Daphne remained relatively silent. She remembered all too clearly Evan's anguished groan at the appearance of his sister. She rather thought Gordon might have a more pressing reason than asserting his authority to send his sister home. There was no doubt that something was going on here, and apparently the danger was more than she had supposed. What would she have to do to persuade the brothers to let her lend a hand? And why on earth should she be so interested in becoming involved in what was, after all, not her business?

She could blame it on Gordon's kiss, but she had become much too involved even before that. She refused to think of Evan's ungentlemanly conduct, and she had no right to consider Gordon's attentions as anything more than a mild flirtation. Surely a London gentleman would have heard all the rumors about her mother and herself and would assiduously avoid her were he considering anything but a flirtation. So she couldn't take his attentions seriously.

Yet she shared the twins' concern over their sister's arrival. It was preposterous, of course, but she could not encourage what she knew would dismay the elder Griffins. She wasn't even certain if it was for Gordon's or Evan's sake that she was reluctant to press Miss Griffin to remain. It was confusing to the extreme.

That night, while Daphne debated the wisest course, she heard the sound of rapid hoofbeats on the road outside. Carrying a candle to the window, she wished she could see out, but the night was no more than a velvety darkness broken by an occasional gleam from window or lantern. The moon was in the wrong portion of the sky for her to even discern it.

But she could hear perfectly well over the nighttime silence. The hoofbeats thudded from the road onto thick turf, and now there seemed to be more than one set. Surely Evan wasn't chasing some poor victim across Aunt Agatha's property.

She caught herself, wondering why she would grace a common thief with the courtesy of a gentleman. That thought was interrupted by a violent explosion. Daphne jumped, startled, and tried once again to scan the night. A horse whinnied, and she thought she heard a man's curse. The heart-stopping noise sounded again, and this time she identified it clearly. A pistol!

This wouldn't do. This wouldn't do at all. Hastily, she sat down and tied on the slippers she had just discarded. Thank goodness she had not yet begun to undress. It would have been better if she had not given her maid the night off, but she could make do without her. She doubted if her aunt or the servants in the far side of the house had heard the noise, but perhaps someone was still up and about.

She slipped hurriedly down the stairs, wondering if she ought to rouse a groom or footman to accompany her since none seemed to be still awake. Not that she knew where she was going or what she was looking for, but she sensed something terrible was happening, and she had to find out what it was.

The house was dark. Everyone had retired long before her, when Aunt Agatha did, as was their custom. It didn't matter. She could find her way out without trouble. She had learned all the obstacles that might interfere with her progress and how to avoid them.

She slipped out the side door, which required only a turn of the key in the lock. Aunt Agatha's lax security could be found in every house in the shire. A true thief would have no trouble stealing a king's ransom in a few ambitious nights if he felt so inclined. That was one case in favor of the band in the woods. They couldn't be real thieves and ignore the wealth lying around to be had for the taking.

Outside, the night breeze tugged at her hair as Daphne hurried along the garden path she had learned by heart. She heard voices now, muffled and indistinct, but definitely more than one. She tugged her shawl more closely around the thin muslin of her gown and slowed her pace. She could do nothing against a band of men. What was happening out there?

She halted in the shadows of a tree and watched as a horse and rider emerged from the shrubbery to return to the road. Even in the darkness she could discern the glitter of steel and the blur of a red coat. Soldiers!

Heart in throat, Daphne watched as several more figures emerged on foot from behind the high hedgerows along the road. The man on horseback cursed at them, and gathering her courage, she crept closer. She had to know what had happened.

The men in the road wore uniforms, too, and she could hear one of them protesting, ''We shot at him, just as you said to! Henry and me both shot, but he kept on going, flying that great black beast over a wall it woulda taken wings to fly. If you'd a' let us use the rifles . . .''

''We don't want him dead, you bloody fools!''

Daphne recognized that commanding voice at once. Captain Rollings. It didn't take much of a stretch of the imagination to know what had happened here tonight. The soldiers had set another trap, and Evan had ridden right into it. They had shot at an unarmed man!

''We winged him, I know we did. I heard him curse as that beast of his got away. Want us to start beating the woods after him?''

''And have his gang come out and make fools of us all? You don't know these parts as they do. We've lost our chance to take him this night. Let's head back.''

Daphne trembled as the sound of voices trailed off down the road. Winged him? Did that mean what it sounded like? If he were wounded, would he head toward the Griffin estate and help? Or would he hide himself in the woods to prevent pursuit? Foolish question.

Agonizing inside, she picked her way back across the lawn. How could she possibly find him at night? The darkness pressed around her as it had that long-ago night, and it needed only the crack of thunder to bring her quivering to her knees. She might walk as far as the hedgerow dividing lawn from pasture and woods without harm, but beyond that, she would be at the mercy of the unknown.

Remembering the dance they had shared just the night before, Daphne felt tears prick at her eyes. Perhaps Evan Griffin was misguided and ill-humored and many other things, but he could be kind, too, and gentle. She wouldn't let him die in the woods. She had to get help for him, somehow.

Hurrying back inside, she picked up the candle she had left by the door and went in search of her aunt's medicine chest. She knew there were all kinds of salves and ointments in there, but she was too terrified of her own daring to stop and examine them. There were a few folded bandages, too, she remembered. Perhaps she ought to bring some old linen from the mending basket, just in case.

By the time she had filled a basket with all the supplies she could think of, the candle was ready to gutter out. She couldn't carry it outside, but perhaps a lantern . . . ? The soldiers had said they were going home. Would a lantern hurt? It would feel so much better out there if she could have some light. One day she might grow accustomed to these nighttime fears, but not just yet.

Deciding a lantern would be the most practical course, Daphne lit one she found in the kitchen, then set out for the woods. Her teeth chattered with fear, but she could not possibly return to her room and sleep and leave a man lying injured somewhere in those cold woods.

She tried desperately not to jar her weakened knee as she maneuvered gardens and pasture carefully. The shadowed outline of the trees ahead gave her direction and she concentrated on them and not the darkness around her. She could have no idea where to go once she got there, but she would think of something. If they were any kind of thieves at all, they would see her coming.

As it was, they did better than that. Before she was halfway across the field she met a shadow coming toward her. Not until he was practically in front of her could she discern the limp and know his identity. Breathing a sigh of relief, she waited for Rhys to catch up with her.

"I was coming for you, miss. It's not bad, but he needs looking after." Rhys glanced down at the basket on her arm, and then up to the remarkable woman holding it. She was no more than a slip of a girl, and the way she held her head, he knew she was terrified, but she had come blindly all this way without being asked. An emotion he had not felt in a very long time threatened to crack his composure, and he hastily reached for the basket. "Let me take this. Can you find your way back to the house safely?"

"You may carry the basket, but I'm coming with you. I'll be the judge of how bad it is. He's a stubborn man, and I daresay whatever your position is, it won't allow you to go against his orders. I have no such qualms."

The limp betrayed her as she stumbled over a grassy tussock. Rhys grimaced and hurried after her. He could have argued with her. He could have outrun her and left her to wander alone, but she had the right of it. Evan might not listen to anyone, but he couldn't keep Miss Templeton from acting as she saw fit. If a physician was required, she would be the one best able to arrange it.

Silently, Rhys took the lantern and closed it, then placed her hand on his arm for support over the rugged ground. "Lights attract too much attention, Miss Templeton. It will be safer this way."

They moved cautiously across the fallow field to the shadows of the trees. Daphne no longer shivered now that she knew what to expect. She didn't know why this Llewellyn person came to be here at this hour of the night instead of filling his post on the Griffin estate, but she wouldn't quibble with fate. She was grateful for his company.

A guard rose out of the bushes to intercept them, but recognizing Rhys, he stepped aside, and they went on, entering a small clearing. A fire had been built inside the entrance of a small cave where it couldn't easily be seen, and a lone figure lay propped in front of the flames, preventing more than a corona of light to escape. Daphne bit back a gasp of dismay at thus seeing last night's gallant gentleman once more reduced to a thief in the woods. She would never read another Robin Hood tale again. The romance did not erase the reality.

Evan glanced up and at the sight of his visitor, cursed and tried to scramble to his feet. Rhys hurried forward to hold him down.

"Deuce take it, man, I told you to sit still!"

The authoritative ring of the Welshman's voice caught Daphne by surprise, and she watched him with a new respect as he settled Evan back to the blankets. Cautiously, she approached bearing her basket.

"Are you out of your mind to bring her here? The place is probably crawling with soldiers. Get her out of here right now," Evan hissed, deliberately ignoring Daphne's presence.

"They've returned to town. It's much easier to drink a pint of ale and talk about the one who got away." Daphne moved into the circle of light and brushed Rhys aside as she lowered herself to the blanket to examine the hastily tied bandage on Evan's shoulder.

"Besides, she was already on the way out here when I found her. Should I have left her wandering about alone?"

"Damn it, yes!" Evan cursed as Daphne lifted the crude bandage. His gaze flickered over the pale oval of her face, the flash of her lovely eyes hidden behind long lashes as she pried the blood-caked rag from his shoulder. She was undoubtedly furious with him, but he read no disgust in her expression. With a groan, he surrendered and gestured for Rhys to bring the water heating over the fire to help her loosen the bandage.

"Why?" Evan demanded through clenched teeth as she pried at the last piece of thread, ripping it from the wound.

"So I could say I told you so," Daphne replied serenely. "Now all I have to do to tell you from your brother is punch your shoulder. The one who flinches will be you."

Rhys chuckled as he sifted through the basket of supplies. He held up one or two to the firelight and shook his head as he considered the odd assortment, wondering what they could do with sal volatile and rheumatics salve, but he held his tongue. The feverish light in Evan's eyes had very little to do with a rise in temperature as yet. It did him good to recognize his own mortality for a while.

"I didn't think you had much difficulty telling us apart in the first place," Evan muttered thickly as Daphne sponged the wound. The pain in his shoulder was as nothing to the pain in the rest of his body as her breasts brushed against his arm and her delightful scent filled his senses. At any other time had she dared to come this close he would have pulled her onto his lap and covered her with kisses. That behavior didn't seem particularly appropriate now. "Everyone else has confused us for years. We're experts at avoiding trouble because no one is ever willing to identify which of us was the culprit."

"I'm certain all they had to do was name you. Undoubtedly your parents could have taken it from there." Experienced at dealing with the injuries of her father's tenants for lack of anyone else to do so, Daphne knew enough to keep her patient talking to distract from the pain.

Evan winced as she probed the wound for damage, then grimaced at the knowing chuckle coming from the other side of the fire. "We're better than that. Gordon always insisted that he was the guilty party, and I always insisted he was innocent, until they never knew whom to believe. Perhaps their convictions were not so firm as yours," he added dryly.

"Perhaps they found it hard to believe that their sons would lie to them. I have no such misapprehension." Daphne accepted the jar of salve that Rhys handed to her. The bullet had evidently gone right through without damaging any bone, but the amount of blood he was losing was frightening. She worked hastily to stanch the flow. "You're both lying rogues and I shall wash my hands of you as soon as I figure out why you're playing the parts of utter idiots."

"Llewellyn, don't you have guard duty or a mare in foal or something?" Evan threw his friend's grinning features a look of irritation.

"You planning on taking the lady home yourself?" he inquired innocently.

"Insubordinate muddlehead," Evan muttered, throwing his head back against the wall and closing his eyes. Even not looking at her caused him pain. Her fingers were gentle against his skin, soothing wounds more raw than the one caused by a bullet. He clenched his teeth against the desire driving through him.

"Rhys, make certain I have missed nothing before I wrap

the bandage.'' Daphne spoke softly, thinking perhaps Evan had gone to sleep or slipped into unconsciousness.

Both men heard the faltering uncertainty in her voice and looked to each other in surprise. She may have spoken of cowardice upon occasion, but she had never evidenced it to their knowledge. Rhys sent her a puzzled glance and came over to inspect her work.

"It looks a fine job to me, lass. Let me hold the cloth while you wrap it.'' He pressed hard where she indicated, and Evan jerked at the pain.

They finished the work in silence, Daphne occasionally giving a glance to Evan's pale face. She could not read his expression, however, although this close, she could more clearly examine the angles and planes that had eluded her in the darkness. She ached to stroke the hollow of his cheek, but she kept her hands busy where they belonged.

When they were done, she glanced down at the torn and bloody shirt hanging from one elbow, concealing the masculine chest she so longed to lean upon. Her grimace caught Rhys's eye, and he hastened to assure her.

"I'll get him clean clothes in the morning. It's time I got you back to the house.''

Evan finally stirred himself to mutter, "And don't bring her back again. Daphne, get the hell back to London, now. And take Melanie with you.''

"When you see fit to explain why, I'll consider it,'' Daphne replied sweetly, rising from the blanket with the aid of Rhys's callused hand.

Evan glared at her, but Daphne refused to see his fury. Muttering another curse, he closed his eyes and let the pain in his shoulder mix with the pain of her departure into one swirling black maelstrom of guilt.

TEN

"Where on earth are you going at this hour of the morning?" Agatha looked up from the breakfast table with incredulity as her niece came into the room wearing an old brown pelisse and a sadly unfashionable bonnet.

"It's such a nice day, I thought I'd go for a bit of a walk." Daphne picked up a roll from the sideboard and contemplated the array of steaming hot dishes. The men in the woods would have nothing so delectable to eat, but she could not imagine how she would smuggle these out.

Since the day had looked gray and drizzly the last time Agatha had looked outside, she gave her niece a speculative stare. "You'd best have boots on," she admonished.

"Do you think Cook would mind terribly if I took some of these rolls and muffins? They smell frightfully delicious but I'm not hungry just yet. They'll taste good after I've walked a way."

Definitely suspicious now, Agatha tried to follow the convoluted byways of Daphne's mind. Undoubtedly there were poor families in the village who could use a good meal, but Daphne hadn't ordered the pony cart, and she doubted if her niece intended to walk all the way to the village in this mist. The possibility that she might actually eat all those things that were disappearing into the damask napkin was not even worth considering. Daphne ate little more than a bird at the best of times. This was most extraordinary behavior, but Agatha could not believe it was in any way dangerous.

She picked up her cup of tea and answered lightly, "Some of that fruit would be good for you, too. Why don't you make a basket and have a picnic of it?"

Daphne threw her aunt a surprised and grateful look. There wasn't any way she could read Agatha's thoughts, but her tone was that of understanding. Hurriedly, she did as told, gathering anything portable that she could find while keeping in mind that the servants would breakfast from this bounty, too. There looked to be plenty for all.

She wished she could bring something to guard against the damp, but there was little remedy for that. The house did not come provided with tents and oilcloths and any of the other things that men who live in the weather required. She ought to be angry with herself for bringing even the comfort of breakfast to men who chose to live by thievery. But she could not bring herself to acknowledge that Evan was actually a thief, and she was beginning to have her doubts about Mr. Llewellyn, too. Now that he was cleaned up and wearing proper clothes, he had almost an air of respectability to him.

She found a thin young man wrapped in rags waiting for her at the edge of the woods. He eyed the aromatic basket she carried hungrily but said not a word as he led her through the thicket of vines and rhododendrons to the concealment of the small cave on the riverbank. He disappeared quietly into the trees when Rhys hurried forward to take the basket from her hand.

"We'll eat like kings!" he announced happily as he examined the contents. "I haven't been able to get word to Lord Griffin yet, but you needn't risk doing this again. I don't doubt that he'll see Evan gets whatever he needs."

That answered a few of the questions in her mind, but not enough. "And the other men, will he provide for them?" she demanded.

"Of course, as best as he is able without arousing suspicion," Rhys soothed her.

As they approached the cave, Evan appeared to be asleep. His unshaven jaw was shadowed and pale in the gray light, and his golden brown hair fell in tousled clumps about his face, speaking of a restless night. He wore a clean shirt over the bulky bandage, and his frayed coat was thrown over his shoulders in protection against the damp mist. Daphne

frowned at the battered coat, but remembering the rags the
other men wore, she surmised the reason.

He opened his eyes as she sat on the blanket beside him,
and for a brief moment, she felt the power of his gaze. Then
he averted it to the wall above her head.

"There was no reason for you to come back. Rhys is well
experienced in tending the injuries of war."

"There is only one way you will be rid of me, you know,"
she said conversationally as she peeled back his shirt to
examine the bandage. "Have you eaten yet?"

"I'm not hungry."

Rhys came forward with a pot from the fire. "I've been
making some meat broth, but he refuses to eat. He'll need
it to get his strength back."

"Honestly, you're worse than a child." Daphne took the
napkin covering the basket and tucked it in at Evan's neck.
"If you don't eat, I'll take that basket of Cook's best rolls
back with me and your men will have none of them. Do you
wish to be responsible for a riot?"

Evan's glance returned to Daphne's fair face. How anyone
could look so helpless and sound so much like a drill sergeant,
he could not quite fathom. At the image of all that feminine
beauty ordering a battalion of men to step in line, he grinned.

"If I'm ever called to duty again, I'm taking you with me,"
he murmured.

Daphne cast him a worried look and glanced up to Rhys.
Was he fevered? She touched a cool hand to Evan's brow
and thought it might be a little warm, but not enough for
hallucinations. Grinning now, Rhys shrugged and walked
away with the basket, leaving Daphne to deal with their
recalcitrant patient alone.

"I'll not go," she announced defensively, just in case he
was speaking in riddles. "Now open up and have a bite of
broth."

"I can't bite broth," he replied irascibly. "Give me one
of those rolls."

"Rhys took them all away. You can't have any until you
eat your broth."

Evan glared at her, then appropriated the pot and defiantly sipped from its brim. Unperturbed, Daphne sat back and waited patiently for his temper to cool.

Managing more than enough of the foul brew, Evan set the pot aside and contemplated the stubborn female who had about as much regard for propriety as he did. The folds of the old pelisse disguised the slim curves he had held in his arms just a few nights ago, but the memory of them was still strong. Besides, she could be as bony as a rail and she would still fascinate him. He had never met a female who could be as blunt and direct as a man, and who didn't have the vapors or giggle when he displayed his errant humors. Apparently he had been looking in the wrong places for his match. He should have taken to holding up coaches long ago.

Remembering the sight of her in his brother's arms, Evan tried to shut out these thoughts. "I'm still alive, as you can see. There's no need for you to linger in this damp any longer. Your old war wound won't suffer it gladly," he said sardonically.

He was very likely right, but Daphne wasn't about to admit it. "And there's some need for you to stay here courting pneumonia? Would Gordon keep you from going home?"

Evan looked pained and leaned his head back against the cave wall. Drawing one knee up, he rested his uninjured arm over it and tried to sort out how much he could and couldn't reveal to this persistent female. Perhaps if he told her enough, she would go away and take Melanie with her.

"He's in enough danger without adding my presence. Can't you just take my word for it and get out of here before you are caught up in it too?"

"I don't doubt that you're in trouble up to your ears, but I cannot believe that courting pneumonia will solve it. I will need the whole story before I am convinced to leave you here." Daphne hid her shiver at her own temerity. The buckskin-clad knee just inches from her nose had much to do with that shiver. She had never been this close, this *intimate*, with any man. She could feel the warmth radiating from him, sensed the virile strength in the tension of that muscled leg, and wondered at her boldness in not removing herself at once. Instead, she wished to clasp those brown fingers in her own and feel their heat and strength and texture against her palm. She was quite simply losing her mind. This time, the thought did not startle or alarm her.

As if hearing her wishes, Evan lifted his long fingers to wrap a straying curl of her hair around them. His rough knuckles brushed against the velvet smoothness of her cheek, and he stared at her fascinated. What would it be like to feel those moist, full lips against his own? His body lurched in response, and he hastily diverted his thoughts.

"There is naught to tell that makes any sense." He stared at the wall but kept the silken strand of her hair wrapped in his hand. "My father was the heir to my grandfather's earldom. He had little interest in his inheritance, so Gordon took over his responsibilities at an early age, and I went off to make a profession of war. Besides my father and Gordon and myself, there were numerous other uncles and cousins who might inherit should we three give up the ghost, so no one was overly concerned with my dangerous choice of professions. Among ourselves, it was more or less expected that Gordon would marry and provide the next heir since the others were a rackety lot without a responsible bone in their bodies. Besides, Gordon has always had a way with the ladies, and it was to be expected that he would be married with children well before my father and grandfather stuck their spoons in the wall."

Daphne waited patiently through these family chronicles. The story was scarcely a new one. Born to wealth and aristocracy, most families bred few with the ambition or interest to perpetuate that status. It was much easier to fritter the money away than to earn it. Fortunately, every other generation of most families seemed to produce at least one heir serious enough to take care of the family fortunes. The others were generally content to live off his bounty. The Griffins didn't appear to be any different.

Not noticing her silence, Evan tried to find the right words for the rest of his tale. Idly, he pushed back Daphne's concealing bonnet so he could better see her face. Dew sparkled on her dark lashes and rose-tinted cheeks, and he rubbed his knuckles thoughtfully against her cheek again.

"My father died a year ago, when Wellington and Napoleon were decimating the Belgium countryside. I had no word of it until months later, when I lay seriously wounded in some desolate military hospital. I had responsibilities I couldn't desert, and the letter was so old that I thought there was no need to hurry. Gordon and Grandfather would be well in control of the situation. When the next letter finally found me, I was recovering and well enough to travel. It took time to sell out and arrange for what few of my men remained and to make the journey in midwinter."

Daphne wondered what the second letter said that had caused such haste when the first had not, but she daren't interrupt for fear he would suddenly close up on her again. Daringly, she rested her hand on the arm lying limply across his lap. She shouldn't have underestimated his strength despite his injury. He instantly turned his arm to grasp her hand.

"I didn't arrive until mid-February. I had notified no one of my arrival. It seemed the wisest course given the contents of Gordon's letter." He hesitated, watching Daphne's alert face with curiosity. "I really have no business telling you any of this. It's not a fair reflection on our family."

"I have met you and Gordon and Melanie, and I think I'm a fair judge of human nature. I'll not believe ill of you, and I'll not reveal your secrets without your permission."

He already knew the truth of that. He would not be lying here still were she one to tell all she knew. Resting easier, Evan resolved to tell her the whole miserable tale.

"Gordon's letter said there was some question as to whether my father's death was accidental. It had been assumed that he had taken a fall in a freak jumping accident, but later events called for further inquiries. The saddle had already been mended, but the groom who replaced the girth straps agreed there was some chance they might have been deliberately damaged. The saddle's slipping could have caused my father's fall."

Daphne's fingers curled tighter about Evan's as she stared at him in shock and disbelief. Things like that just didn't

happen except in the worst sort of novels. The strap had undoubtedly been flawed, but what did any of this have to do
with Evan's sleeping in the woods?

"What were the events that made Gordon go back and look
at the saddle?" she asked cautiously, not wanting to voice
her doubts just yet.

Evan sighed and tried to arrange his aching shoulder more
comfortably against the wall. Daphne moved as if to help
him, but he kept a firm hold of her hand. "He found is own
saddle cut, a stray shot while hunting nearly took his life,
the axle of his phaeton came loose—a number of suspicious
accidents occurred. Gordon isn't given to flights of fancy,
as you can imagine, but he was quite certain someone meant
to kill him."

Daphne drew in a breath at the certainty in his tone. That
wasn't really possible. People didn't do that in this day and
age. This was positively medieval. "Why?" she finally
asked. "Why would anyone suddenly decide to do away with
your family? You said yourself there were none other
interested in the estates but Gordon."

"They might not be interested in the responsibilities
entailed by the estates, but in the money they represent.
Haven't I said enough to show you there is danger here? Will
you take Melanie and leave now? Dream up an excursion
to Bath or to visit relatives in the north or anything but linger
here. I have my hands full looking after Gordon. I cannot
watch more of you."

Daphne was still working her way through the pieces of
the puzzle. "When you came home they shot at you too?
Is that why your horse went into the river?"

"Yes," Evan said curtly. "Only I daresay they thought
I was Gordon. I was supposed to be dead on the Continent
since no one had heard from me."

"So you couldn't go home or the murderer would have
two of you to kill. That's gruesome. I cannot imagine it. Does
your grandfather know of this?"

Impatiently, he replied, "My grandfather is not well. We'll
not add to his worries. Obviously, whoever is behind this
thinks Grandfather will not live long, and if he should die

for a book. She would find the book and he could go to the devil.

He had danced her to the far end of the room, and the unfamiliar territory combined with the dusky light suddenly heightened her fears. In her haste to escape, she tripped over a knee-high stepladder, tried to catch herself on what turned out to be a spinning globe, and would have fallen had her nemesis not cursed and come out of the shadows to catch her.

"Why in hell don't you behave like a cripple so a person knows the difference?" Evan caught her by the waist and held her steady. The scent of her light perfume wafted around him, filling his senses and making him incapable of doing more. He remembered clearly her reference to an "old war wound"—indeed, he remembered clearly everything she had ever said—but he had never thought of her as imperfect. And still didn't, he realized, as he pulled closer.

Angry at herself, angry at him, Daphne tried to jerk away, but he wouldn't let her go that easily. "I'm not a cripple," she replied testily. "Do you wish me to sit in a corner and whine and demand that I be waited upon hand and foot?"

"Not any more than I expect Rhys to do the same. What in heaven's name persuaded you to find him employment?"

"I should have known he was a friend of yours." Finally shaking loose of his hold, Daphne reoriented herself. Finding the library table, she started in that direction, still shaken by the encounter. Odd, but it was no longer the dark she feared.

"More than a friend, but that is beside the point. He was a complete stranger of the most disreputable kind to you. Whatever possessed you even to speak to him? Do you do that kind of thing often?"

"What business is it of yours?" She swept her hand along the table, looking for the solidness of a book.

"I'm making it my business." Evan stepped forward and watched her quizzically. "What in the deuce are you looking for?"

Exasperated, Daphne straightened and glared at him. "Your language, sir, is abominable. If you cannot keep a first, there might be a mad scramble for the inheritance. Gordon could rush out and marry, or I might have left a wife and child on the Continent, or some such flummery. Twisted minds might think like that. But if we're out of the way, then the title goes back to Grandfather's next direct descendant. I've told you more than enough, Daphne, it is time you promised to leave.''

''Why should I be in any danger? I am not related to any of you. I can see that Melanie might be harmed in any incident that involved Gordon since the two of them will undoubtedly be much together, but I should think I would be able to help you without anyone suspecting otherwise.''

Thoroughly exasperated, Evan tugged on her hand and brought her to sit closer, where she could not avoid his eyes. ''Daphne, you cannot be so maggot-brained as that. If even I have seen you and Gordon together, surely you must realize that the entire area is aware of your attachment. This is the worst possible time for Gordon to finally settle on a suitable wife. It will make our killer frantic to be rid of both of you before there is still another heir to stand in his way.''

Daphne stared at him in disbelief. ''You are quite mad, Evan Griffin. There is nothing between us. How can there be? Any sensible person can see that. How can you conceive of such a fanciful notion?''

Evan's mouth twisted in a wry grimace as he watched her lovely face framed by a cap of silken brown curls. There didn't seem to be a duplicitous thought in her head, but females always knew these things. She couldn't be totally blind. ''I saw him kiss you, Daphne. If he didn't declare himself then, he certainly should have. It is only this confounded masquerade that prevents him from doing so, I'm certain.''

''That is absurd.'' Daphne tugged to free her hand and rise from his dangerous proximity. His grip was stronger than she expected. ''It is just the mildest sort of flirtation that you have seen. I am certain Gordon is quite bored out here and he looks for a little amusement. I am old enough that he need not be worried that I'll take offense or that he will engage my affection. There is nothing at all between us. Anyone can see that it would be quite absurd for him to fix his interest on a female who rumor has it has not the wits or sense to see if her gown is buttoned correctly.''

That startling statement brought Evan's fascinated gaze in the direction of her bodice, but the pelisse adequately disguised any errors in fastening. Mischief combined with desire as his hand slid from Daphne's cheek to wrap around her waist. It was not fever that smoldered in his eyes as he drew her cloer.

''Just a flirtation?'' he murmured deep in his throat as her wide-eyed gaze came closer. ''Perhaps I have forgotten how to flirt. Refresh my memory.''

She could not tear away. It wasn't just that his hold was strong as he pulled her forward, but a fascination with the sight and sound and smell of him that she could not resist. Beneath the linen of his shirt, his chest was warm and hard where she braced herself against him. His cheeks smelled of whatever soap he had used for shaving that morning, and his hair held the fresh scent of rain as she leaned forward to touch her lips to his.

She could not protest that he forced her. She was a willing victim. She wanted the sensation of his lips on hers, craved the closeness of his kiss, needed the searing surrender of being taken in his arms. What she hadn't expected was this, the savage passion of a hungry man, the flood of desire and heat that swept between them so completely that she could only bend to his will as Evan crushed her against him and parted her lips.

Daphne's head swam with the discovery of his possession. She could not brace herself above him anymore but fell before his persuasive and passionate grip, curling against his chest and giving herself up to his hungry demands. A kiss should never be like this, some disconnected part of her brain warned, but she could not respond to the warning while he held her like this, while she could feel the pounding of his heart beneath her hands and the fire of his mouth on hers. Her hand slid to his neck, and she parted her lips willingly.

It was only when Evan used his injured arm to begin searching the enveloping folds of her pelisse that Daphne realized how far she had gone. With dazed shock, she pushed away, searching the familiar angles of his face for some clue as to his intentions. He let her go without protest, and she could read nothing into his silence.

"That is not how a gentleman treats a lady," she murmured, sitting up and trying to adjust her dignity.

"That is how a man treats a woman," he said without an ounce of regret as he watched her flushed face and nervous gestures. He had nothing to offer her. At that moment, he was a wanted criminal with soldiers seeking him. At best, he had no title and a small trust to support him now that he had resigned his military career. She belonged with Gordon, but she seemed to be singularly blind to her attractiveness. What was that comment about her wits? Perhaps now she would realize what a man's kiss meant. Pity Gordon was too damned polite to teach her.

Daphne backed out of reach of his dangerous arms. The fatalistic tone of Evan's voice warned that he could be expected to treat her like so again if she did not stay away. Yet how could she stay away? Her mouth burned where his had touched her, and her body seemed to tingle with the unexplored sensations he had taught her. She was in sad danger to linger in his company. Her reputation would be damaged for all time should word of her presence here get about. But she could not find it in her to leave.

"A very simple lesson, thank you," she replied acerbically. "I shall remember it in the future, but it does not change the present. I am no more likely to marry Viscount Griffin than his Robin Hood brother. I am destined to be a spinster, so leave me to enjoy my few pleasures while I can. And I can assure you, they are not to be found in London."

Evan ran his hand through his rumpled hair and glared at her. "You promised to leave when I told you our reasons."

"I did no such thing. I only said I would consider it. Besides, it seems to me you have left out the most important part. Whom do you suspect to be the guilty party and how do you intend to stop him?"

ELEVEN

"**D**aphne, had I full use of both hands, I would wring your neck." Evan reached for the pot of broth as the only available substitute for placing his hands on her delectable throat.

"I see his mood hasn't changed for the better." Rhys stomped cheerfully through the bushes like some modern-day Red Riding Hood, carrying Daphne's basket on his arm, now nearly empty of its contents. "You're supposed to sweeten his disposition, my lady, not sour it."

"One can sweeten lemonade, but not bad apples," she retorted. "I don't suppose you would care to explain how he means to help his brother by skulking in the woods and courting pneumonia?"

"Certainly. He doesn't believe his uncle will do the dirty deed himself but will hire someone. He rather thought to set himself up as evil respresentative for hire. Any other questions?"

Rhys had lost any trace of his uneducated accent and respectful behavior. Daphne stared at him in as much perplexity as dismay. The plan he recited sounded far-fetched to her, but she could not think of a better one. She turned to Evan to see if he would offer further explanation.

"Uncle? So you know who it is?"

"I didn't say that. Mackle-mouth did. Now it's time you left. Your aunt will be looking for you, and your suitors will be camped at your door."

His sarcasm fell on deaf ears. Now that she had almost reached the root of the plot, Daphne began to feel the excitement of the chase. No one had ever let her become involved in anything more complex than charades. She had always been left out of the planning and doing and had only been allowed to be listener to cries of triumph or throes of despair after the fact. Now she was almost as much a part of the plot as everyone else, and she refused to be cast aside like a helpless infant. Her brain worked feverishly to find her advantage.

She had already gone over the circle of her London acquaintance trying to place the name of Griffin to anyone she might know. It was not that common a name. She was quite certain she had never been introduced to either of the twins or Melanie, but she did remember her brother's mentioning an unusual acquaintance of his who had that name. She thought the man was considerably older than her brother, and since Michael was so much older than she, Daphne had dismissed the man from her mind. But if it were an uncle whom Evan sought . . . Something of the older Griffin's reputation came back to her, and she threw his name out just for a reaction.

"Is Robert Griffin one of your relatives?" she inquired innocently without rising as ordered.

Evan's face went blank, and Rhys whistled a single note behind her. Daphne felt satisfaction as she sensed the sudden tension around her.

"How do you know Robert?" Evan demanded harshly.

"He's an acquaintance of my brother's. They belong to the same club, I believe, though Michael isn't in London much anymore. I take it he is one of your relatives, then? Michael is a good deal older than I am, and this Robert is older than he. I'd judge him at about forty or so, old enough to be an uncle, I should think."

Evan ran his hand over his face. "I had forgotten how small a circle the *ton* is. Should I know your brother? I didn't even know you had one."

"He is not of the Corinthian set. We're of very modest means, after all, but he went to Oxford. I daresay you were at different levels, though. Michael is some years older than you."

"I am rapidly catching up with him, though." Evan stifled a moan and shifted his shoulder. He refused to think about this connection. His only goal right now was to get Daphne out of here. It was becoming obvious that that wouldn't be an easy task.

Rhys didn't have the same compunctions. He gazed on Daphne with a delighted smile and handed Evan a roll to keep him quiet. "So your brother knows Robert? How very interesting. We need to draw the cad out, prove his intentions, but he hasn't been on speaking terms with the rest of the family since the earl refused to pay any more of his debts. He couldn't show his face around here without rousing suspicion."

He drifted into thought which Evan rudely interrupted. "Whatever you're thinking, Llewellyn, don't. I'll not have Daphne involved any more than she is. Get her out of here, preferably to the other end of the country."

Rhys beamed. "And if I could do both?"

"You'd be a magician. What do you mean, 'both'?" Evan crumbled his roll and watched his friend with suspicion.

"Bring Robert out of the woodwork and get Daphne out of here. Wouldn't that work?"

"What would work?" Easing her aching knee, Daphne sat herself more comfortably on Evan's blanket and watched Rhys with doubt. She didn't want to be sent away, but if it would help resolve this mystery, she was willing to listen.

"Using you to draw Robert out and sending you away so you don't become involved when we expose him. Come on, Evan, you know this is better than sitting here waiting for something to happen." Rhys nudged Evan's leg with his wooden stump.

"I know no such thing. You've become the rogue you mock, Llewellyn, to even consider involving a lady in this," Evan growled, no longer looking at the slight female at his side. He wouldn't involve her. He couldn't.

"Well, then, we shall go to Gordon and see if he isn't more reasonable," Daphne said intractably. "I'm certain he will see the advantage in bringing you out of here as swiftly as possible."

She made as if to rise, but a hard hand reached out to grab

her arm and jerk her back. Evan glared at her. "Don't you
think he has enough on his mind without adding this mad
scheme to it?"

"You don't even know the scheme yet, Griffin. Don't go
up in the boughs until you've heard it out. We can be all
that is discreet and send Miss Templeton and Miss Griffin
away and corner the fox without any interference, providing
we have the assistance of Mr. Templeton. And since it would
be a rather unwitting assistance, I shouldn't think that would
be denied."

Even Evan became curious, and with a sigh of defeat, he
signaled for Rhys to continue.

Rhys took that as a signal to make himself comfortable,
also. Sliding down the cave wall, he sat cross-legged before
them like some pagan story-teller. "Miss Templeton will
write to her brother with private word of her betrothal to
Lord Griffin. In the letter, she can explain there has been
a bitter estrangement between the family and Robert, and
she would like to bring peace to the family again. She can
ask him to make the announcement of her marriage to Robert
privately, before the public announcement, and see if he is
willing to accept offers of amity."

Rhys ignored Evan's angry grumble and continued
inventing his plan out loud. "Of course, by the time her
brother receives the letter, Miss Templeton and Miss Griffin
will have gone to Bath or somewhere. Miss Templeton, is
your brother likely to act upon your request with any
alacrity?"

"To see me married to a viscount? Do you have to ask?"
Daphne answered wryly.

Rhys grinned. "Loving families are all alike. Will you do
it?"

"How are you going to explain to her brother if Daphne
doesn't marry Gordon?" Evan asked irritably.

"There is some doubt that she won't?" Rhys raised a
sarcastic eyebrow. "We'll cross that bridge when we come
to it. The main concern is to give Robert an excuse to appear
here in person. He'll have to, if our theory is correct. He
can't risk this marriage happening."

"But how will you stop him from hurting Gordon?" Daphne could follow the plan well enough to that point, but she couldn't see how a ragtag band of thieves in the woods could protect a viscount in his mansion.

"We know his ways, Miss Templeton. You are not to worry about that. It is just for you to agree with the rest of it. Is there somewhere you can go and take Miss Griffin while we straighten this out?"

Evan didn't even have to look at Daphne to know the signs of rebellion flashing in those glorious eyes. He caught her hand and squeezed it, causing her to turn that glare on him. "That's the only way I'll consent to this charade. Otherwise, I shall sit here and rot until Robert finds another scheme, and Gordon can turn gray with worry waiting to see where the next attack will come from."

"That's unfair," Daphne muttered bitterly. "It is little more than blackmail, Evan Griffin."

"You would do the same in my place," he replied unrepentantly. "Do you mind deceiving your brother just a little while, if deceit it is?"

"I do not want Gordon placed in a position where he feels obligated to marry should Michael and my father appear on his doorstep, which they are very likely to do. Perhaps I could just hint at the possibility of marriage in my letter, and indicate that reconciling the family would convince your grandfather of my suitability."

Rhys grinned, and Evan gave her an admiring look. "Very clever," Evan admitted. "But I expect Gordon won't appreciate the finesse. Never mind that. Will you do it? And will you take Melanie with you when you leave?"

Daphne sighed and sat back in resignation. "It seems a very poor thing to do under the circumstances, but I suppose I am not precisely the swashbuckling type. I have an aunt in Bath at this time of year. Who is to explain all of this to Melanie and Gordon?"

"Miss Griffin needn't know," Rhys hastily intervened. "I'll make it understood to his lordship so when you extend the invitation, he makes certain his sister agrees. How soon can you write your letters?"

They both waited on her anxiously. Oblivious to their stares, Daphne shrugged. "I shall do it tonight. I have always wondered what it might feel like to be a fiction writer."

They looked relieved, but Evan's voice revealed its concern as he reminded her, "No one must know of these plans. Robert is quite likely to have spies in every household."

Daphne looked startled at the thought. "Spies? How perfectly horrible. He cannot be in complete need of money if he can go to that much trouble."

"Little do you know the workings of the moneylenders, then. Before we trample your innocence any further, you had best leave to compose that letter. Then start packing your bag and saying your farewells. I want you out of here as soon as the letter is posted."

Daphne rose reluctantly, brushing her skirts and wishing for some means of delay. She felt more comfortable in these woods with these outlandish men than she ever had in the houses of society. And she had just agreed to leave them to some deadly danger she could not even envision.

"I cannot be so forward as that. Aunt Agatha would question such speed and think she has offended me in some way. And there would certainly be gossip over such impetuousness. Gordon will have to visit my aunt and ask if I will accompany Melanie to Bath. If he says she is not feeling well, that will give us excuse for some haste. If we say the journey will be only a brief one, it would require only the packing of a trunk or two. More than that, and the house will be in an uproar of washing and ironing and sorting and folding and it would be a week before we could get away."

With a despairing curse, Evan eased himself upright until he towered over her again. There was not an ounce of fear in her eyes as she gazed up to his undoubtedly disreputable visage. Had she been any other female, he would have terrified her into departing simply by his glare. He had caused field-hardened artillery men to shake in their boots when he turned his glare on them. Daphne Templeton merely stood

there with moist lips partially open, tempting his kiss all over
again.

His stifled groan had nothing to do with the pain in his
shoulder, and Evan grabbed her hand as she reached to
comfort him. "Go, at once. Buy a new wardrobe in Bath.
Invent ailing relatives. Do anything, but get yourself out of
here," he commanded harshly.

She couldn't read the anguish in his eyes, but she heard
the anger in his voice. Shoulders stiffening, she nodded
curtly. "Of course. Who am I to intrude where I am not
wanted?"

As she marched away and a slight youth ran to guide her,
Rhys sent his friend a speculative look. To his surprise,
Evan's shoulders were shaking with what very much
appeared to be mirth. Rhys felt anger rising at this disrespectful treatment of Daphne's obvious pain, and he
clambered to his feet to confront his arrogant companion.

"How could you, you bastard? Just look at her! She's
offered to place her life and reputation on the front line for
you, and you . . . you impudent jackass, you laugh!"

Evan wrapped his arms protectively around his chest as
the spasms of increased laughter sent shards of pain through
his torn shoulder. He shook his head as he gasped, "Not
intrude, she says!" He wiped a tear from his eye with the
back of his hand and let the memory of her proud stance ease
the anguish ripping through him. "Not intrude where she
isn't wanted! Bigad, I have never met a more contrary woman
in all my life."

Rhys shot him a skeptical look, then glanced back to where
Daphne had disappeared into the trees. However she had
done it, she had turned his cynical, battle-hardened officer
into a laughing, crying human being again. Perhaps it was
fairy dust. Mayhap if he ever got out of these woods again,
he would re-read his Shakespeare. He remembered a scene
in *Midsummer Night's Dream* . . .

Rhys shook his head. Evan might be a jackass, but he was
no dunce. Things would start happening now.

* * *

The rain began in earnest before Daphne returned to the house. Her aunt and maid scolded and ordered her to bathe and change before she could even begin the arduous task of composing the letter. As she soaked in the warm water, she realized she really would have to show the letter to Gordon before she posted it. It was very well and good to plan these things, but the carrying out of such wild schemes entailed a good deal more detail. She couldn't embroil Gordon without knowing for certain that he approved.

Since speed was obviously of the essence, she hurriedly dried herself and dressed in the gown the maid held out for her. Then, left blessedly alone at last, she took up pen and paper and contemplated the words she could use to deceive her brother.

Michael would be in London by now. He had written he would be joining her there, but she had left before he could arrive. She hadn't wanted to hear any more sermons about her unfilial behavior. The difference in their ages had kept them from ever being close, but she was conscious of all his superior qualities. He had always been all that was respectful, proper, and dutiful, while she had always been rebellious, proud, and cynical to a fault. She didn't need her flaws thrown in sharp relief by his proximity.

But Michael's flawless character would undoubtedly lead him to rush to carry out her request, out of pity if nothing else. To find a husband for his invalid sister had been his intent when he had agreed to help Daphne escape to London. If he thought she had enticed some obscure country nobleman into marriage, he would dance to her tune, then rush to investigate her prospective bridegroom. She could imagine him thinking she had fallen for some rogue who would steal her money and leave her cold. Perhaps by praising Gordon's virtues she could stave off any such precipitous journey.

In any event, the laborious task of forcing her pen across paper limited her praises to her usual terse minimum. Besides, Gordon would have to be shown the letter, and she could not embarrass him with more. The request to talk to Robert she left to the very end, so Michael would remember it. It was difficult to convey her urgency, but just the fact that she had actually written should startle her brother into action.

By the time she had sanded the final version, the rain had momentarily returned to mist. With resolution, she sought out her aunt and requested the carriage, ostensibly to visit Melanie.

Melanie greeted her with open arms. The tedium of idling away a rainy day in the country loosed her already fluent tongue, and Daphne soon began to wonder if she would ever find the opportunity to speak to the viscount, let alone see him privately.

Gordon solved the dilemma for her. Coming from his office to discover Daphne's visit, he sent Melanie in search of his new volume of Scott, then hands in pockets, he turned to face the tense lady nervously clasping her reticule.

"I have just spoken with Rhys, Daphne. He tells me you know all. I cannot approve, but I thank you for coming to Evan's aid. He has never been one to sit still and wait for events to happen. I fear this masquerade of his is his most deadly escapade of all. I cannot wish you involved in it."

Daphne relaxed under his soothing tones. Evan always succeeded in making her angry and eager to throw things. Gordon was just the opposite. She smiled with relief and reassured him. "I cannot think I am involved enough. While he lies injured in the misery of this rain, I can do little. I am willing to do whatever it takes to restore him to his home. Did he tell you of the letter?"

Gordon came to sit beside her and take her hand. "Even the letter is asking much of you. I cannot feel it right to deceive your brother and compromise your reputation. If there were any hope . . . Could you ever think of me as . . ."

Hearing the sound of Melanie's laughter floating down the hall, Daphne hastily retrieved her hand and produced the letter. "It is only a very small deceit. Please look at it, if you will." She hesitated, biting her lower lip before adding, "Perhaps you will recognize the address. My mother . . ."
She had to say it before Gordon could embarrass himself by making any sort of declaration. She did not know how much Gordon knew of her history, but she could not have him

offering for her out of obligation. She tried to make herself clear, ''Please, forgive me for deceiving you, but I . . .''

Gordon took her hand again and squeezed it, rising as he, too, heard the sound of his sister approaching. ''I am well aware of your difficulty, Daphne, and it does not deter me in the least. Unfortunately, Melanie does. We will speak again soon.''

He looked up and greeted his sister with a smile, with the letter now safely concealed in his coat pocket.

All the way home, Daphne played and replayed his words. ''Aware of your difficulty?'' could mean anything. ''Could you ever think of me as . . .'' What? Brother? Friend? Did she dare think: lover, husband? It was too preposterous. He couldn't mean that. She daren't believe it, or even think it. Not after all these years to prove her unsuitable. Not after a few weeks of acquaintance. It was only wishful thinking.

Sighing, she sat back against the squabs and watched the rain rolling down the pane of glass. Somewhere out there a man very similar to the one she had just left sat in a miserable cave with his shoulder swathed in bandages staring at this same rain.

Why was it Evan she thought of as Gordon's words of hope rang in her ears?

TWELVE

The rain poured steadily throughout the night, and Daphne began to glance worriedly to the road every time she passed a window the next morning. Aunt Agatha's front drive had turned to a muddy river. What could the lane at the bottom of the hill look like? And how high had the river risen during the night?

Perhaps the letter hadn't gone out in last night's post. Gordon might have decided against mailing it. Or the weather could have been so bad he hesitated sending anyone out in it. But remembering Rhys working in the stables, Daphne felt inclined to believe otherwise. Rhys would have gone looking for Gordon and the letter as soon as she had left.

So haste was of the utmost importance, but she could do nothing until Gordon arrived to ask Aunt Agatha for permission for her to accompany Melanie to Bath. And looking at those roads, she doubted even Gordon's expensive steed could wade through the muck.

The rain poured in torrents throughout the day, making it impossible for anyone to come or go. Daphne thought of Evan and his men shivering in the woods and prayed they had the good sense to retreat to someone's barn.

The knowledge that no one else could travel in the downpour reassured her. There would be plenty of time. Even if the mail coach made it to London in a day, which was very unlikely despite their speed, no one could come from the city while it rained so heavily.

Gordon arrived in a break of the storm the next day. Agatha exclaimed at his daring to brave the roads, but he modestly claimed that he had taken the fields quite safely.

There was no polite way he could send his hostess to another room as he had his sister, and he sent Daphne an

imploring look over her aunt's head. Overly conscious of
the proprieties under the circumstances, Daphne could think
of no means to ask for privacy. A walk in the gardens was
out of the question in this mud. Perhaps it was better this
way. She really must think of putting an end to Evan's
dangerous masquerade before even considering Gordon's
courtship, if courtship it were.

She made a gesture of futility and, resigned, Gordon spun
his tale of Melanie's desire to go to Bath. As Daphne had
known she would, Agatha left the decision up to her. The
arrangements were quickly made, with only the date of
departure left uncertain. The rains made travel too dangerous
in Agatha's opinion, and she insisted that they wait until the
roads were clear.

Hearing the muted torment behind Gordon's agreement
to this delay, Daphne surmised the letter had already gone
out. A bit of fear lodged in her middle and twisted, but she
refused to acknowledge it. It would take time for the letter
to reach London. Michael might have already left. Even if
he had not, it would take time for him to call on Robert
Griffin, time for Robert to act on it, time for anyone to travel
all the way to Devon. They would be well on their way by
then.

She walked with Gordon to the door, but a servant waited
with his hat and gloves and they still could not exchange
private words. Gordon squeezed her fingers as he bent over
her hand.

"Persuade her soon, Daphne. I cannot like this delay,"
he murmured in farewell.

"Have Melanie begin packing. Surely the rain cannot be
so bad elsewhere."

Gordon's smile was stiff as he gazed down on her slight,
brave figure. "I am going to write my grandfather. I daren't
take any more chances now that you are involved."

Daphne looked mildly alarmed. "If he is ill . . ."

Gordon brushed the objection aside. "I'll not tell all, only
just enough to see you safe. The terms I shall use will make
him quite happy."

Unable to say more within hearing of the footman, Gordon

bowed and went out, leaving Daphne to stare, wonderingly, after him. What could he possibly say of this hideous affair that would make the earl happy?

Captain Rollings lifted his mug of ale and sipped it as he stood in the tavern's front window and gloomily stared out at the mud-filled streets. The rain had let up enough to ease the steady river of water that had flowed earlier, but not enough to carry out his duties with any hope of success. He damned the weather and the stupidity of his troop and wondered how a highwayman spent his days in weather like this, particularly an injured highwayman.

His eyes narrowed thoughtfully as he considered how best to use the information he had purchased from the inn's stable boy. It didn't seem very reliable. He could not imagine a man like the Viscount Griffin being involved in the petty larceny of a highway robber, but there could be another story behind the tale. As much as he would like to believe it of the viscount, it was more likely the viscount's servants who were the guilty parties. The estate had been long neglected before this summer, he understood. Mayhap the servants meant to make up the sums the viscount's arrival had deprived them of from petty theft from the estate.

It was time to set his trap and put an end to it. The letter received from his superior officer showed his growing impatience with the delay. His failure at both his schemes would bring an end to life as he knew it, and he was not yet ready to give up all his hopes. Gazing up the street to the hedge concealing the squire's house from the village, Rollings drained his mug. It was early yet. Now that the rain had stopped, he could pay a brief afternoon call.

Just as he called for his bill, a mud-splattered barouche rolled grandly through the village street. Rollings stared at the gilded lanterns, the haughty, liveried servants, and the high-stepping horses, then fastened his gaze on the crest embossed on a once-gleaming ebony door and cursed. Beneath the filth of travel he could just discern the crest of the house of Griffin, the Earl of Shelce.

* * *

Daphne listened in dismay as Agatha read aloud the hasty invitation. Had Gordon taken leave of his senses? After three solid days of rain, the roads were only just now starting to dry. She had hoped the message would say the carriage would be at the door in the morning to take them to Bath. An invitation to dinner to meet the newly arrived earl was not at all what she had expected.

She had thought Gordon's grandfather an ill old man. What was he doing traveling in this kind of weather, if so? What had Gordon put in that letter to bring him out with such haste? She didn't want to know.

Her thoughts turned instantly to the man in the woods. The *men* in the woods, she quickly amended. She had not dared venture from the house again to see to their welfare. What would Evan think of this new development? She had a sinking feeling that he wouldn't be at all pleased by the news of the earl's arrival. That meant one more person to be endangered in the vicinity.

She would have to go. Perhaps she could determine the earl's reason for being here and convey the information to Evan so he wouldn't worry. The fact that Rhys was much better placed to do so completely escaped her. The need to see how Evan fared was greater than logic.

So she garbed herself carefully that evening in a lilac jaconet that ended in a small ruffled train. The slightly daring bodice had matching ruffles on the tiny sleeve but no other adornment. Daphne wondered if she should have chosen something more elaborate, but she disliked frills and cared nothing for delicate embroidery, so she limited her wardrobe to styles she could appreciate. She had no idea that the elegant lines and fabrics she chose could be appreciated even at a distance, making her entrance into any room a very effective one.

The effect came into play as Daphne entered the viscount's salon that evening slightly ahead of her aunt, who was still busily disposing of her various articles of travel. While servants gathered up cloaks and bonnets and veils and umbrellas behind her, Daphne drifted to the entrance and hesitated, trying to form a picture of the room and its inhabitants.

As she lingered there, her slender figure swaying like a lilac in a spring breeze, the eyes of several of the male inhabitants of the room were drawn to her. Daphne recognized Gordon first as he hurried toward her, and gratefully, she held out her hand to him, accepting his gentle guidance, keeping her knee stiff enough to bear her weight without limping. Perhaps Gordon had meant to say he knew of her infirmity—that was something Evan could have told him. Surely he could not know of her mother and still dance attendance on her as if she were an eligible *partie*.

"I was afraid you wouldn't come," he whispered as he led her toward the far end of the stately room where the earl held court. "I couldn't warn you. Please do not act surprised by anything my grandfather says. We will straighten this all out later. For now, your protection was most important."

This whispered warning served to terrify Daphne. Gordon wasn't inclined to impetuous acts and daring lies like Evan. What could he possibly have done to speak to her so? She glanced hesitantly up to his square jaw, wishing she could trust him. What if this were really Evan and not Gordon? A smile curved her lips as she realized she need only punch his shoulder for proof. Wouldn't that incite a little excitement for the evening?

The smile acted as buffer as she was introduced to the tall, distinguished, gray-haired gentleman sipping port by the mantel. He immediately set his glass aside to take her hand and look her over thoroughly. Daphne felt as if she were a horse at market, but she bore his scrutiny gracefully.

"So this is the one you would wed, eh?" The earl sent his heir a sharp look. The two were much of a height, and they understood each other very well. When Gordon didn't quite meet his eye but looked instead to Daphne by his side, the earl snorted and returned his gaze to her. "Templeton? Some relation to Lord Templeton of Northampton?"

"My grandfather, sir." Daphne's fingers continued to cling to Gordon's coat. Wed? What had he done? She tried not to stare as she gazed up to the earl. What could the man be thinking at news that his heir meant to marry a distant relation of a very minor title? Or did he recognize the name from the infamous tales of her mother?

"Ahhhh, yes, of course." The earl nodded his head and apparently traced her family tree through the Debrett's of his mind, but his face never revealed his thoughts. "Where is your father? Is he here now?"

"No, my lord, he is at home. I reside with his sister, my Aunt Agatha. Are you acquainted?" Daphne asked this nervously. It was one thing to suddenly discover you're about to be married without knowing of it, but to have the news announced to a family not previously forewarned brought staggering visions of hysterics and congratulations and a trap never to be escaped.

Gordon hastily intervened to reassure. "Not a word, sir. I have promised Daphne. I have told you, the roads have been such that I could not ride out to ask Mr. Templeton's permission. You have been very precipitate in coming here before I could arrange the formalities."

Instead of reproving his heir for this disrespectful rebuke, the earl barked with laughter and raised his head to watch Agatha approach. "My spoon's not in the well yet, you young pup. I'll not have any more of this havey-cavey nonsense out of you. I'll be at the bottom of it soon, no doubt." Without disturbing a note of his voice, he made an elegant leg as Agatha came up beside her niece. "Ahh, my good lady, we meet again."

Daphne felt as if she had just been run through a thresher. Distinguished earls of her grandfather's age or older weren't supposed to speak common cant and hint that their heirs weren't to be trusted, particularly when their heirs were someone as proper and staid as Gordon. Then to start a flirtation with a lady obviously twenty years his junior and well into her dotage, also—well, that was beyond the bounds of any behavior she knew.

With relief, she felt Gordon lead her away as her aunt and the earl engaged in the animated conversation about a garden party that had obviously taken place in the last century. This really could not be happening. She would wake up and find it all a dream soon. She had meant to retire to a quiet life in the country, bury herself in the wilderness of the moors. How was it that she now found herself temporarily affianced to a viscount and conversing in the same circles as earls? Not to mention hob-nobbing with thieves and plotting against murderers.

Gordon felt a twinge of sympathy at Daphne's dazed expression, but he had other guests and could not neglect them long. Covering the hand she kept trustingly on his arm, he said reassuringly, "It will be fine. My grandfather can be very discreet, if somewhat disconcerting. He only wished to meet you to be certain I am not about to do something remarkably out of line. I am certain he will be gone shortly. I have explained that you and Melanie have made plans to travel. The sooner all of you are gone, the better I will feel, if you will excuse my sentiments under the circumstances."

Daphne managed a smile, but she did not feel his same certainty. She very much suspected the earl knew his grandsons only too well. She doubted if this were the first mad escapade they had engaged in, but if someone didn't act soon, it could very well be their last.

Anxiously, before Gordon could escape to his duties, she asked, "Has Evan been notified? Is he well? With all this rain . . ."

Gordon patted her hand. "The innkeeper is a trusted friend. I insisted that he stay there so we could communicate with more ease. And his men are housed in various barns and sheds and are not likely to die of starvation. There is nothing you need worry yourself about but having a good time and getting off to Bath."

She really would like to scream at him, or perhaps beat him with a parasol as she had his brother. She didn't know which was more infuriating, Evan's arrogant courage or Gordon's unflappable assurance. Both assumed she was little more than fragile porcelain to be protected and wrapped in cotton wool. Perhaps she ought to seek out Rhys. He at least had the insolent attitude that she could be used for something.

But a lady did not cause public scenes, and she really did

not need to draw more attention to herself than she already had. Her smile did not reach her eyes as she dismissed the viscount and turned to Melanie for conversation. It was going to be a very long evening.

"She's what!"

"Daughter of Maria Templeton, sir," Gordon replied patiently after their guests had departed.

"*The* Maria Templeton? The one who drove her perfectly good horses off the cliff? Have you lost your mind as well? I thought the chit behaved as if a cat had leapt down her back, all jumps and starts. She's her mother all over again. One look at those eyes will tell you that."

Gordon held onto the shreds of his frazzled nerves. At the moment, he would rather be Evan and sleeping in the woods and dining off berries than dealing with his cantankerous and only too sharp grandparent. He poured himself a small brandy and offered the decanter to the earl.

"Daphne had reason to be nervous after what you put her through. You have not even given me time to obtain her father's consent and already you're setting her to your paces," Gordon grumbled, sick with irritation. "And there is nothing wrong with her eyes. They're lovely eyes. It is her leg that pains her, as I understand, a result of the accident, I believe."

The earl gave his grandson a scathing glance and drained his glass before continuing to stalk up and down the floor. "And you wish to marry this poor creature you have scarcely known a fortnight? I find that deuced suspicious. Her mother was quite mad, you know. Does madness run in the family? What can you be thinking of to introduce tainted blood to the line? Can you imagine a legacy of mad earls? It will not do, Gordon."

Gordon stiffened. "I have not been so rude as to inquire into the family's weaknesses. The mother's fault is not the daughter's. Daphne is far from being a poor creature. You cannot know the courage and compassion she has revealed to me. A few earls with a backbone like Daphne's would serve this family well."

Shelce grunted at this revelation. It sounded very much as if his grandson were truly smitten, for the very first time. It would pay to examine this issue a little more closely. "Very well. Then you will not mind if I stay a while to get to know her better. You have had the pick of all of London's finest, and you have chosen an unremarkable nobody who cannot stand still without jumping at every little sound. I wish to learn what it is that she possesses that the other ladies did not."

Gordon ground his teeth together and wished he had not agreed to any of this. He had never believed his grandfather would stir himself to come to Devon because he mentioned he was considering marrying. He was eight and twenty and quite capable of choosing a wife without anyone's help. He had thought the earl knew him well enough to accept that.

No, there was something else bothering his grandfather besides the impending betrothal. He watched the earl's irritable pacing of the room and resigned himself. Sooner or later it would all come out. He would just much rather it be later.

"Daphne and Melanie have made plans to travel to Bath, sir. Perhaps you ought to accompany them."

The earl sent his heir a shrewd look and finally accepted the decanter offered. The night had only just begun. His heir just didn't know it yet.

He refilled his glass and, smiling wickedly, asked, "And just where does Evan fit into these arrangements?"

THIRTEEN

Daphne sent the overcast skies a despairing look, then opened the formal note from Gordon. It had been addressed officially to herself and her aunt, so she could not expect it to say all she wished to hear, but even a stiff message was better than none.

When the note was read, her vexation did not ease. Delaying another day so the earl could rest before traveling with them did not sit kindly on her already frayed nerves. Undoubtedly the earl's luxurious barouche would be more comfortable, but the company of that irascible old man would not ease her mood. She just might blurt out the whole story to keep him from testing her like a prize mare, and then they would be in the basket for certain.

She wanted to talk to Evan. He would be as furious and irritable as she over this delay. But the note contained more of an order than an invitation for tea, and Daphne dared not ignore it. Perhaps if the rain held off, she would be able to make a quick trip into the village afterward. The clouds made evening seem to come earlier, but there would be sufficient light for some hours.

The earl presented a certain gruff charm over tea, but Daphne felt as if she were present under false pretenses and said little. Gordon's attentions were so pointed that even Melanie and Aunt Agatha noticed, making Daphne even more ill at ease.

She liked Gordon very well. He was everything that she had ever thought a gentleman should be: kind, thoughtful, undeterred by her flaws, intelligent, considerate, attentive . . . The list could go on into infinity without even adding attractive and wealthy. Why, then, wasn't her heart pounding with expectation whenever Gordon touched her hand or looked upon her? She had wanted a flirtation to remember. She had wanted to experience love even if unrequited. Why, then, couldn't she take advantage of this once in a lifetime opportunity to play the part that Gordon offered her?

She tried. She smiled into his eyes when he sat beside her as he sipped his tea. She was quite certain he was a very exciting and handsome man and that women had swooned over him for years. She let him offer her a plate of cakes, and when their fingers touched, she was quite positive she felt a small shiver of something interesting. She walked with him about the perimeter of the room as the others conversed in the center, and their conversation covered dozens of appealing topics. She really did enjoy Gordon's company and his ability to make her feel like someone important, but her thoughts kept straying disobediently to the injured man at the inn and the visit she planned to make as soon as this was over.

"Your thoughts are a million miles away," Gordon finally whispered as they reached the far end of the long drawing room where they would not be heard so easily. "Has the delay made you as nervous as I? I thought nothing weakened your courage."

He wasn't wearing blue today but a forest-green cutaway over buff kerseymere pantaloons that fitted neatly to his long, powerful legs. Even Daphne could see he was a fine figure of a man, and her heart pounded a little stronger.

"I am worried about having both your sister and the earl here. If Evan isn't indulging in flights of fancy, that could be very dangerous. Do you think we will be able to leave on the morrow?"

"I'm certain. It has all been arranged. Do you object too strongly to traveling with grandfather?"

"No, of course not. It is only the delay I mislike. Did you really have to give him the impression we are to marry? I feel so deceitful like this."

Gordon's grasp tightened on her hand where it rested on his arm. "Then agree in truth and there will be no deceit."

Daphne sent him a startled glance but they had once more strolled within speaking distance of the others, and a question from her aunt diverted the subject back to the general.

She was quite certain that Gordon knew of her lameness, if not her mother's crime, Daphne decided as they rode back to her aunt's afterward. How, then, could he possibly carry his flirtation so far as to actually sound as if he wished to marry her? His wife would be a countess someday. A lame countess didn't sound quite the thing. Surely he realized that. No wonder his grandfather was scrutinizing her so closely. She really hadn't thought Gordon meant any of this.

"You are terribly quiet, my dear." Agatha interrupted her reverie. "Are you worried that Gordon has been too precipitous in his addresses? He has, of course, but once a man of his age finally makes up his mind, he becomes quite impatient. I am not at all certain that going to Bath now is the wisest idea. Perhaps you ought to wait and give him time to press his suit."

Alarmed, Daphne shook her head and refused to meet her aunt's eye. "I do not know what has come over him. Perhaps if I go away a little while he will return to his senses and look among more suitable ladies. I am conscious of the honor he does me, but I cannot believe I am all that I must be to be a proper wife."

Agatha looked amused as she watched the emotions on her niece's lovely face. It was a pity the child could not see her own charms, but Gordon was scarcely blind to them. His gaze had seldom left Daphne all afternoon, and for good reason. Her niece was all that was fine in a woman: charming, demure, attractive, and intelligent. She would make an excellent countess. That slight streak of rebelliousness and stubbornness would add to her authority some day. They would make a lovely couple, although she expected Daphne might just give the staid viscount a real run for his money upon occasion.

"You do yourself no favor to speak like that," she admonished. "And you do Gordon a grave injustice. Are you certain it is not missishness that makes you think this way? A woman should be proud and honored to accept the suit of so fine a gentleman."

Missishness? Ordinarily, Daphne would have laughed at

the thought. She had always thought of herself as forthright
and above the vaporish whims of ordinary females. But
perhaps Aunt Agatha was right. She had never seriously
received a gentleman's attentions before. It had been quite
easy to laugh off the inanities of those few gentlemen who
had politely kept her company. Gordon wasn't so easily
dismissed.

That called to question all of her behavior. Had her own
proposal in London frightened her into retiring to the country
where she would never have to face such a predicament
again? Did the prospect of marriage and all that it entailed
so terrify her that she had resolved to be a spinster? Perhaps
all her actions in London had been such as to deliberately
frighten away suitors, and only when she thought herself not
pursued did she find someone to see her as she really was.

Daphne didn't think she was frightened of marriage, but
she really had not given it much thought. Girls grew up to
be married. That was what she had assumed when she went
to London. Now she knew differently, but she still had a
secret longing to be loved and cherished. And she wasn't
at all certain that a platonic friendship would suit.

Remembering the heat of Evan's kiss, Daphne blushed and
looked out the window. Would Gordon kiss her like that if
they were married?

Rather than sink in these disturbing thoughts, Daphne
ordered out her pony cart as soon as she had changed her
clothes. She needed some kind of exertion to divert her
thoughts away from herself. The sky had been overcast all
day without rain. It would very likely wait a little longer.

Going out without a maid was a little more difficult. Tillie
had the sniffles and couldn't come out in the damp weather,
but Marie looked disappointed not to be asked. It didn't
matter. What she was about to do didn't need witnesses.

Agatha had retired to her room for a rest before dinner,
so there was no one about to protest when Daphne donned
a pelisse over her walking dress and called for the cart. The
groom offered to accompany her, but she politely declined.

She felt a drop or two fall as she rattled over the bridge

to the village, but she was too close now to turn back. If it rained too hard, she could always stop a while with the Dalrymples until it was over. Jane would enjoy a good coze to discuss the earl's arrival.

The main problem was being inconspicuous. That wasn't a problem; it was an impossibility. The whole village would know she was there just from the sight of the pony cart in the street. Drastic measures were called for.

Before reaching the village proper, Daphne turned the pony down a hedge-lined lane. Evan had to be able to come and go from the inn somehow without being seen, and she rather imagined the river running parallel to the village street had much to do with it.

In triumph, she discovered a path along the riverbank. She daren't risk her pony and cart in this narrow terrain, but they would be safe enough tethered to a tree out of the way. If someone saw them later, they might think her maid had borrowed them for an errand or some illicit tryst. She tied the reins and set out to maneuver her way between hedge and river in the direction of the inn. Evan would no doubt ride his horse back and forth through here to the stables behind the inn. How would he enter the inn without being seen from there?

She would cross that path when she came to it. If nothing else, she would use the same ploy as earlier and pretend she was faint and in need of water. Female vagaries were always overlooked and forgiven.

As it was, she found the garden empty as before and entered it through the kitchen gate. If anyone saw her browsing through the flowers, they would think her eccentric and nothing more.

Before Daphne could devise a plan for entering the inn to search for Evan, she caught the flash of a red coat over the fence in the side street, and she stepped behind a large mulberry bush. The sound of steps did not go directly to the inn but seemed to amble down the alley toward the stables.

"What's our chances of catching a highwayman on a night like this?" a voice asked scornfully.

"Not much of a highwayman if you ask me. More like

a bloody Robin Hood. Did you see that widow weep when she found the bolt of cloth on her doorstep? Fair makes a fellow shiver to think how the rogue got it there without none of us seeing it.''

''Well, if the captain's right, we'll find how he does it tonight. But I still don't think he's fool enough to come near the only inn in town. We might as well find ourselves a dry spot and wait it out.''

The voices traveled on until Daphne couldn't hear them anymore. She was momentarily frozen to the spot, but her fear couldn't allow her to linger. Evan had to be warned. If only she knew more of their plans.

She hesitated, wondering if she ought to take a chance and find Captain Rollings first or just hurry to warn Evan. She feared the likelihood of going from the soldier to Evan safely was small. It would be better to do it the other way around and make some arrangement to send the information back to him.

With that plan in mind, Daphne waited until she sensed there was no one about, then cautiously crossed the garden to the side door of the inn. The sound of the captain's voice coming from the back room where she had once met Evan sent a ripple of fear coursing through her. She had hoped to find Evan there as before. That had been an idiotic notion. Now that it was dashed, she was at a loss.

Hugging her pelisse closer, Daphne slipped into the side hall and listened to the sounds around her, searching for any indication of Evan's presence. A public inn seemed a foolish hiding place for a known criminal, particularly one who was so identifiable. His resemblance to Gordon would cause marked suspicion in strangers. The villagers would know instantly that a hoax had been perpetrated.

The sound of heavy boots leaving the parlor sent Daphne's heart into a racing panic. Without thought, she dodged into the shadows of the back stairs. When she realized where she was, she caught her breath, looked upward for any sign of movement, then lightly hurried to the upper story.

The uneven floor boards made walking tricky. The lack of any source of light but a dirty window at either end of the narrow, low-ceilinged hall gave her pause, but she had come here for a purpose. She would not forget it now.

Skimming her fingers along the wall and watching for the darker rectangles of doorways, Daphne sought the room that might conceal an injured Robin Hood. Few strangers ventured through these parts. The rooms were seldom taken except by travelers caught by darkness or the weather, or an occasional drunken farmer unable to make it home after a long night of ale-swigging. The two open doors near the top of the stairs would not conceal what she sought. Daphne eased herself down the hall, ever alert for approaching voices or feet.

When she found the closed door to one of the front rooms, she hesitated. Her sense of the impropriety of what she was doing had fled long ago under her fear of the soldiers surrounding and filling this place. She had gone well beyond propriety the night the dratted man had appeared in her bedroom. She could only repay the favor in kind.

With that resolve of sardonic humor, Daphne tapped lightly at the worn wooden panel.

She heard a stirring inside, then a quiet voice that made her heart turn over in her chest.

"That you, Beckworth?"

She couldn't answer, not with soldiers just yards away in the hall below. Gently, Daphne turned the latch. It was locked.

Biting back a cry of frustration, she scratched lightly again, damning him for not opening the door at once. At any moment someone could choose to amble up either of those staircases, and she would be well and truly caught. How could she persuade him to turn the key?

She heard a mutter just the other side of the panel, and knew he was closer. "Open up, hurry," she whispered, praying he could hear.

On the other side of the panel, Evan stared at the cracked and peeling wood and wondered if his fever had returned. Had his boredom and wishful thinking created phantoms to whisper through the cracks of the door and haunt his lonely hours? He could almost imagine the fresh scent of apple blossoms wafting around him, and he rested his forehead against the old wood while a surge of longing swept over him. He remembered well the last time he had held a bundle of soft curves and feminine vulnerability in his arms, and the scent of apple blossoms had taunted him then. He was growing quite mad for lack of action, and he damned Rhys and Gordon for imprisoning him here.

The sound of boots on the stairs registered the danger of allowing his mind to wander, and he stepped back, but not before the unladylike hiss on the other side of the door caught his full attention.

Jerking open the door, Evan reached through and grabbed a handful of damp wool and jerked his visitor through the narrow opening, then closed and solidly bolted the door.

They stared at each other in fear and fascination. Evan sought the shadowed bruises beneath the lovely wide green eyes and cursed, then couldn't help allowing his gaze to travel over the trim figure displayed by the tight fastening of the fashionable spencer beneath the damp pelisse. He took the heavy garment from her shoulders and threw it aside. It was as conspicuous as a fur muff on a summer day. His lips twisted at her naive attempt at disguise.

"Is there a battalion of soldiers on your heels?" he inquired wryly.

Daphne's mouth was too dry to reply. She could see the white of Evan's bandages beneath the untied neckline of his open linen shirt, and for the first time, she acknowledged the manly chest beneath layers of gentlemanly clothing. His tightly tailored buckskin unmentionables were partially unbuttoned, and she jerked her gaze back to his face before she could look further.

A day's beard roughened Evan's shadowed cheeks, and his golden hair fell in tousled disarray across his forehead, but she was scarcely aware of these defects. She felt her eyes held by his, and her tongue froze in her mouth as his hand caught her shoulder.

"Speak, Daphne, or I shall die of heart failure here and now. What has driven you to this madness?"

The sudden crack of thunder and burst of heavy rain on

the tile roof overhead jarred her back to her senses, and the fear coursing through her roused her to action. This was Evan, the despot of the woods. She must warn him and get out of here.

"Captain Rollings has something planned for tonight. There are men below and stationed along the river. It seems to have something to do with the inn. I didn't know what to do."

"Had I been consulted, I would have recommended staying home." Evan's dry answer did not reflect the turmoil inside as he turned away and strode toward the rickety table that served as washstand and dresser. He poured a tumbler of water and returned to hand it to her. She looked paler than he had ever seen her. "Drink this, then tell me what the deuce you are doing out in weather like this, and without a maid."

Daphne sipped gratefully at the water, then glanced around at the room, gradually fading in the dying light of the storm. She could make out only the shape of a wide cot and the washstand, and the window on the far wall—dismal surroundings for the grandson of an earl, but a notch above the cave.

"I wanted to talk to you. Gordon told me you were here. And then I heard the soldiers talking . . ."

"And you hied yourself up here into an impossible situation. Did anyone ever tell you that you're a fool, madam?" Evan turned and strode away before her anxious face made a fool of him, too. He gripped the window frame with both hands and glared down at the darkened shrubbery below. The river was just beyond that line of trees. With a little imagination he could almost see the red coats through the leaves and the torrential rain.

Anger replaced anxiety as Daphne glared at his back. "Pardon me for being concerned. If you have the situation well in hand, I shall be happy to leave." She turned to unbolt the door, but his words halted her.

"It's pouring again. Where do you think you will go? Had you some notion of gaily flitting downstairs, twirling your parasol, and displaying yourself to a tavern full of randy soldiers and asking for a ride home?"

She had half a mind to fling the glass at him, but water

was not nearly as satisfying as ale. Instead, she refilled the glass and handed it to him. "Here, wash your filthy mouth. 'Tis a pity it cannot wash the dirt from your mind."

He swung around and glared at her, but she was halfway across the room now, and he could not keep his anger. She looked so fragile in this gloom, that it took all his strength to keep from reaching out to her. "That's the world the rest of us live in. Are you such a saint that you haven't noticed? What could have possessed you to come here when every precept of society warns against it?"

Daphne wilted beneath the harshness of his voice. He was right, of course. Their other encounters, while improper in the extreme, were also very private. This was something much different, and she had done it to herself.

Twisting the fingers of her gloves, she spoke to the floor. "Melanie and I are leaving with your grandfather for Bath in the morning. I wanted . . . I didn't know if Gordon . . ."

Voices broke out in argument on the front stairs, and Evan's head jerked up. With a despairing glance around he groaned, caught Daphne's shoulders, and pushed her toward the bed. "Take the jacket off, let your hair down, and get beneath the covers. Try to look as if you're asleep."

Not understanding what he meant to do but understanding his urgency from the vociferousness of the argument below, Daphne hesitated only a second over his orders. When it became obvious that Evan was releasing his breeches in preparation to removing them, she blanched and turned away. It scarcely made any difference if they were caught with or without clothing at this point. She was well and thoroughly ruined. Shakily, she reached to remove the pins holding her hair.

She heard Evan padding about the room behind her as she hurriedly unfastened the short jacket and threw it over the wash stand. She glanced at the narrow bed and down at her double layer of lovely skirts, and setting her lips, she hastily released the tiny buttons holding the eyelet overskirt in place.

She tried not to hear Evan's intake of breath as she let the hampering cloth fall to her ankles. She was still fully concealed beneath the thin muslin of her gown, but it had been designed to be worn beneath the concealing skirt and spencer. The bodice was low and the fabric, very frail. Telling herself he had seen more when she wore her night-rail, Daphne slid beneath the thin wool blanket of Evan's bed.

Evan had to force his gaze away from the shimmering waterfall of nut-brown tresses cascading down a slim, barely-clad figure sliding hastily beneath his covers. He had never tried to picture what she would look like in his bed. He was not a man given to flights of fancy. But the sight of her there stirred images no man could be blamed for having. He grabbed his brandy flask and sprinkled it liberally over his shirt. That was a trick he had learned well from his lady-love, though it had never fooled her. He did not think the intruders below were so perceptive.

The boots sounded alarmingly loud on the uncovered wooden planks of the hallway. Evan combed his hair into his face with his fingers, turned to see that Daphne was facing the window with only the wild tangle of her hair revealed, and held his breath as the pounding of fists rattled the bedroom door.

"Open up in the name of His Majesty!"

FOURTEEN

The rain pounded against the roof and thunder crackled overhead as Evan slowly slid the bolt open. He daren't turn for one more glance at the woman in his bed. If his plan failed, she was ruined for life, and he would be in no position to save her. Not even Gordon would be inclined to rescue her. He had to play his part well; her life as well as his depended on it.

The gloom of the storm clothed the room in darkness, and Evan breathed a sigh of relief as he realized the man outside carried no candle or lantern. For all practical purposes, it was early evening. Beckworth wouldn't have wasted good oil and tallow by setting out lights yet. Evan could scarcely discern the gleam of brass buttons as he peered warily around the door's edge. He crouched low to disguise his height, keeping his gaze fastened at the level of the soldier's chest.

"What's the meaning of this?" he demanded in the querulous tones of a Cornish squire aroused from sleep. He'd had a sergeant once from those parts. He'd learned to mimic him well.

"We have orders to search this inn for a wanted criminal. Who are you and where are you going?"

The soldier on the other side of the door tried to shove his boot through the crack, but Evan held the latch firmly while appearing to use it for drunken support. "I'm a merchant, sir, traveling with the wife. Can't a man have a decent night's sleep? Listen to that weather out there. Your criminal would have to be a madman to be about on a night like this."

"Let me in, you old fool, so I can search the place, and then you can have the comforts of your bed again."

The soldier shoved harder against the door, and Evan

allowed it to give just enough for the man to get a glimpse of the feminine form in the bed. He chuckled as the soldier stumbled and gasped. "Ain't she a rare one? Just wed, we are. The brandy's put her right off to sleep, and I'm like to hear about it in the morn, but not now, sir. So if'n you'll excuse us . . ." He stepped in front of the soldier's view.

The man muttered a curse, gave Evan's stooped and shirt-clad figure a disbelieving look, and clattered down the hallway again. Evan gently closed the door, straightened to slide the bolt home, and leaned against the wood with a sigh of relief. "Well, wife, you had best make room for me in there. It's going to be a long night."

Daphne sat up hurriedly, pulling the covers to her chin and staring into the gloom at the white ghost of Evan's shirt. "Long night? I cannot stay here any longer. I'll have to sneak out and go to the Dalrymples', tell them I was caught in the storm."

Evan advanced on the bed with a mirthless smile. "And what, pray tell, will you tell the soldier no doubt stationed at the end of the hall? That you've decided to run from your brandy-soaked bridal bed?"

"Surely, they haven't . . . " She stared in disbelief as Evan deliberately sat down on the mattress beside her and reached for his discarded trousers. His shirt came down to his stockings, and she couldn't stop her gaze from straying lower. In the semidarkness she could see little of the long, muscular legs disappearing into the buckskin, but just the knowledge of his near-nakedness caused her to blush profusely.

Evan watched her with growing amusement. This episode had its farcical side. If only dear brother Gordon could be here now . . . That wasn't a thought he wished to contemplate. "Did you hear him go down the stairs?" he demanded, forcing her to recognize their plight.

She hadn't. Daphne stared at him in dismay. "Perhaps he'll fall asleep?"

"When? Midnight? You wish to sneak past him then and pound on the Dalrymples' door?" Evan stood and pulled his trousers up, calmly tucking his shirttails in while she watched. He didn't know how much she could see, but it was too late for modesty for either of them now. He was just beginning to realize the full extent of damage this night had wrought.

Daphne pulled the pillow behind her and sank back into it. Her hair spilled over the short sleeves and drawstring neckline of her gown, and she impatiently caught the thick mass and pulled it to one side, absently braiding it with her fingers.

Evan stayed her hand, leaning over to release the silken mass and spread it across her gown again. "I like to look at it. If I were your husband, what would you say to me now?"

Daphne stared at her irritating and forceful companion, and opened her mouth to give him a scathing reply. Something in his touch and the tone of his voice caused her to close it again. Mischievously, she replied in the same spirit as his question, "You smell of strong spirits, sir. I wish you would bathe."

He laughed low in his throat and sat down beside her, folding his hands behind his head as a pillow against the wall's hardness. "What do you think our soldiers would say should I call for Beckworth to bring me a bath?"

"You needn't worry about the soldiers so much as what I would say," Daphne replied acerbically. "Be the tub shallow or deep, I would find some means to drown you in it."

"That's not fair, Miss Templeton. You speak as if this is all my fault. I did not invite you here, if you'll remember."

His genial tone did not ease her flush of guilt and confusion. She was quite old enough to know the extent of her rashness and the consequences, but she refused to think of it until she was certain there was no escape. What she had more difficulty ignoring was the man's large body seated so intimately beside her, in such a compromising place. She feared she knew what he was thinking, and she hastened to stamp out such notions.

"Your rash and criminal actions invited this outcome," she admonished him in as severe a tone as she could summon.

"Had you not set yourself in such a position as to be wounded and hunted down like an animal, I would not have been compelled to act as I did. I only hope this convinces you and Gordon to put an end to this charade and go to the authorities with your complaint."

She was good. She was very, very good. She could not have done better had she dumped a pail of cold water over his head. Evan gritted his teeth and stared at the far wall. "One does not go to the authorities with accusations against family. I take it you have met my grandfather?"

He did not need to say more than that. How could the twins accuse the earl's only surviving child of such heinous treachery? Particularly without proof. They had reached some kind of verbal stalemate. Daphne wrinkled her nose and gave a sigh.

"I was really not meant to be a viscount's wife at all. And heaven forbid, never a countess. Your grandfather is quite awesome in his authority. What was your grandmother like?"

Evan bent his diminutive companion a startled look. "Is that why the earl condescended to leave his noble tower? Has Gordon asked you to be his wife?"

Daphne threaded her fingers together and wished his gaze were not quite so intense. She was having difficulty enough adjusting to being alone with him. She refused to think of the miserable piece of furniture they were sitting on as a bed, preferring to pretend it was a parlor sofa where they conversed. But she couldn't pretend away his proximity, particularly when he stared at her like that.

"No, not in so many words, but I fear his sense of honor will require it. He had some notion of protecting me by announcing his intentions to your grandfather. I fear your masquerade has made Gordon very nervous. He did not mean for the earl to come down and inspect me, but I believe I have failed inspection."

Such bluntness from a female was a novelty to Evan, but a riot of emotions in his breast kept him from fully admiring her honesty, or her extraordinary cynicism, whichever it might be. He wanted to throw Gordon a facer, curse his interfering relations, and offer this tender morsel his eternal protection, all of which would be absolute faradiddle under the circumstances. Evan gritted his teeth against the words that threatened to come out.

"This night with me will certainly have you court-martialed should it ever be known. I'll make it right with Gordon, and he'll ignore the old man's decrees. Gordon's got a good head on his shoulders and doesn't blow with the wind. If he's made his mind up, he'll not change it."

He pronounced these words with a certain satisfaction. He knew his twin. Gordon would take Evan's word for what happened. Evan could offer Daphne this happiness in exchange for her mad attempts to save his worthless life. Of course, after the wedding, he might blow his brains out, but that was all part of a dim future. First, they had to get out of this predicament and run his Uncle Robert out of the country.

Evan's words had a dampening effect on Daphne's spirits, although she couldn't say why. It was good to know Gordon wouldn't think badly of her, but she couldn't help thinking it of herself.

"I'll not cause a rift between them. Can you imagine what the *ton* would think of me as countess? Me, the daughter of Mad Maria? No, I'm quite content to remain as I am, providing you make very good explanations to my aunt so she'll allow me to stay. Should I take a look at your shoulder? You seem to be favoring it more than earlier." Daphne turned inquiringly to him.

If she touched him, he would have her flat against the bed with her skirts about her waist in a trice. Evan didn't know what she rambled about and didn't care. It took all his concentration to keep his hands off her. He dropped his hands and swung his feet over the edge of the bed, clutching his fingers into fists as waves of desire smote him with the explosive force of breakers against a cliff. Lord, give him strength, for it wasn't his neighbor's wife that he coveted, but his brother's.

"It still aches when I'm weary. Why don't you get some sleep? I think I'll keep an eye on the river awhile."

"Sleep?" Daphne stared at Evan's broad shoulders with

incredulity. "I am trapped in a room with a notorious thief, surrounded by soldiers, my reputation is ruined, and you wish me to sleep? You may as well ask me to sing songs."

Evan grinned at the window as he rested his arm along the frame and stared out. "That should be amusing, too. Do you think we would keep the inn's inhabitants entertained if we lapsed into drunken song for the remainder of the night? Where would we start? Ballad or ditty?"

"Well, as a bridal couple, I should think it ought to be something jolly, but I am more inclined toward something doleful. Should we wail loud enough, mayhap they will all go home."

"I rather favor 'Johnny, I hardly knew ye,' but they may accuse us of being Jacobite traitors or some such. I suppose that eliminates 'Loch Lomond,' too." Evan tried to imagine the reaction of the man down the hall if these laments hit his ears, but the soft laughter behind him said it all. He tried not to watch her image in the darkened glass of the window.

"If I were able to sing, I would try those just out of curiosity. We would at least go laughing to the gallows. But since I cannot sing, you will need to tell me tales. How did you and Rhys meet? I think there's a story between the two of you."

Evan gave up and turned around. He was a gentleman and she was his brother's affianced wife. It was his duty to protect her. He would do his duty or die trying. Duty was something he understood. These other emotions now smothering him were foreign to his nature.

He sat at the end of the bed and leaned back on his elbows. "I don't think it's a story that can be told without Llewellyn's permission. I'll tell you a story about Gordon if you'll tell me one about you."

That was better. The taut energy that had been emanating from Evan seemed to relax to a cautious stance, and he was almost managing a smile. Daphne pulled her legs up under her and encouraged him to continue.

They talked the better part of the night as thunder rumbled and rain beat against the roof, drowning out all noises but their voices soft against the darkness. They talked of London and the things Daphne would have liked to have done and the ones that Evan missed and discovered they were both the same. Evan spoke uncertainly of a future he might never see, and Daphne encouraged him, knowing she had no future beyond these moors.

Laughing in the darkness, they made up a future in parliament for him as a candidate from Gordon's pocket borough. He would provide funds for needy soldiers and their families, and Daphne insisted that he provide equal funds to train all those who could not find employment due to their physical disabilities. Evan laughed and asked if he should provide equal training for those with mental disabilities and inquired whether she would join the program then and learn to be a sheepherder.

Her sudden tears at this suggestion brought Evan apologetically to her side. "What is it I have said? I meant only to tease."

His concern brought another rush of tears, but Daphne took a deep breath and determinedly wiped them away. It was more than evident that Evan did not know all the tales about her, so no doubt Gordon had never heard them either. It seemed quite preposterous when she was certain all of London had nothing better to talk about, but perhaps she was overemphasizing her importance. And then, Evan had been on the Continent these last years. He hadn't been near London to hear the tales.

"You hit too closely to home, sir," she finally replied. "There ought to be some help for people with mental disabilities, but sheepherding and Bedlam are not what I have in mind."

Puzzled, Evan touched her chin and turned her to face him. "I will agree to that, but there is no reason for my facetiousness to cause your tears. There is something you have kept from me. Isn't it time I have the whole?"

Daphne sighed and looked away. Her little charade of normalcy had to end sometime. Much better now, before Gordon could say or do anything foolish. It would be easito tell Evan and let him pass on the story. Then she wouldn't have to meet Gordon's eyes when this was over. "You have not heard of Mad Maria?"

At his shake of the head, Daphne clasped her hands on her lap and gazing straight ahead, continued as if repeating a bedtime story. "My mother was a loving, charming woman, but even when I was a child, I can remember how emotional she would become if I came to her with a bloody knee or if we laughed too long over a silly game. She would cry or laugh until she was ill and my father would have to come and send her to bed with her medicine. There would be days she would never come out of her room, but there would be weeks of sunshine and laughter, too. She was my mother and I just thought that was how mothers acted."

Hearing the painful catch in her voice, Evan tried to halt this speech, but Daphne held a finger to his lips and hurried on.

"No, I want to tell you the truth, before someone tells you the rumors. My mother was a beautiful person, and no one can take that from me. I am not at all like her, but there are times when I wish I could be. When she was well, she enjoyed every minute of life with a fullness I may never possess. Unfortunately, when she was not, she visited some hell where no one could follow.

"The physicians supplied her with medicines to calm her when she became uncontrollable, but there was an incident when she took too much, and my father had to lock the medicine away where she could not find it. He tried sending her to her family in London, thinking she would be happier in the social world where she had grown up, but she always came home after a few months.

"That last time she came home, she wasn't well at all. Nothing returned her spirits. I think it hurt my father badly, and he stayed away from home much of the time. Anyway, I was the only one home except for the servants the night she took out the chaise. Even our stableboy was gone. It had been drizzling all day and I knew the fog would rise in the valleys, but there was no one there to warn her or stop her but me. And it had begun to thunder and lightning. It wasn't a safe night to drive. There wasn't time to saddle a horse to follow her, so I took father's gelding, the one he kept a bridle on all the time. I fastened the reins and found a fence I could stand on and rode it without a saddle.''

Daphne ignored Evan's intake of breath. She had been young and impetuous, but she dared say she would do it again. Now that she had begun the story, there was no point in stopping it to examine the full extent of her youthful stupidity.

''The chaise was going too fast down the fell, and I had difficulty catching up with it. It all happened too quickly. I saw her horse run in one direction, and the carriage went the other, off the road and toward the tarn. I must have screamed, or perhaps it was the lightning striking just ahead. My horse reared. And then I knew nothing else until I woke in bed in excruciating pain.''

Evan started to gather her into his arms, but Daphne placed a hand against his chest and held him off as she spoke against his shoulder.

''I was in horrible pain and didn't understand the import of what I was saying when I tried to explain what happened. But my father did. And the physician did. And before long, the whole village had heard some version of the tale. They knew my mother had to have deliberately unhitched the horse for the accident to have happened as I said. Of course, someone checked the harness, as they never would have done had I not told what happened. My mother's carefuly planned accident became known as the suicide it was. She had been known as 'Mad Maria' before for her lively manners and eccentric emotions, but now the whole world knew she was mad in truth.''

Evan stroked the thick silk of Daphne's hair and let her continue. He knew of nothing he could say to comfort old wounds.

''My accident kept me invalided for almost the length of our mourning. The physicians said I would never walk again, but I knew I would follow my mother to the grave if I were bedridden for life. So as soon as my leg was healed enough, I began moving it, a little at a time, more each day. I would get up at night when no one was watching and practice walking again, holding onto the furniture. When I could stand on my own, I walked out of my room in daylight, and they finally had to consent to let me downstairs for a while each day. It is a tedious story, but suffice it to say, when it came time for my come-out, I went to London, against my father's wishes.''

She wasn't done yet. Daphne lifted herself from the tempting comfort of Evan's arms and stared at the faded mirror across the room. "I am afraid of so many things. After the accident, I was terrified of horses. And carriages. Rain. Darkness. Thunder. Lightning. Anything could return the nightmare of that night. People began to whisper I was as crazed as my mother. I was determined to prove them wrong.

"My mother's family tried hard to be kind. Before I arrived, they prepared everyone to be all that was amiable for their poor, invalid relative. The tale of my mother's death made the rounds again. Everyone watched and listened, waiting for me to give evidence that I was all that they expected, while being sympathetic. I'm afraid I was rather rude to some, and lost my temper with others, and the rumors didn't go away as I had hoped. Whatever I might or might not be never really mattered. The gossip was so much better.''

The cynicism had returned to her voice as Daphne pulled away and sat with arms folded across raised knees. She didn't look back at Evan as she concluded, "So, you see, I am rather sensitive about jests as to my state of mind. I am also a coward, and somewhat lame when it rains, and none too certain on my feet when it does not. A far from perfect specimen in anyone's book.''

"Coward,'' Evan snorted scornfully from behind her. "You are the least cowardly female I have ever had the misfortune to come across. Name me one woman who would have taken that ramshackle cart out at night, in the rain, and driven it to the river. I cannot think of even one who would dare that much, no less all the rest. Coward, you are not. Fool, quite possibly.''

Daphne turned on him with rage, but Evan caught her small fist before it could beat his sore shoulder. "Pax, little heathen. This is neither the time nor the place to judge ourselves. Let us save that for others to do when we escape this little scrape. I have a feeling recriminations aplenty will fly then. Sit back, and I will tell you of my unfortunate father, of if you prefer, I'll create lies of my hectic social life in London. What story would you like to hear?"

The tears and the tension leached out of her with these rough words, and Daphne had to smile wryly at the half-dressed man in the bed. He was not the polished viscount at all, but a rogue and a warrior with no polite words of comfort to offer. But he offered what he had with a sincerity that made her feel at home in this preposterous situation. She hadn't felt at home anywhere since her mother died. Sighing a little in relief, she went back to Evan's comforting shoulder and scraped a finger daringly over his bristly cheek.

"Robin Hood. Tell me the story of Robin Hood."

"And Lady Marion," he added.

Their easy companionship in the dark made the night comfortable. As their stories lapsed into fewer and fewer words, and Daphne struggled to keep her eyes open, Evan found it easier to pull her closer until her head rested comfortably in the curve between his shoulder and chest. By dawn, she was sound asleep and curled against his side and Evan held her securely wrapped in his arms, his cheek resting against her soft cloud of hair. It was as close to heaven as he would ever come, he reasoned, but he took no advantage from it.

He watched a rosy dawn break through the grimy window, and glanced down at the long sable lashes spread across fair cheeks in sleep. The dawn spilled a fresh hue across Daphne's skin, and her moist lips parted in sleep stirred longings he tried to set aside. She was warm and softly curved in his arms, and he ached with more than just physical longing. He had never spent a night like this in his life, and he could easily imagine a lifetime of such nights and more.

Evan wondered what it would be like to have the right to

kiss those lips every night. That led him to wonder all manner
of wondrous things, and before he was quite aware of what
he was doing, he bent to cover her mouth with his.

He only meant a gentle kiss, but Daphne's lips seemed to
wake beneath his, gradually dawning to the delights of this
tender touch, and their mouths began to blend with a will
of their own. Evan gathered her closer, feeling the soft curve
of her breast beneath his hand as he lifted her to him, but
she made no protest. Her arms slid willingly around his neck,
and he was lost in the tender delights of her charms.

The sound of voices rising in the hall below did not disturb
them immediately. Too engrossed in the discovery of what
lips and hands can do, they were beyond considering the
outside world. Daphne shivered with previously
undiscovered need as Evan's hand slid from her waist to
reverently touch uncharted curves, and her lips parted in a
startled "oh," allowing him full access to further explora-
tion. Her body quivered with taut expectation beneath his
unhurried caresses, and she scarcely heeded the noises
indicating the inn was awake and bustling.

Only the sound of a familiar voice rising in cheery greeting
belowstairs penetrated their haven. As Gordon's voice
battered at their senses, they drew apart and stared at each
other in dazed incomprehension.

This wasn't like it was supposed to be. Evan caught his
fingers in the curling silk of Daphne's hair and gazed down
in disbelief at the fathomless depths of her wide eyes. He
winced at the sight of her reddened cheeks where his beard
had chafed her, but her kiss-swollen lips beckoned him to
further mischief. He had not touched the drawstring of her
gown, but one sleeve had slid aside and his wandering hand
had pulled the fragile material to expose the creamy curve
of her skin beneath. She was thoroughly compromised, and
he could see the knowledge of that fact rising in those glorious
eyes.

He gently straightened the bodice of her gown and set her
back on the mattress, grateful he'd had the sense to don his
trousers before climbing into bed with her.

More to himself than to her, he said, "At times like these,

I wonder how much it is you understand, and actually find myself praying that it is very little. I'm not certain that I know myself this morning."

Daphne knew the feeling, and because she did, she raised her hand to stroke Evan's bristly cheek. "I know enough, my gallant Robin, to know we are both a sight. That does not bode at all well for your explanations to Gordon."

"No." Curtly, Evan rose and checked the water in the pitcher. "There's enough here that you might freshen yourself. I don't know what Gordon plans, but he knows where this room is. I have no doubt that he'll be here shortly."

Daphne reluctantly rose from the rumpled bed. She did not at all feel herself, but she wasn't certain who she might be either. She just felt as if she were a stranger to herself as she rose from this man's bed and crossed the room to wash away the evidence of what they had been doing.

She didn't dare scrutinize their behavior too closely. It had seemed perfectly right at the time, but now, with the sun shining across the room and Gordon's voice speaking cheerfully below, it suddenly seemed rather sordid. She sent Evan's profile a quick glance as he stood by the window, but as usual, she could read nothing of his expression. Only his stiff stance told her he felt much the same as she.

She scrubbed at her face and used Evan's comb to pull some of the tangles from her hair. To search for her pins would be futile, so she hastily made a loose braid and tied it with a ribbon. She had donned her spencer and overskirt and was fastening the tiny buttons when Evan finally swung around to face her again.

"I cannot offer you the wealth and title that Gordon can, but I can offer you what little protection my name affords. Do not worry on that account. I just wish I were in a better position to protect you from the embarrassment that will follow."

"You are scarcely to blame. We would be better concerned with how to keep you from the gallows. I cannot believe this is a safe hiding place any longer."

The rapid knock at the door prevented further reply.

Stealing himself, Evan crossed the room and threw the bolt, placing himself between the visitor and any sight of the room as he opened the door a crack.

"Let me in, you devil, before I call Rollings up here myself." Gordon's normally affable voice, even though spoken in a harsh whisper, came all too clearly into the room. There was nothing of affability in it now.

Daphne stifled a moan of dismay and stepped forward to stand firmly beside Evan.

FIFTEEN

Evan opened the door sufficiently to allow his twin to enter, then bolted it behind him. Gordon stared at the two of them with their rumpled clothes and guilty expressions, and the anger fled his face, replaced with a quiet despair.

"Rollings's story of finding only a couple of drunken newlyweds in the rooms upstairs rather had me concerned, but this isn't what I had imagined. You'll have to give me a minute to sort this one out. I hadn't expected to have to get two of you out of here. The soldiers below aren't in the best of humors for having lost a night of sleep to the cold and wet with nothing to show for it."

Evan did not move from Daphne's side, but neither did he touch her to lend support. Stoically, he faced his brother's condemnation. "It is not as you think. We'll make explanations later, but first we must smuggle Daphne out. It will not be so easy in the daylight."

Daphne met Gordon's questioning look without flinching. She had done this to herself, and oddly, now that the first shock of discovery was over, she felt no shame. She felt sorrow for any hurt she might have caused, and perhaps later she would regret what she had done, but she did not now. "I came through the garden and up the back stairs. My cart is down the alley from the river. I daresay it will have been seen."

Gordon nodded, but Evan was the one who spoke. "You'll have to smuggle her maid back here, pretend it was the maid who had the cart and abandoned it in the storm. If we maneuver it right, you can make it look as if you brought Daphne here to look for her maid."

The two men exchanged glances. In boyhood, they had

161

played many a trick on their elders by disguising their identity
and seemingly being in two places at once. There had been
incidents with various willing maids and the like, but none
quite like this. Never before had they attempted to deceive
soldiers or hide ladies.

"Daphne, will your maid help? Your aunt is frantic, but
I can think of no other alternative."

"Tillie fancies herself too high in the instep, but Marie
is good for a lark. She's rather silly and giggles too much,
but she'll do whatever you ask." Daphne didn't dare say
more. She wanted to send abject apologies to her aunt, offer
never to darken her door again, propose that a carriage be
sent to take her directly to Bath in disgrace, but she sensed
neither of the twins was ready for that, for all she knew that
was what it would come to. She would let them plan their
strategies and feel as if they protected her. But she knew her
plans of living her life out here had come to an end.

"Fine. I'll go below and mention that I have just
discovered the identity of the 'drunken couple' and say I have
gone to inform you of the sad news." Gordon sent his brother
a sharp look. "While I'm gone, manage to shave, if you will.
And trim his hair up, Daphne. I'll not have him posing as
me looking like that."

He left without further explanation, leaving Daphne more
bewildered than relieved. She turned to the stiff man beside
her. "What does he mean to do? I'll not have Marie's
reputation besmirched because of me."

Evan shrugged and strode toward the washstand. "This
is the way we've always worked. Gordon is good at details.
I'm only good for ideas. You'll have to trust him."

It was Gordon's safety that had put Evan into this position,
Daphne realized. She was just beginning to understand the
strength of the bond between the two men. They would do
anything for each other. But somehow she was beginning
to come between them. She didn't want it to be like that,
and she stared at Evan's turned back with helplessness. He
had grown cold and prickly when Gordon entered the room,
and Gordon had become aloof and unreachable. That wasn't
natural for either man. She couldn't allow this to happen.

Out of respect for her presence, Evan kept his shirt on as he lathered his face. She perched nervously on the window ledge, but it wasn't the greenery outside that held her attention. The broad play of Evan's shoulders as he leaned to look into the wavy mirror did strange things to her pulse. When he lifted his chin to work the straight edge underneath, her toes fairly curled in her boots.

Daphne stared down at her leather halfboots and emitted a giggle that sent Evan's head swinging in her direction. At his quizzical stare, she held out her leather-clad toe. "Do you think Gordon will understand we did nothing if we tell him I kept my boots on?"

Evan watched the sun dance off her hair and in her eyes and gave a ragged sigh, releasing all the minutes of tense guilt and self-condemnation that his brother's presence had engendered. Miss Daphne Templeton was a world unto herself, and he had to grin in appreciation. The rest of the world might very well count her mad, but whatever drummer she marched to, he would like to follow. "He'll only understand if I offer to die with my boots on, and he's allowed to wield the weapon. We're well in the briars right now. It will take some fast talking to bring him down out of the boughs."

Daphne loved it when she could hear the grin in his voice like that. She rather thought Evan used to laugh more than he did now. Perhaps war had taken the fun out of his life, but he needn't be as solemn as Gordon anymore. She felt satisfaction in having relieved some of his tension. "He will fly up into the boughs even higher should I begin talking like that, or Melanie. Your language is quite abominable, you realize."

Evan grew sober at the mention of his sister, and he returned to his task. "Right now my only concern is to get you and Melanie and Grandfather out of here. I don't know what Gordon is about to allow you to linger."

"I should think it would be more than difficult to order the earl to do anything he didn't wish to do," Daphne replied with a trace of acerbity. She didn't wish to be sent away any longer. Her place was here, whether he liked it or not. Of course, if Evan didn't want her here, she would have to leave, but she wasn't prepared to consider that eventuality. "But he was to go with us to Bath this morning. I fear I may have overset Gordon's plans."

"If you're packed, there should be no reason for you not to leave this afternoon. I'll make things right with Gordon while you're gone, and one of us will come for you when it's all over."

Daphne sent his back a quizzical look. Did he truly think this incident could be wiped clean, that Gordon and her aunt would pretend it had never happened? She could not be allowed to accompany Melanie after this. A fallen woman scarcely made a suitable chaperone for a young girl. Evan had made the obligatory offer, but obviously, his heart wasn't in it. The brief hope that had flickered within her died quickly. It was very well and good to imagine two men fighting over her, but experience said that they fought to see which one was stuck with her. It was a good thing she had a level head on her shoulders. Imagination was a dangerous thing.

"I rather think you'll find some objection to that," she replied, "but do not worry. I am quite accustomed to traveling alone and have any number of relatives on whom to call. If my aunt writes them of my disgrace, it will make things a trifle difficult, but I have my own income and need not rely on anyone. I'm certain your grandfather will agree to take Melanie away once you explain to him that there is some danger in keeping her here. Make up a story if you cannot tell the true one. Dangerous highwaymen and drunken soldiers always put fear in the hearts of protective parents."

Evan set his razor aside, wiped his face clean, and stared at Daphne in bemusement. She seemed to have dismissed his offer entirely. She was quite right, he supposed. For all their talk, he had no future, and she no doubt had set her heart on Gordon. Daphne had too much character to settle for a man she did not love or could not care for. Thinking Gordon would abandon her now, she had decided to leave the area entirely. He would have to make things right with Gordon. Of all people, Evan knew how much Daphne needed the home she had found here.

"Do not dwell on it. First, we must get you out. Can you use my knife to trim my hair?"

The task seemed an impossible one, but the chance to touch Evan's thick, golden-brown locks gave Daphne incentive to try. While Gordon raced to smuggle her maid back to the inn, Daphne carefully cut the lightly curling ends of Evan's hair. She did not pride herself into thinking she had accomplished a stylish Brutus cut, but it did not curl about his collar when she finished. If Gordon brought a hat, the top would be well concealed.

The soldiers in the tavern below grinned and nudged each other when the Viscount Griffin arrived escorting a slightly sodden pony cart driven by a lady in silken bonnet and voluminous pelisse. Evidently the lady had reclaimed her cart, for her horse was tied on behind, and the incongruous sight of a thoroughbred trailing a cart pulled by a misbred pony tickled their fancies.

Captain Rollings strolled out to greet the pair, but the lady hurried for the stairs clutching her pelisse closely around her, before he could offer a good day. Griffin stopped to give him a word before swiftly following. Rollings contemplated offering to escort the fallen maid out of town rather than let Miss Templeton suffer the embarrassment, but Miss Templeton had struck him as a rather obstinate-minded young lady. If she had taken a notion to chastise the maid herself, or save her from her wanton ways, he wanted no part of it.

When the aristocratic pair came down again, trailing the brightly smiling maid behind them, Rollings lifted a questioning eyebrow. This time, Miss Templeton saw him. Fastening the silken pelisse, she stopped before him while the top-hatted viscount escorted the maid to the waiting cart.

"Good day, Captain. I hope you are well. Have you seen Miss Dalrymple lately? I have been meaning to stop in and say hello, but the rains have been dreadful."

"Miss Dalrymple has been bemoaning that fact. Do you mind my curiosity in asking why you have come to fetch a maid who obviously shows no remorse for running off?"

Daphne shrugged. "Aunt Agatha is very fond of her and believes she has learned her lesson. I trust you and your men will not speak of this to anyone. The fellow has promised to marry her, so I can only do what is best for her under the circumstances.''

The old rogue his man had described last night scarcely sounded the best kind of husband, but the maid seemed satisfied. Miss Templeton probably had the right of it. It was one way of ridding herself of a troublesome wench. The captain made a polite bow. ''Many would not be so kind. Your generosity is to be applauded.''

Daphne smiled and offered her hand in farewell, then tripped lightly into the overcast day when her escort waited anxiously on his stallion and her maid sat, giggling, in the cart. The soldiers returned to their seats as the trio rode off, leaving the village street empty.

Some while later, a soldier making use of the necessary behind the inn noticed a gentleman striding through the kitchen garden toward the stables. The man wore the same beaver hat and elegantly fitted navy frock coat as the viscount had earlier, and the soldier scratched his head in puzzlement.

Returning to the tavern, he mentioned the viscount's appearance and inquired the reason for his return. Captain Rollings heard the inquiry and slowly came to his feet, a troubled expression on his wide brow. With a curt word, he sent a man upstairs to check on the prospective ''bridegroom,'' then he hurriedly turned his own feet in the direction of the stables.

The viscount was leading a suspiciously familiar bay mare out of the shelter when the good captain intercepted his path. Griffin halted at the man's approach, patting the mare affectionately as he waited.

''You seem in a hurry, Rollings. Is there something I can do for you?'' The viscount's good-natured drawl seemed unhurried and relaxed as the officer stopped in front of him.

''Is that not Miss Templeton's mare you have there?'' Perplexed, Rollings watched the viscount's expression carefully. The young nobleman seemed truly unaware that he was doing anything unusual in returning to the inn so shortly after he had left it in the company of two women.

''Mine, actually. I gave Miss Templeton the use of her

when she arrived. Lady Agatha's stables are rather on the dull side. Did you have some interest in her?'' Gordon played the game with good cheer, reading the captain's suspicions easily from years of experience in such looks. He was only grateful that Evan had had time to disappear down the river path on foot after boldly returning the mare to the stable in the guise of viscount. He should be well on his way back to the lane and the waiting stallion by now.

The captain had the grace to look slightly embarrassed. ''No, it seemed odd you just returned after leaving with Miss Templeton. Was there some trouble?''

''As a matter of fact, yes. The mare seems to have loosened a shoe. Miss Templeton insisted that I return to have it looked at. Actually, I rather think she meant to give her maid a good scold before returning to Lady Agatha's and thought the shoe good excuse to be rid of me. Old Abe says the mare is fine.''

Something was not quite right here, but Rollings couldn't put his finger on it. There was nothing he could do, however, and he let the viscount go on. Not until his man came down to report the ''bridegroom'' had disappeared did Rollings curse and swear and stare at the empty road. He didn't know how they had done it, but he knew he'd been had.

Some miles away, a tense trio drew within sight of the tree-lined drive to the Griffin estate. Rather, a tense duo, for Marie thought the adventure a great lark and laughed and chattered the whole way. Daphne sent her a look of irritation, but her grip on the reins relaxed slightly as they halted on the ridge overlooking the estate. Cautiously, she watched Evan's proud back garbed in the same navy as his brother as he halted to overlook the home he was finally able to return to openly after so many years away.

''Will you go in? Or must you continue this silly charade a little longer?'' Unable to bear the silence, Daphne voiced the most important question on her mind.

Steeling himself for the inevitable confrontation, Evan edged his horse down the road. ''I'll not leave you to face the consequences alone. Gordon said he took Lady Agatha to meet with Grandfather. We'll go there.''

Daphne felt a shiver of apprehension at the implacability in his voice. She was beginning to understand that Evan abided by a very rigid sense of duty that allowed him to overlook any number of relative trivialities, such as the law and people's feelings. She supposed a man could have worse flaws, but this one could be very uncomfortable to live with. She sent him a surreptitious look, but all she could see was the breadth of his back as he approached his home. She found it difficult to believe this was the same man who had held her and kissed her not more than a few hours ago.

The servant who opened the door stared at the man doffing his hat and assisting the lady from the cart. Everyone in the kitchen knew the viscount had gone in search of the missing lady, and here he was returned all right and proper with the lady and her maid unharmed. But it wasn't the same man who had left here earlier this morning. Lord Griffin never wore his hair in such an abominable manner, and his complexion was of a gentlemanly fairness, not this weathered color of a gypsy. Lines of suffering pulled at the corners of this man's mouth, but lines of laughter etched his eyes. It did not seem possible. It could not be. The servant stared as the lady took the gentleman's arm and traversed the steps. A never-to-be-forgotten wink of the gentleman's eye sent the servant's spirits soaring, and a grin broke out on his solemn countenance.

"Master Evan! It is you! May God preserve us and welcome home, sir!"

The smile forming on the gentleman's lips transformed his face to the youthful merriment of years ago. Daphne clung to Evan's arm in astonishment as the staid butler beamed and spouted more words than she had heard from him in a month. She couldn't help noticing Evan's lighter step as he entered his boyhood home and gazed around.

"Nothing's changed, Emery. I suppose there are still kittens in the coal scuttle and tarts in the pantry?"

"They're old enough to scamper about the kitchen, sir. It's time they go to the barns. And Cook just took them out of the oven. Shall I bring you some in the drawing room?"

Dazed, Daphne wondered if the tarts were going to the barn or the kittens to the drawing room, but Evan seemed to understand. He chuckled and nodded and clasped his fingers warmly over her arm.

"You had best show us to the earl and Lady Agatha, Emery. Then bring the tarts. We've neither of us broke our fast, and it's deuced difficult to be scolded on an empty stomach."

The servant grew solemn, aware from years of such confrontations that the young master was in the briars again. The explanation of his appearance months after his funeral would somehow filter down to the staff sooner or later. Properly trained, Emery turned and led the way to the formal salon where the earl paced and Lady Agatha worked sedately at her embroidery.

Both older people glanced up as the young couple entered. Lady Agatha gave a cry of relief and rose to embrace her niece before stopping and staring, puzzled, at Daphne's escort. The earl scowled, took a step forward, then glancing closer at Evan's face, gave a curse that reddened Daphne's ears.

Evan forced a smile to his lips as he released Daphne to her aunt and made a polite bow. "It is always good to be welcomed home, sir, although you could have saved your exuberance until the ladies were out of hearing."

"I ought to box your impertinent ears," the earl growled, taking another step forward as if to carry out his threat.

"Shelce!" Agatha interposed with a warning, clasping Daphne's arm and preventing her niece from rushing back to the young man's side.

To the surprise of both women, the men held out their hands and shook warmly, Evan wincing at the older man's rigorous tug on his injured arm.

"Damned pup, I'll wring your neck this time." The earl still spoke harshly, but there was a hint of some softer emotion behind his words. "Where's that other young rascal? I warrant I'll do more than ring a peal over his ears. It's inexcusable for my heir to behave like this at his age. The pair of you deserve a caning, always did. I'll have my explanations now, boy, and they had better be good ones or you'll be out on your ear in a trice.''

Evan sent a glance to Daphne and her aunt, then shook his head. "We had best wait until Gordon returns. It might be best if I saw the ladies home, first.''

Lady Agatha straightened to her full height. "If that is you, Evan Griffin, I'll not be shunted off like some ailing caper-wit. I've watched your mischief from afar for years, but now you've involved my niece, I'll know the meaning of this one.''

Before the argument could continue, a slight figure in sprigged muslin careened into the room, hesitating only briefly before flinging herself into Evan's arms.

"Damn you for a lying rogue, Evan Griffin! You ruined my come-out for naught and I shall kill you for this! To imagine the servants must tell me of your arrival!''

Evan's dark features puckered with laughter as he gathered his suddenly grown-up little sister into his arms to prevent her flailing fists from causing grave injury. "Whoa, twirp! Do I deserve no last words before you lay me out?''

That laughing question cut too close to the core and resulted in a sudden wail as Melanie fell, sobbing, against his shoulder. Evan paled slightly and threw Daphne a pleading look. She did not need further explanation to know his plea.

Releasing herself from her aunt's hold, Daphne gently took Melanie by the arm and disentangled her from her brother's embrace. "Go see what is keeping the tea from being served. Evan is still weak and in need of nourishment,'' she whispered as she led the younger girl away.

Melanie's sobs dwindled to a sniffle, and hugging Daphne, she did as told. When Daphne turned back to the room, both men were staring at her as if amazed by the miracle she had wrought. Unaware of their stares, she gratefully lowered herself into the nearest chair to ease the weight from her aching limb. Adventures might be wildly exciting, but they were a trifle hard on a person.

"I have never seen a watering pot turned off faster,'' Evan marveled. Without realizing, he moved next to Daphne's chair, catching himself only when he lifted his hand to touch her hair. Knowing the mistake such a possessive gesture would be, he hurriedly rested his hand on the chair back and leaned against it for support. This interview would be more trying than he had imagined.

"You're injured!" Agatha exclaimed. "You poor boy, sit down! Wherever could those servants be? Daphne, did you send Miss Griffin to find them? Perhaps, Shelce, you should offer him a little brandy?"

By the time the tea tray arrived, Agatha had whipped her troops in line. Evan sat in a chair beside Daphne, and the earl presided over a decanter of brandy. Melanie was ordered to serve as soon as she returned, and a rather stilted tea party was in progress when Gordon finally burst through the drawing room doors.

SIXTEEN

The normally sedate viscount appeared slightly rattled as he came upon the seemingly harmonious tea party. Ready for battle himself, he found it difficult to rearrange his rampaging emotions. Sending his errant brother a glaring look, he refused Melanie's offer of a cup but accepted the brandy from his grandfather.

The earl watched in amazement as his heir swallowed the strong liquor without flinching. "It is morning yet, as I recollect. Are you in the habit of imbibing heavily before noon?"

Gordon grimaced and set the glass aside. "Only when my twin arises from the dead. I wish to speak to the two of you when you have finished your repast. I'll be waiting in my study. I don't believe I make pleasant company at the moment."

As Gordon started to leave, Melanie gave a shocked cry and glanced from brother to brother with a worried frown. Daphne struggled for some way to ease the situation, but not at all certain that she understood the argument, she felt helpless. She wanted to rise and go to Gordon and somehow reassure him, but he must certainly think her a fallen woman now. She was not certain she could bear his scorn.

Instead, she set her cup aside and offered, "I think it best if I return to my aunt's and finish packing. Melanie, perhaps you ought to go upstairs and do the same."

Having no idea that her friend had been caught out all night and wishing only to hear how Evan had returned from the dead, Melanie appeared prepared to protest. Rising at the same time as Daphne, Evan confirmed her suggestions.

"There are urgent matters Grandfather and Gordon and

I must discuss, brat. You'll be duly informed of my misdeeds later, I promise. Now be gone with you.''

Daphne felt his hand briefly brush hers with a quick squeeze, but she disliked leaving him here to fight the battle alone. She looked to Aunt Agatha for support, but the old lady seemed to be enjoying herself hugely, without any notion of removing herself from the family squabble. Unable to order her elder around, Daphne took herself to the door, with Melanie trailing behind.

No one raised any objection to their leaving, and once outside the drawing room, Daphne gave a small sigh of defeat as the door closed behind her. Melanie glared at her accusingly.

"You knew Evan was alive! Why didn't you tell me?"

Daphne shook her head, feeling a small ache forming between her eyes. "It was not my place to do so. Evan and Gordon had their reasons for keeping it a secret. I'm certain they'll explain all when the time is right."

Melanie looked doubtful as voices rose in the room behind them. "They are very angry. They'll think I'm too young to understand. But I'm not too young. I'm old enough to be wed, aren't I?"

Daphne managed a tired smile. "Men never think we're old enough. We have to find other ways around them. I'm sorry that our trip to Bath has been postponed, but I believe the earl will be ready to go soon. Perhaps he will explain things if you ask."

She knew she wouldn't be there when they went. It would be back to her father's house for her. Perhaps an invalid's lot was fitting punishment for allowing herself to think she could manage her own life. She had grown so bold in the idea that she had all but thrown herself into a man's arms to prove she was as much a woman as any. Perhaps her wits were to let after all.

Sending for Marie and parting from Melanie, Daphne set out for her pony cart. She couldn't wait any longer in the hall, listening to the argument over her fate. She had no intention of marrying Evan out of obligation, but they weren't in any humor to hear that yet. They could argue and explain and work things out until everyone was calm again. When they were ready to come to her, she would have her say.

Holding tightly to that thought, Daphne barely waited for Marie to settle in her seat before urging the pony into a small canter. If nothing else, she had brought an end to the neighborhood Robin Hood. The news of Evan's return would be all over the shire before nightfall.

Before she was scarcely out of the drive and on the road, a familiar figure stepped into her path. Marie gave a squeal of fright, but Daphne calmly brought the cart to a halt and gave the one-legged ruffian a chance to catch up.

"I heard some talk in the village, and Evan wasn't in his room. I just wanted to make certain everyone was all right." Rhys had tipped his disreputable hat before he spoke, but he made no other indication of servility as he boldly accosted his better.

Daphne did not find his attitude in the least odd any longer. She spoke with him as an equal and a friend. "He's explaining things to the earl right now. I think Captain Rollings has come too close for comfort. You'd best warn the others."

Rhys nodded, then cast her shadowed eyes a concerned look. "And you, Miss Templeton? Is there aught I can do for you?"

At this rare expression of sympathy from the cynical thief, Daphne had to smile. "Can you wave magic wands and make us perfect? If not, there really is nothing else you can do for me."

Rhys shook his head. "You are already more perfect than any other lady of my acquaintance, and I think you know that. If I can ever be of service to you, please call on me."

She did not find his gallant bow any more odd than his refined speech. Daphne thanked him and sent her pony on down the road. Rhys Llewellyn was an exceptional man. 'Twas a pity he could not find a place among the landed gentry where he so obviously belonged, but he had no right to throw himself away on thieves, either. Still, she had more problems than she could deal with on her own as it was. She didn't need to borrow more.

As she turned the pony cart up the drive to Aunt Agatha's home, a coach and four rolled wildly down the hill in her direction, and she was forced to take the grass to avoid it. A shouted curse and a cry from the driver as he slowed his horses followed, and Daphne watched in amazement as the equipage swayed to a halt just beyond her. There was something vaguely familiar about that curse.

A sensible female would have taken to her heels and fled for safety from the madman on the coach, but Daphne waited in curiosity as the door flew open and a slim, compact figure leapt out, followed by a slower, sturdier one. Rather than running to them in greeting, Daphne continued to sit and stare in dazed recognition. This really could not be happening to her. No day could be as bad as this one. Surely whoever was in charge of punishment had meted out more than enough justice for one day.

"What in the name of all that is holy are you doing in that cart, daughter?" The sturdier man shoved forward to confront his frozen child.

"Father?" Questioningly, Daphne stared into the face of the man she had seen every day of her life until she turned nineteen. She had seen him briefly on holidays since then, but the distance between London and Gloucester was too great to cover frequently. She had not quite realized that distance was cut in half by her move to Devon. "What are you doing here?"

"What am I doing here?" he exploded. "Can I not come to see the man my daughter intends to marry, even though she doesn't have the respect to tell her own father? There is something havey-cavey about all this, and now your aunt's addlepated servants tell me you've been gone all night and half the neighborhood's out searching for you, and you come riding up like the Queen of May, if you please. And you want to know what *I'm* doing here?"

"Father, please." The younger man put a steadying hand on his father's shoulder. His parent's voluble tirades were well known but not conducive to explanations. Michael turned an expressive look to his sister. "Perhaps we ought to allow Daphne to return to the house and refresh herself before we bombard her with questions."

"I would be grateful for that," Daphne managed to murmur politely, if not actually gratefully. She was much too tired to think of explanations quite yet.

"Then get in the carriage with me and let your brother drive that dangerous contraption. I knew my sister was all about in her wits, but what she could be about by allowing you to—"

Daphne picked up her reins and adamantly refused to budge. "Leave off, Papa. I am in less danger here than you are if that's William driving the coach. I'll not be bullied and set upon like a child."

Leaving her father ranting and raving and Michael to comfort him, Daphne urged the pony into motion. If Gordon was surprised at his grandfather's overweening concern over their supposed marriage, she was doubly so by her father's appearance. She really had not expected Michael to break the news without her permission. She had insisted on privacy. How could he abuse her trust so?

While the carriage was lumberingly coming about, Daphne sent the pony into a sharp clip and reached the house first. She intended to wash and don fresh clothes before this interview. It would be lovely to have a few hours sleep, also, but she could see that wouldn't be on the agenda any time soon. The ache behind her eyes grew a little fiercer.

She could hear her father's roar from her room as she hastily undressed with the help of a disapproving Tillie. She washed more quickly than she had intended as she imagined the confrontation should Evan come riding up to make his obligatory offer. She shuddered at the prospect. It was one thing to reject the man who had compromised her when she was the only one affected. It was quite another under the stern eyes of father and brother.

By the time Daphne was done, had she a black gown to wear she would have worn it, so low had her spirits sunk. Instead, she found a particularly drab brown and pinned her hair in a coronet of braids rather than allow even a hint of curl to escape. She had set out to be a spinster and so she would be. Her father would have to see that somehow.

Wondering how on earth she would explain away her letter and Gordon's fictitious suit, Daphne trailed down the stairway to her aunt's front drawing room. There didn't seem to be any feasible way of sending her family off before Evan arrived. Even should he take the time to get some rest first, they would still be here when he came. And she knew he would come. His sense of duty would not allow him to act otherwise.

Michael was staring out the front window at the rolling moor while her father sat edgily in Aunt Agatha's favorite horsehair chair. He rose instantly at Daphne's appearance, giving her dowdy attire a scathing look.

"I sent you to London to dress like that? Where's that yellow thing you had on? If you're to wed a viscount, you ought to dress the part."

"Papa, I'm not to wed a viscount." Daphne sent her brother's back a murderous look.

Michael turned in time to intercept it and gave an apologetic shrug. "Father was visiting when your letter arrived. A letter from you is such an auspicious occasion that I could not keep it from him without causing undue concern."

Daphne sighed and sank down in the nearest chair. Never in her life had she ever done anything the least little bit improper until she met Evan Griffin. And her one attempt at doing anything just the tiniest bit out of the way had not only been caught out, but blown into a fiasco far out of proportion to the error. Never again would she try to be something she was not.

"I don't suppose you took the time to find Robert Griffin before you came galloping out here?" she asked with resignation.

"Of course I did. He was at the club the night the letter arrived. He seemed amenable to the suggestion, but we made no definite plans. I thought it wisest to talk to you first."

Daphne allowed the horror of this knowledge to slowly seep through her. Robert Griffin, the twins' dangerous uncle, now thought she and Gordon were to be married. Despite the heavy rain, Michael had had time to arrive from London. That meant Robert had had an equal amount of time to arrive. And the entire Griffin family was neatly ensconced in their home, all in one place. Could anyone be so devilish as to . . . ? Surely not. She stared wildly at her brother.

"What kind of man is he?" she demanded.

Michael looked vaguely startled. "I scarce know him, Daph. He's considerable older than I and belongs to a fast set that I have never aspired to. He did not cut me for my daring to intrude in his affairs. He even seemed vaguely amused. Why do you ask?"

Daphne rose and nervously clasped and unclasped her hands as she paced the faded carpet. She ignored the vague ache in her leg as her thoughts tumbled about. Surely the twins knew the urgency of the situation, but they did not know that Michael had carried out his task with such alacrity. They might not even know the roads to London were open now. Caught up in their argument, they might not even consider it until it was too late. And if Evan came riding over here alone . . .

It did not bear considering. As her brother and father watched her in amazement, she straightened her shoulders and started for the door. "We must notify the Griffins at once. If your horses are weary, I'll send for Aunt Agatha's."

"Daphne Elaine! You come back here at once, do you hear me?"

Her father's roar scarce made an impression as she went in search of someone to bring a carriage around. Perhaps she ought just to send a message. To unleash her father on the already disturbed Griffin household was not an act of kindness. But she acted on an intuition that she could not explain, even to herself.

Her father and Michael followed her into the hall, but Daphne was already calling for her bonnet and gloves, and the carriage that had just arrived with her family was now pulling up to the door once more.

Michael caught his sister's elbow as she tied her bonnet strings. "What's this all about, Daph?"

"It's not for me to explain. Why don't you and father rest and have some tea or something? I will be right back." She could only try. It really did not matter if she failed to dissuade them.

"Rest!" her father roared behind them. "Do you think me some senile invalid that I need rest while my daughter gallivants about the neighborhood without so much as a chaperone?"

"Aunt Agatha is there. I'm certain she makes quite an adequate chaperone." Daphne took the umbrella the servant handed her and started for the door.

"We're coming with you!" Lord Thomas Templeton hurried after his impetuous daughter and, shrugging his shoulders, his son followed in his footsteps.

Daphne did not try to speak as she stared, white-faced, out the carriage window as it traveled the lane she had just traversed. Perhaps she was just overwrought and seeing goblins in the shadows, but she could not help but search the hedgerows as they passed by. Mayhap it would be better if Captain Rollings stationed his men around the Griffin estate, only she could think of no way of persuading him to do so.

None of this seemed quite real. Yet she could not imagine a man like Evan living the desperate life of a criminal in the woods without reason, nor Gordon allowing him to do so if he had not thought it safest. She had to trust the twins and warn them.

"Daphne, you will scare us half to death if you do not tell us what is wrong," Michael said, intruding cautiously upon her reflections. His father's stiff-lipped silence did not bode well, and he sent the older version of himself an anxious look.

"There is naught wrong," Daphne replied absently. "I am quite fine, if rather annoyed."

"Annoyed, she says. Ha!" Lord Thomas snorted *sotto voce*.

Daphne ignored him. "I pray you will not cause a scene. The Griffins have suffered several hardships in past months, and tempers are not of the best. If you should make mention of my private confidence, I shall never speak to either of you again.''

"Havey-cavey, that's what it is," his lordship continued muttering.

"It does not sound quite the thing, Daph," Michael objected. "Why should the viscount keep his suit a secret? Father is right. He has not conducted himself at all with honor.''

"Oh, do be quiet, Michael," Daphne finally snapped, turning to face her stiff-laced brother. None of her family was of any great stature, but Michael was a well-looking man with an air of pride and self-assurance. That he was also so high in the instep that he couldn't see the ground had always been the barrier between them, but she knew he meant well. "I never said Gordon had proposed. I am certain when and if he wishes to do so that he will be all that is proper. But not now.''

She said it with such finality that they traveled the rest of the distance in silence.

Evan was just mounting his horse as the carriage rumbled up the drive. He halted his stride as he caught sight of Daphne's pale face in the window and handed the reins back to the stableboy as the reckless driver rocked the ancient equipage to a halt. He glanced at the surly, slouch-hatted coachman in surprise but hurried forward to assist Daphne as the door flew open.

To his further surprise, a slender man with broad shoulders and chestnut hair descended first. A feeling much like that of the one before battle gripped Evan's stomach, but he came to a stiff halt beside the carriage door and engaged in a bout of eye-to-eye combat with the stranger as Daphne started to step out.

Both men held out their hands, but Daphne could only see Evan. She reached for him gratefully, taking solace from the strength of his clasp as he helped her to the ground. He did not release her immediately as she turned to wait for the third passenger to descend, and they waited in silence as Lord

Thomas clung to the carriage door, cursed the coachman, and descended with an angry thump, glaring at Evan all the while.

"I suppose you're the bumptious wretch who means to ruin my daughter," were the first words he spoke.

Daphne hid a resigned smile at Evan's jerk of shock. She pressed his fingers reassuringly and made the introductions.

"Papa was with Michael when he received my letter," she explained hurriedly. "They've already spoken with your uncle."

Evan's jaw locked in a tight knot at this news, but he managed a grim bow of greeting. "Your haste is to be commended, my lord. Do come in. I'm certain my grandfather will be pleased to meet you."

Evan longed to pull Daphne aside and question her privately, but the time for that was past. Her father's arrival actually made things easier. He could ask for her hand and arrange to have her spirited to Bath all in one day. The only difficulty might be that Lord Thomas had come expecting his daughter's betrothal to a wealthy viscount, not a near-to penniless ex-soldier.

"Grandfather?" the irascible old man grumped. "What the deuce do I want with your grandfather? It's you I've come to see. There's something havey-cavey here and I mean to get to the bottom of it. Where's that sister of mine? Fine idea she has of acting the chaperone while her niece is all about the countryside endangering life and limb in that ramshackle vehicle."

Amusement began to dance about Evan's lips as he listened to the older man's complaints and watched the exasperation on Daphne's mobile features. If only he could take her in his arms and tell her everything would be all right . . . But he had not yet earned the right for that. He contented himself with keeping her hand on his arm as he directed the Templetons toward the drawing room, where his brother and the earl waited.

SEVENTEEN

Gordon swung around in surprise as his brother re-entered the room after so recently leaving it. His eyes widened at the sight of a primly unhappy Daphne on Evan's arm, trailed by two men whose family resemblance marked their names even before introductions were made. As he realized their purpose here, his resolve firmed, and he swiftly came forward to greet both men.

The Templeton men stared in some dismay and bewilderment as a duplicate of the man they had just accosted came forward to take their hands and stand beside Daphne. She stood between these twin giants, her hands resting familiarly on both their arms much as if she were perched between the arms of a comforting chair. Despite the concealment of her bonnet and pelisse, she appeared quite natural and proud there, not at all the diffident invalid they thought her. And the looks the twins gave her delicate beauty were not that of pity or sympathy. Lord Thomas harrumphed loudly, and Michael stepped aside to greet his aunt.

"Which one of you is the viscount?" Daphne's father demanded.

"What's it to you?" The earl strolled from his corner, brandishing his walking stick as if it were a riding crop.

The sturdy Lord Thomas swung around fearlessly. "She's my daughter and I've a right to know!"

Gordon stepped into the breach, clasping Daphne's hand firmly with his and tugging her gently toward their elders, away from Evan. She had no choice but to follow without making a scene, and he seized the advantage. "I'm Gordon Griffin, sir. Your arrival is a timely one. I have just been discussing with my grandfather my desire to marry your daughter."

Daphne felt her knees give way, and she clutched Gordon's arm desperately for support. She sent his serious mien an aghast look, but he never turned to notice it. Why was he doing this? She had enjoyed their flirtation, toyed with the idea of being a viscountess, but she had known it was only a fancy. Did he really think that one silly letter had placed him in this position?

Lord Thomas harrumphed again and gave the young viscount a considering look. He was a handsome devil, but then so was the man behind him, glowering like an evil genie. He hadn't missed his daughter's expression, either. A woman didn't look at the man she wanted to marry as if she had been poleaxed when he asked for her hand. His nose for the suspicious twitched mightily.

"Is that so? And have you discussed it with my daughter?"

Gordon's lips tightened. "I have tried, but it was not seemly to ask too much when I was not in a position to ask your permission first. We have known each other but a short while. I thought it wisest to give Daphne time to consider the idea."

The other young man seemed prepared to explode, Lord Thomas noted with satisfaction. He turned to acknowledge the earl standing silently beside him. "You know aught of this? The girl's my daughter and one of a kind, but as much as I love her, I can't fancy you're happy with the idea of your heir marrying into a country family like ours."

The earl's mouth opened and clamped closed. He looked from one twin to the other and shook his head. Evan had just overridden all his brother's objections a moment ago to insist that he was obliged to offer his name to the girl. But Gordon's suit had first brought him here and his heir seemed most vehement now. This was one fracas where he wouldn't intervene, as much as he was tempted to.

"My grandsons are old enough to know their minds," Shelce announced, praying fervently that was so. He looked to Agatha for confirmation, and she nodded smilingly.

Taking up her needlework, Agatha leaned comfortably back into her chair. "I'm happy to hear you believe your brother's story about last night, Gordon. I knew Daphne could do nothing improper. And Evan is a gentleman, after all. He would never harm a lady, particularly his brother's intended."

She could not more successfully have exploded the waters had she shot a cannonball into their midst. Lord Thomas turned a wrathful gaze on the darker twin, and Michael stepped forward as if to demand immediate satisfaction. Thinking he had neatly rescued the situation without Daphne's impropriety being revealed, Gordon appeared resigned. Only Evan stoically showed nothing of his thoughts as attention swung to him.

His gaze met and held Daphne's as he spoke. "I would never do anything intentionally to harm Miss Templeton. I should hope that I would only act in her best interests. Daphne, perhaps you and your aunt would join Melanie to prepare for your journey to Bath. I think it time that Gordon be apprised of the news you have brought."

For once, Daphne felt only relief at thus being dismissed, and she gave Evan a grateful, if somewhat weary smile. He looked as tired as she, and she felt a small measure of alarm at the thought. What if Robert were somewhere outside now, looking to cause harm? Evan was the only one with any training to deal with such a situation. He had to get some rest.

"I can leave with my father. Do you think Captain Rollings might escort Lord Shelce and Melanie as far as the toll road? You must get some rest and have someone tend your shoulder."

"Wait just one moment, young lady!" Lord Thomas roared. "You'll not be going anywhere until I get the meaning of this. What have you and this damned upstart got to say to anything? I'll hear this whole tale before I ove myself an inch further!"

Evan sent his twin a speaking look, and gauging the urgency of the situation, Gordon acted. "Explanations will come, but with all due respect you must bear with us a moment. Daphne has made a very good point. If you will excuse me, I shall be back directly."

Daphne breathed easier as he left, no doubt to summon Captain Rollings. This foolish argument over her betrothal had delayed their departure to inordinate lengths. It might even be dangerous to leave now. Surely there was safety in numbers. Her gaze returned briefly to Evan, but he had turned his back to stare out the windows overlooking the park. Recognizing the wisdom of that, Daphne went to take a seat beside her aunt. She didn't know why Agatha had done what she did, but she supposed her misbehavior had to come out sometime.

While Gordon was gone, Evan began a very expurgated version of the events leading up to last night for the benefit of Lord Thomas and Michael. It was evident that his grandfather had already heard it. There would have been no other way of explaining how she had come to be in Evan's room all night. Daphne wished she could read the earl's expression, but it was as closed as Evan's. Michael's honest visage expressed surprise and alarm as the story unfolded. Her father's face she did not need to read however. He was quite capable of making his thoughts heard even as Evan spoke. His mutters and curses filled every pause in the story.

Gordon returned to the room just as Lord Thomas rose to his feet with a shaking fist and a loud curse in reference to Evan's origins, and a demand for immediate reparations to his daughter's honor. With Gordon returned to the line of fire, he set his artillery on the viscount, too, until all the room filled with the shouts of men demanding to be heard.

Michael tried to press his father to silence. The earl vehemently protested the insult to his grandsons. And the twins rose to the defense of each other and the protection of Daphne. The cacophony was tremendous and pointless, for none heard a word of the other.

Agatha sat smiling into her embroidery. Daphne gave her an amazed look and started to rise to lend her pleas to Michael's, but her aunt held her arm.

"Let them bluster and let it out of their systems. Then we'll have some sense. Have you decided which of them you prefer? I should think you would have your choice when the fur stops flying."

Daphne shook her head. Choice? She had come here a month ago prepared to be a spinster. She was not at all certain that she was prepared to give up that decision in favor of men who thought her incapable of directing her own life. Her gaze fell thoughtfully on the darker twin, who had retreated to watching the window again. It was evident he had already resigned her to his brother without a protest. She didn't see much choice in that.

"I don't give a devil for your reasons!" Lord Thomas shouted above Gordon's reasoning protest. "My daughter's been compromised and I mean to see her wed. Dashed if I care which of you does it, but it will be pistols at dawn if one of you don't step forward. My Daphne's a good girl. I'll not see her ruined by your frippery notions. Murderin' bounders and highwaymen! The devil take the lot of you. I ain't certain there's a one of you deserves her.''

Evan smiled at that, though only his reflection in the window noted it. The blustery old man might just be right. He and Gordon had played a fool's game from the first, and Daphne had been the innocent victim. She made a lovely victim, he had to admit, with her delicate beauty and wounded eyes and defiant spirit that had turned both him and his brother head over heels. He turned and placed his back to the draperies so he could better observe her reaction to the scene swirling around them.

She seemed quite confused and bewildered by all the shouting. There were shadows under her eyes from the late hours they had kept with their foolish talk of nonexistent futures. He noted again how frail she was, the thin skin pulled tight over cheekbones of the most delicate grace. Her fine, longfingered hands clasped and unclasped in her lap, forbidden the outlet of needlework that her aunt used. She needed the comfort and security of a home where she could be protected and treated gently as she deserved. And he could not offer it. He had meant to try, but Gordon was making it all too obvious that he was the better choice. Even now, he was pacifying their growling elders, bringing order out of chaos, and restoring peace to Daphne's drawn features. Evan's only inclination had been to spirit Daphne off to Gretna and put an end to the argument once and for all. He could see already that that was not a satisfactory solution.

"My heir is right." The earl spoke into a sudden lull in the roar. "The choice should be Miss Templeton's since both my grandsons have shown their desire for this marriage. I cannot but think there ought to be more time before making such a momentous decision, but if you insist upon it, Templeton, I'll not stand in the way."

Daphne felt the sudden silence and realized she had become the center of attention. She had not been seriously attending to the conversation, having already made up her own mind. To be set abruptly in the midst of it left her even more bewildered.

Gordon resolved her confusion by coming to kneel beside her chair. His coat of blue superfine fit superbly over strong shoulders and fell gracefully over narrow hips. The white linen at his throat was still immaculate despite the day's activities. A gold watch fob was the only adornment on his discreetly striped buff vest. He was every inch the nobleman from the crown of his golden head to the tips of his polished Hessians. And he lifted Daphne's hand with great respect and gentleness as he spoke.

"I realize we have been arguing your fate with all the selfishness of our natures, but it's time that you make your desires known, my love. I've tried to tell you of how I feel. I think you are not unaware of it. Could you possibly find it in your heart to forgive my slowness in speaking my mind and accept my suit?"

Gordon was all that a lady could want in a husband. He was kind, generous, intelligent, respectful—she had run over the list in her mind a dozen times. And now he was opening himself to public rejection for her sake, to give her a choice. She did not know if he did it out of sympathy or honor or a misplaced sense of gratitude, but none of these were enough to base a marriage on. Yet she could not bring herself to reject him in front of all these people. She owed him that much for his consideration.

Daphne clasped his hand between hers and tried to express with her touch what she could not say with words. "I am more than honored, my lord. I am overwhelmed. But I do not think this is the time or the place to decide. You must see to the care of your family first. You, of all people, know that any harm that has come to me has been of my own doing. I would not have your suit from fear of the consequences I must face. I am quite content to face them on my own.''

Evan felt a wave of both pain and relief wash over him as the room broke out in a babble of angry voices once again. But this time, he was able to avert it. Giving the window another quick glance, he stepped forward and with a voice that carried on the field of battle, he announced, "I believe Captain Rollings has arrived. Shall I turn myself in now or wait until he is introduced to the company?''

The almost ascetic features of the older man were reflected in the carriage window as he stared pensively out on the rolling moor. His blond hair had grown somewhat thin and receded with age, but his slender height and aristocratic features showed none of the ravages of time. His thin lips were pressed together as if in anger, but his companion disregarded the expression.

"After all these years, why are you doing this now? You said yourself you made a bundle on that last roll. Why grovel at their call when you don't need to?''

The older man returned his attention to his son. Hugh was a well-looking lad of four and twenty, the dark locks he had inherited from his mother framing a face not quite handsome, but certainly striking. There had been very little wealth with which to spoil him, and certainly little in the way of attention or affection from either of his parents, but he had grown up passably enough despite this neglect. There might be hope for him yet.

Patiently, Robert explained, "Since I am in need of nothing, I am arriving at their request, not mine. I do not know what it is that they want, but I will not be the one groveling.''

"Well, it seems deuced odd that they acknowledge your existence after a score or more years. If it were not for mother's insistence, I would not have joined you. We've lived without them all our lives. I, for one, have no need of them now.''

190   *Patricia Rice*

Hugh's father suddenly looked weary, but his hands continued resting easily on his elegant walking stick. "Family and connections can be important. Your brother has already discovered that, to his grief. I'll do what I can to make it easier for you. You should not have to continue paying for my mistakes."

The young man grimaced irritably but did not belabor the point. "I don't see why my cousin Gordon did not make the request himself. It's deuced shabby of him to go through his fiancée's brother."

"My nephews were still in leading strings when last I saw them. I cannot know their minds. It could very well be a mad-cap notion of his fiancée's. Women have strange fancies. You have only to consider your mother to know the truth of that."

"Do not bring my mother into this. She has done the best she could, under the circumstances."

Robert Griffin sighed. "Neither of us has ever done the best we could, but it is too late now to correct that. At least give me credit for having married her. I have yet to see her reasoning in refusing the name it cost me so much to give."

Hugh knew they had touched upon the one sensitive issue that still rankled after years of separation. His parents had kept different households since his birth, for excellent reasons on both their parts. The idea of two such self-centered, arrogant, irresponsible people living together was far beyond his limited ability to imagine, but he had spent the better part of his life speculating on the question between them now.

Carefully, he voiced his opinion on the matter. "I do believe she was trying to protect you, sir. All the *ton* thinks her your former mistress. There is no credit in being leg-shackled to a common actress."

Robert sent his younger son a skeptical look, then leaned back in his seat to consider the scenery once again. The damned fool woman in a fit of temper or passionate loyalty might have thought to protect him once, but it was at a high cost to his sons now. The time had come to rectify the mistake.

Trying not to hope, he cursed the miserable wilderness around them and gave no thought to the next few hours.

EIGHTEEN

Captain Rollings let his gaze roam over the respectable occupants of the elegant drawing room. Scattered about on satin settees and velvet upholstery, illuminated by crystal lamps, protected from the dreary weather by silk-lined walls and brocade draperies, they possessed all the trappings of the wealth and indolence he craved. He could not believe half their tale, and his gaze strayed back to the one man who remained standing.

Damn Evan Griffin for making a bloody fool of him. An officer who bought his commission was no trained soldier. Captain Evan Griffin must have nine lives to have survived the war. Rollings swung his gaze to the pampered heir sprawling in the chair beside his fiancée, watching his every move. They were lying to him, he felt certain, but what was at the root of their lies he could not comprehend.

The wily old earl the captain disregarded entirely. He was too old to be of consequence, and his conniving days were past. The women he disregarded, too. The younger two were good to look upon, but his tastes ran to the lively miss back in town, not the elite atmosphere of these fragile creatures. Women had no thoughts of their own, so he would find no truth there.

He briefly considered Lord Thomas and his son but could not quite place them in the way of things. The older man appeared ready to burst a blood vessel, and the younger posed little threat. He was obviously no Corinthian, and of little influence.

That left the twins. It was always the twins. Even now, seeing them together, he found it hard to believe they were so much alike. They had tricked him, but he was not exactly certain as to how yet. It didn't matter. Time was growing short, and they had left him only this one opportunity. It wouldn't be the same as nabbing the highwayman, but with the two of them alive, there was little else he could do. He heartily regretted the murderous rage that had set these events in motion, but it was too late to turn back now.

Rollings nodded reluctantly, his gaze returning to the viscount and his fiancée on the settee. Miss Templeton didn't appear too happy about being sent away. He had been of the opinion that all females preferred the fashionable districts of Bath to the isolation of Devon, but that was none of his concern. She was harmless enough, as was Miss Griffin. The task should be quite simple.

"If the matter is as urgent as you say, my men and I will be ready within the hour, my lord." Rollings made a formal bow to the earl.

"Good, good." The old man rose to dismiss the young officer. "The gels will be waiting. I'll have the carriage brought 'round."

Rollings stepped quickly from the room, leaving a vacuum of silence behind. No one seemed pleased with the decisions made here today, but now that they were made, none dared risk further argument. Daphne glanced at Evan, but he seemed a million miles away. She could only be content that he had been persuaded from making a confession of guilt. The captain had obviously believed very little of his story of his return from the dead, but that was of no consequence for the nonce. What mattered was putting an end to the danger to Gordon. She wasn't at all certain they had found a satisfactory conclusion to that problem. And it was obvious the twins weren't happy about the earl's decision to remain with them, thereby increasing the number of targets. But she had no influence in their argument. She could only agree to accompany Melanie to safety and hope for the best.

They decided for the sake of convenience and comfort it would be best to take only Daphne's maid with them in Gordon's landau. The rest of their baggage and Melanie's maid could follow later. While Melanie went upstairs to complete her packing, Daphne thought to take her aunt's vehicle to gather up her belongings and Tillie's, but the twins became adamant that she not travel anywhere without an escort. Since no one could agree on who that escort would be, it became obvious that she would have to wait for Captain Rollings to return with his men. She had very little left to do. It would just be a matter of carrying down her trunk and listening to Tillie's hysterics for not being given better notice. That was better than watching Gordon and Evan glaring at each other over so small a detail.

She listened in resignation as her father and Michael argued over whether they ought to follow in their carriage or stay to await Robert Griffin's arrival, in whatever form it took. To Daphne, the unknown uncle seemed more a character from a fanciful novel than a real person, and Daphne was finding it harder and harder to believe in him. After all, she had been here over a month and there had been no incidents that she knew of. Perhaps the twins were guilty of overactive imaginations. Accidents happened all the time. Their father's death and Evan's fall could easily have been accidents. That was much easier to believe than that one's family might try to kill one.

But in the end, Daphne acquiesced quietly to being bundled into a carriage with Melanie and her trunk. She needed time to think, and it would be much easier without the pressure of the men pushing her this way and that. Maybe when this was all over they would forget her indiscretion and let her live her own life, but she wasn't at all certain that she even wanted that anymore. Evan's caresses had awakened a longing inside her that she could no longer pretend didn't exist. If she closed her eyes, she could feel him next to her now, and her imagination easily sketched in what might have happened had Gordon not arrived to stop them. She didn't know the details of physical intimacy, but she could feel them inside herself, and she wasn't certain she could live without them forever.

But those were scarcely suitable thoughts for a fashionable young lady on her way to Bath. Daphne discreetly kissed her father and brother's cheeks in farewell, ignored Evan as he ignored her, accepted Gordon's assist into the carriage, and wrapped her fingers primly in her lap as Captain Rollings inspected the carriage harness and supervised the loading. He had two of his men with him, apparently the only two capable of riding or fortunate enough to own horses.

Daphne tried to remember the conversation she had overheard once on the differences between infantry and cavalry, but she could only remember the young ladies of her acquaintance exclaiming over the dashing uniforms of the Hussars. Evan had been a Hussar, she knew, but she had never seen him in uniform. She didn't think Captain Rolling's uniform was that of a cavalry man, and she remembered Evan's saying the soldiers who hunted him didn't have horses. Perhaps Gordon had offered part of his stable for the soldier's use. Captain Rollings had evidently brought his own horse, for she remembered his chase of the highwayman. Perhaps officers were allowed horses.

These ruminations carried Daphne through the final farewells. If she thought only neutral thoughts, she could get through this without a tear. She really didn't think she would ever come back, but that was one of those things she had to try not to think about. She lifted her lace mitten in a last wave from the window as the carriage jolted into motion.

She tried to memorize their faces as they stood there on the stone steps, watching the carriage drive off. Evan stood aloof, his arms crossed forbiddingly across his wide chest, a black frown between his eyebrows. Gordon stood beside the earl, lending his arm in support. Whatever his expression, it was not so easily visible as Evan's frown. Michael stood with hands in pockets beside his father, who held a large handkerchief to his nose. Daphne smiled at that. Perhaps her father wasn't quite so bad as she once had painted him. They might deal well with each other now that he realized she was no longer a child and had no intention of becoming an invalid for his sake.

As the carriage rolled down the drive and into the lane, she looked for the bold uniform of Captain Rollings, but he obviously rode on ahead. She had heard the others ordered to ride behind, and she did not envy them their position behind the mud-spattering wheels of the vehicle. Perhaps they would ride far behind.

Melanie looked solemn as she stared at the seat before them, and her voice was less than its usual exuberant tone when she spoke. "Will you tell me what is happening? I am so tired of being treated as a baby."

It really ought to be one of the family doing the explaining, but the earl had refused to accompany them as originally planned. And Melanie really had a right to know some of the story. How much, was the problem. Daphne turned her attention to this problem and away from her own, and haltingly set out on explanations of events she wasn't at all certain she understood or believed herself.

The carriage pulled to the side to allow another vehicle to pass by in the narrow lane. Both Daphne and Melanie glanced up in surprise for few others in the area possessed carriages and those few seldom had need to come this way. The vehicle looked little more than a hired hackney with the curtains drawn, and they could only speculate on the occupants. Daphne felt a qualm of fear but steadied it by telling herself that a dangerous murderer was unlikely to drive up to the gate in broad daylight in a hired coach.

The carriage traveled faster now, as if the small delay had put them behind schedule. Daphne winced as a wheel hit a rut washed out by the rain, throwing her against the window. She had gradually overcome her fear of carriages, but not of speed, and she clenched her fingers nervously. Such haste was not only unnecessary, but dangerous. Drawing a deep breath to summon her courage, she beat her umbrella against the driver's door for attention. This was as bad as riding with her father's Wild Willie. The two old men were devoted to each other, and they were quite likely to die together if her father didn't pension the coachman off.

The carriage only slid into another muddy rut and lurched and drove on, the driver heedless of her angry rap. Daphne pursed her lips, planning the stiff scold she would deliver once they reached Aunt Agatha's. She might as well take William on as to continue at this pace.

When they rolled right past the drive to Aunt Agatha's, Daphne flew into a rage. This was the outside of enough! Melanie stared in wonder as her mild companion beat furiously at the driver's door, then tried to unfasten the window so she might give vent to her fury. The carriage jostled and rocked so, she was only thrown back into her seat for her efforts.

Melanie attempted to reassure. "Captain Rollings will see the error shortly and come back for us. He must have ridden on ahead and the driver did not see where he went."

Daphne shook her head. "Gordon's driver knows the way as well as I do. And he does not treat his equipage with such contempt. There is something wrong here, but I cannot know what."

Melanie's eyes grew wider. However vaguely informed by Daphne's expurgated explanations, she understood enough to know they could be in danger. She pushed back the curtains and tried to find the reassuring sight of the uniformed soldiers. "Do you think something happened back there when we pulled over? I heard nothing untoward, but I was listening to your tale and not to what was happening outside."

Daphne frowned. "But the soldiers are armed. They could not be replaced without our hearing their struggle. Perhaps we are imagining things. Did you notice the driver when we left? Perhaps he is not Gordon's usual driver but one of the soldiers in disguise." Or Wild Willie, she thought to herself. It would be just like her father to assign his favorite servant to the task of seeing her to safety. Safety, indeed! She caught the carriage strap as the wheel hit a rock and sent them bouncing off the leather roof.

Melanie shook her head. "I cannot say for certain, but I would have noticed had he worn other than Gordon's livery." She pressed her face against the glass, straining for some sign of their guards.

Earlier, Daphne had wondered how this day could be any worse. Now she knew. It was becoming quite obvious this was not any normal ride. Whether they were racing away from something or toward something, she could not detect, but the chances of their getting anywhere in one piece seemed increasingly small. This was no solid wooden mail coach meant for a team of six and high speeds, and this rutted lane was no improved turnpike. The fragile wheels of the carriage and the delicate legs of Gordon's high-stepping horses could not keep this reckless pace for long. Daphne grimly clenched her teeth and hands and prayed rapidly.

Melanie gave an eager cry and grabbed Daphne's hand as she bounced excitedly in her seat. " 'Tis Rhys! Oh, see, Daphne, he's riding over the moor. He must have been a Hussar like Evan! I've never seen anyone take the hedgerow like that. Has he come to rescue us?"

Her companion's excited comments sounded more as if this were some splendid game in which the best man always won. Daphne wouldn't rate Rhys as the best man in any game, but she would take her chances with him before this mad driver. "We'll have to help him. He can't stop the carriage all by himself."

Daphne threw herself into the seat behind the driver and fumbled for the latch to the driver's door. Melanie grew suddenly solemn as Daphne's words took new meaning.

"Surely he won't try to stop the carriage alone. The soldiers . . ." She couldn't express the horror of that thought.

Daphne jerked open the door, caught a glimpse of scarlet and not Gordon's discreet gray and black livery, before a sudden bounce slammed the door shut again. The shock left her breathless, and her mind spun in useless circles. Was Rhys the one they ran from? Could he have been sent to deliver them to the murderers? Or had Captain Rollings gone berserk? Perhaps he didn't recognize the rider approaching. But why would Rhys be so recklessly racing after them if there weren't trouble? And where was Evan?

That thought struck even greater fear in her heart. Evan trusted Rhys. If Rhys had turned traitor, what would he have done to Evan? And the others? It was becoming more than obvious that if they were in trouble, it shouldn't just be Rhys out there chasing across the moor. All the Griffins and her father and brother should be galloping down the road.

The sound of gunfire startled Daphne from her thoughts. Melanie gave a terrified scream and glued herself to the window where the passing landscape had become a blur of motion. Daphne reached to struggle with the door to the driver's box again. She didn't know what she would accomplish by doing so, but she could not sit helplessly and go to her destruction.

Looking out, she could see no sign of the driver's livery, and she did her best to school her rising panic. She could not tell for certain, but from the slope of the land in front of them and the blur of trees, she very much suspected they were heading toward the river. Taking that narrow bridge at this pace was foolhardy to an extreme, and Daphne glanced anxiously at the soldier wielding the reins. Was this his idea of protecting them?

Evan swallowed his fear and rage as the carriage careened down the lane toward him. The driver would shortly be in firing range of his pistol, but he dared not use it while the horses were for all practical purposes out of control. The rain-swollen river lay directly ahead, the wooden bridge appearing little more than a toothpick against the debris of the flood. The man was mad to aim at that, mad or supremely confident of his driving abilities.

Gambling on the latter, Evan gave the signal his men had been waiting for. With yells and curses, the motely band of ragged ex-soldiers began heaving the heavy branch-laden top of a fallen tree across the muddy lane.

It was a gamble that could cost him the lives of those nearest and dearest to him, but it was no worse than allowing them to cross that bridge and the swollen river. Here, he would be in control. Down there, the bastard on the driver's box would have the advantage.

Evan held his pistol steady as Rhys wildly rode between the carriage and its outriders. Gordon came up from behind them, neatly throwing the two soldiers into a quandary. Uncertain who was the enemy, they threw up their hands in surrender, but Evan breathed no sigh of relief. His gaze focused intently on the man with the reins in his hands, and his breath almost left his lungs as he recognized the pale face appearing in the driver's door.

He wanted to scream at her to get down, to take the floor and lie flat, but he was helpless at this distance. He could only watch in horror as the scarlet-coated driver realized what was happening and began to haul at the reins. The carriage could overturn at any minute, and Evan would be the one responsible for sending two innocent females to their fate. Anguish squeezed at his heart for being given two such impossible choices, but his hand never wavered from the pistol.

NINETEEN

The carriage's sudden jerk forward flung Daphne back to the seat. The light vehicle began to sway dangerously. Acting on instinct or feeling the wild fear of Evan's unspoken cry, Daphne grabbed Melanie's arm and pushed her to the floor. Too frightened to protest, Melanie curled in a ball between the two seats, her light pelisse engulfing her from head to toe. Daphne squeezed down beside her, half on top, forming a protective cushion against whatever might come.

She closed her eyes as the horses screamed a protest against the sudden restraint. She felt the wheels sliding uncontrollably on the muddy road and knew a crash was imminent. It was akin to reliving that horrible night so many years ago, only from the inside looking out this time. All they could do was pray.

The carriage tilted precariously as it hit a rut, then righted itself under an expert hand. In the next minute, a wheel spun off into the ditch, the carriage lurched, shuddered, and slowly fell onto its side.

Melanie screamed as they were left hanging feet first over the ditch, the door to freedom above their heads. Any sudden movement might tilt the carriage further, and they would be sliding down the embankment. Wild curses and pistol shots reverberated through the air above them, and both women crouched in panic on the panel that had become their floor.

The door over their heads flew open, and Daphne gave a gasp of relief as she recognized the glittering braid of Captain Rollings in the opening. Before she could offer a word of gratitude, a long, black pistol was aimed at her head, and a menacing growl replaced the polite tones she had learned to expect from the soldier.

"Climb up out of there and don't say a word unless I tell you."

He might as well have told them to part the Red Sea for all they could oblige. Daphne glanced down at her feet where the window showed the dangerous embankment sloping to the river, then glanced up at the opening where Rollings evidently clung to the underside of the carriage. The horses were raising furious screams, but they didn't seem cries of pain. She strained to hear other sounds, but fear limited her abilities. She greatly suspected they could die whether they remained here or not.

The only advantage she could find in the situation was if their movements could throw the carriage into a long slide down the embankment, they would also undoubtedly dislodge the fiend in the doorway.

Daphne glared up at him. "Do you think we are some kind of monkeys to perform acrobatics? The carriage needs to be brought back to the road before we slide into the river."

The captain's curse was quickly cut short by a shout from outside. Crouched on the panel, Daphne hugged Melanie's shivering shoulders and gave praise to the heavens above. Evan's voice. He was here.

Rollings turned so violently that the carriage shook. "Stand off, Griffin, or you and your brother will not see your ladies again."

Evan halted his horse in the road and glared at this man he had known as enemy in his highwayman disguise, but had never considered a danger to his family until now. "Don't be absurd, Rollings. Where do you think you will go from here? The trick is up. Throw away the weapon and no one will be harmed."

"I think not." Rollings clung stiffly to the carriage containing his hostages. "All I want is a share of the fortune. You may argue all you like, but the ladies stay with me until my demands are met. They are likely to grow quite uncomfortable shortly, and if the rain begins again, they could be in some danger. I suggest you consult your top-lofty brother and proceed to find a satisfactory sum posthaste. Since it seems I will now have to leave the country to enjoy it, it had best be a sum large enough to persuade me to let these very attractive ladies go.''

Evan could feel the first dribble of rain begin again, and despair took root in his bones and began to grow. He didn't dare look to the men crawling from the woods and along the embankment. Rollings had to know he didn't act alone, but there was no reason to let him know where the others were. If only there were time before the rain began in earnest . . .

"Gordon!" Evan shouted in the direction of the line of trees behind him. The sound of a horse cantering in his direction was sufficient to let him know that his twin was not far away. Together, they could tackle the officer on the carriage, except his pistol was not aimed at his antagonists, but at the innocent women inside.

"This gentleman seems to think we possess a fortune in which he wishes to share. How much do you have on you?"

Gordon shrugged his broad shoulders against the damp superfine of his tailored coat as he rode up. "I didn't come prepared for travel. Will my watch and fob suit?"

Rollings's pale face grew dark with anger. "Do not play the fools with me. It is only your damned almighty luck that I'm not the next heir to your title, and I can arrange it still. But I can live without names and titles if wealthy enough. I suggest you hurry back to our holy grandfather and find out how much gold you can uncover if you wish to see the ladies alive again."

Less than an hour ago, Evan had learned of the existence of his Uncle Robert's two sons and the fact that they lived under the name of their actress mother—Rollings. It had taken only a few additional words to realize they had sent Daphne and Melanie out in the dubious care of an embittered, melancholy young man. It had scarcely taken his uncle's warning that the Shelce coach was moving at remarkable speed to send Evan flying after it; he had already been halfway across the room in the direction of the door.

Now Evan held his gaze on his newly found cousin as Rhys surreptitiously slid beneath the carriage with a stout limb in his hand. A few more of those and the carriage would be steadier, if not upright. He prayed the cousin he knew now as Gregory Rollings wouldn't notice the difference until it was too late.

The stealth of the ex-soldiers as they slid logs and debris down the ditch to balance the carriage made Evan proud of their training. They were good men, all, despite the fact that they had come home with parts of them left behind on the battlefield. Somehow, he would see them well rewarded. In the meantime, he must keep Rollings distracted from their presence. Why had it never occurred to him that his uncle might have sons?

"Would you have us sign over the deed to the estate? Or drive the contents of the stables down here? How do you propose that we raise funds while our sister and Miss Templeton dangle over a riverbank? It could take days. Be reasonable and come down from there. Your father is back at the house with the earl. Come talk with them and let us get the ladies out of that wreck."

"You think I want to hang? Do you think for a moment that my father cares if I do or not? Had he cared, he would have seen to it that we had the same wealth and respect and name as the pampered favorites. But all he cares about is his own selfish pursuits. He would not even fight for me when they asked me to resign my commission. I've earned this rank. I've made my way despite him. And I'll not let my life be thrown away because of him. I'll not follow in his footsteps and live on the edge of poverty when there is all the Griffin wealth to be had for the asking. Go back to the earl and demand my rights!"

From below, Daphne heard this outraged speech and felt her spirits sink lower. They had reached an impasse of a certainty. From the anguish in Rollings's voice it was apparent that the loss of his commission had been the final blow to his precarious hold on respectability. Without even the life of a soldier to uphold him, he had no future at all. Daphne hoped Evan realized the dangerous despair behind this admission.

She glanced down to the window where they had already discovered the quiet activity below them. Rhys was struggling valiantly with a large timber, and to Daphne's surprise, even her brother was crawling through the mud to prop the carriage in place. If they could only stabilize it, the windows could be removed and they could crawl out the bottom. How long would it take to balance a carriage?

As if sensing the activity, Rollings swung around and pointed the gun at the interior again. Daphne swiftly lifted her arm to balance against the seat, blotting out the view of the window with her pelisse. With any luck, at this angle, Melanie would hide the other window.

Rollings glared down at the two fragile women quietly crouching against the carriage side, their light summer silk pelisses glowing in the dusky light, their prim bonnets still perched fashionably upon their curls despite the upheaval. He had no grudge against women. This had not been his choice of revenge, but they were leaving him with little enough to live for.

"Quit rocking the carriage or you'll be in the river before I am," he warned them firmly.

"We cannot sit or stand like this," Daphne protested. "Can no one right the carriage? Or at least help us out? I do not know your argument, but it cannot be gentlemanly to allow us to languish like this. Miss Griffin has been recently ill, and the damp may irreparably harm her. Can you find no other means to have this discussion?"

Daphne cried her lament for as long as she was able, hoping to give the men beneath the time they needed. Rollings's frown warned she had pushed far enough.

"This isn't a picnic, Miss Templeton, and I am not the local Robin Hood. Perhaps you should speak to your lovers out here and persuade them of your desperate plight. They do not yet seem convinced."

The insult flew right by her head. Daphne heard something else in his voice, and she tested it carefully. "If you found that Robin Hood, would they allow you to keep your commission?"

That tactic startled Rollings, and he stared move carefully into her upturned face. "I had some hopes of that, but it is too late now. Unless you wish to climb up here and speak with my cousins, you would do best to sit there quietly."

"I would like to climb up, but I cannot move without disturbing the carriage. Evan can help you find the thief. He has been on his trail all along. That would be a much more honorable solution to the problem, would it not? And then Miss Dalrymple would have reason to be proud of you. She is inordinately fond of you, you must know."

Rollings desperately wished to believe her for he knew he was in a more than precarious situation, but the hard experience of his youth warned that the honorable way never won him riches. His reply was bitter. "Once the squire learns I am no more than an unnamed son of a common actress, he'll no longer welcome my suit. It makes no matter that by law I have my father's name when he does not admit it to anyone."

"Don't be daft, Gregory," a new voice intruded with bored languor. "Your mother thought her stage name more suitable than mine. If your argument is with me, come down from there and leave the ladies out of it."

Rollings swung around to confront the tall, handsomely tailored gentleman who was his father stepping out of the hackney they had passed earlier. An older version of his father joined him, the earl's dark gaze avidly sweeping over the scarlet-suited soldier without heed to the twins in the road beyond him.

Before Rollings could answer, Evan's anger boiled over. "Your argument is an old one, sir. The villain will face me for his deeds this day and in the past. I have lost a father due to his vile actions. I would have lost my own life and that of my brother had he had his way. And now he threatens my sister and my fiancée. I will see him hang first."

Being labeled Evan's fiancée did not give Daphne the thrill it ought for her attention was solely on the anguished man clinging to the pistol pointed at her head. She could not see who had arrived, but she had heard the carriage and could hear something of the newcomer's words. Could this be the infamous Uncle Robert they had feared?

The captain's furious outburst at Evan's words halted further inquiry. "Your father! What in hell had I to do with

your father? Are you that desperate to see me hang? Thanks
to my own loving father, I was stationed at White Hall when
he died, instead of on the Continent where I belonged. He
can use his influence when he chooses."

Even the bored gentleman raised a golden eyebrow as he
regarded his mounted nephew. "What bee have you in your
bonnet? Your father broke his neck in a drunken riding
accident. Have you come all the way home from the wars
to accuse us of murder?"

The hint of amusement in his voice brought furious color
to both men in the saddles, and they turned their attention
fully to the man they had originally labeled villain.

"It was no accident, sir," Gordon replied with dignity.
"The straps of my saddle were cut in a similar incident. I
was fortunate enough to survive. My father was not."

The newcomer looked startled, then grim. He turned to
the earl beside him. "You told me nothing of this."

The earl snorted. "I knew nothing of it myself, and I
certainly wouldn't have told you if I had. You haven't
concerned yourself with your family in years. Now look at
the results of it standing there on the carriage like some
blasted tobyman. Get down from there, boy, and let us
discuss this like gentlemen."

Daphne gave a sigh of exasperation at this irascible
command. Did the earl truly think a desperate man would
bow to being treated like a child? What did they mean by
standing there arguing while she and Melanie were in
imminent danger of sliding down the hillside? It was time
someone put an end to this impasse, and if no one else did,
she would.

Kneeling gingerly, feeling the carriage rocking only lightly
with the movement, Daphne ran her fingers over the window
frame, searching for the mechanism that removed the window
when the top was down. From below, Rhys reached up to
guide her search, and between them, they unlatched the
leather hood and gently urged the window from its frame.
A rush of cool air swept Daphne's face, and she took a deep
breath. She had not known how stifled she had been in there
until now.

Melanie grasped her arm and glanced nervously upward to where the head and shoulders of Captain Rollings stood framed in the doorway, but his attention was fully on the irate argument outside. Daphne shook her head and carefully sat down on the edge of the open window frame. She hoped the men below had the decency to avert their eyes from her ankles as they dangled out the opening.

To her surprise, two strong hands reached in to lift her out, and she was suddenly crouching beside her brother as the carriage teetered overhead. She gave a gasp at the rocking motion caused by her departure, but Rhys and several of his men were already grasping the vehicle to hold it steady while Melanie edged toward the opening.

Daphne crouched low and moved out of the way as Michael reached to lift Melanie down. The loss of this last weight sent the precariously balanced vehicle into another groan and shudder, and a shout from above warned all was not well. Rhys grabbed her arm and Michael grabbed Melanie's, and everyone scampered for the relative safety of the muddy hillside.

Evan noted the first lurch of the carriage with nervous expectation, praying Rhys and his men knew what they were about. When the second lurch jarred Rollings's hold on the undercarriage, Evan was ready. Kicking his heels into his mount, he raced forward, raised his riding crop, and swung it viciously at his cousin's upraised gun hand. The move called for a careful maneuver and perfect timing to hit the target and bring the horse out of the carriage's wheels without harm. Evan felt a jolt of satisfaction as the crop connected and Rollings screamed. The gun exploded behind him as he jerked his horse to the left, but Evan ignored the mass confusion he left behind. With a cry, he raced toward the hillside and the muddy figures emerging from beneath the carriage.

TWENTY

Daphne dashed into Evan's arms as he dismounted and held them out. Her cheek scraped against the smooth weave of his coat, and she breathed deeply of the scents of starched linen and horse sweat and bay rum, reveling in these sensations she had feared never to experience again. Hard arms clenched her fiercely, briefly, and she had time to feel the swift beat of his heart before they were torn asunder.

"Unhand my sister," Michael intoned tersely, his pale but muddy face a picture of fury at the sight of the reckless adventurer crushing Daphne against him.

Evan obediently released her, knowing he had no right to stake his claim. He had just needed the reassurance that she was unharmed, he told himself, and his gaze strayed guiltily to his sister.

Melanie was staring adoringly into Rhys's grim but awestruck visage. Were he not in such pain, Evan would have to chuckle at the Welshman's expression. Instead, he turned his attention back to the chaos he had left on the road, ignoring the emptiness at his side when Daphne reluctantly took her brother's arm to find safety on level land.

Gordon had successfully relieved Captain Rollings of any other weapons and brought him down from the carriage to face a jury of his peers—his family. The boredom had been wiped from Robert Griffin's face as he came to stand before his eldest son, but the arrival of an erratically driven ancient barouche ended any opening for hostility or peace.

Daphne gripped her brother's arm and sighed in exasperation as her father's coachman nearly ran over the earl, sideswiped the hackney, and came to a halt in the ditch. The various scars on the vehicle's wooden sides told tales of more than one such landing, and Daphne waited impatiently for the tirade of mutual curses to end as her father leapt out and berated the impudent Willie. To her surprise, a second figure jumped from the overturned barouche and stood expectantly surveying the scene of chaos.

Finding the figure in scarlet, his eyes lit and he strode forward shouting, "Gregory!" The resemblance between the two was such that they could almost be mistaken for twins.

Before Daphne could reconcile all these events in her spinning head, Gordon was at her side, appropriating her other arm and returning Michael's glare with equanimity. "I think the ladies should be escorted home immediately. The hackney is still upright and Llewellyn can maneuver it around while the others are righting my carriage, if that is all right with you?"

Before Michael could murmur an assent, Daphne jerked her hands from the arms of both men. "You might ask if it is all right with me. It isn't. Nothing has been settled yet, and it appears very much as if Evan is about to come to fisticuffs with both your cousins at once. I know upon occasion I misunderstand people's intentions, but I don't think I am so bad as to mistake that particular stance. Perhaps all three of them ought to be bound and gagged for safety's sake."

That startling announcement brought her companion's gaze swinging back to the road, and with a curse, Gordon hastily leapt to his brother's side.

As the cousins dived into the fracas and the muddy lane became a sprawling free-for-all of flailing arms and legs, the older men watched with resignation and a touch of sorrow.

"Gregory didn't do it, you know," Robert spoke idly, poking his cane into the mud of the road. "He was at White Hall, just as he said, raising hell and demanding his transfer to Brussels. I'm not saying he wouldn't have tried it if he had thought of it, but I rather believe George's death coupled with the end of the war is what started him resenting his cousins."

The earl wearily attempted to maintain his noble carriage as he watched his heir plant a facer squarely in the center

of the captain's nose. He winced at the crunch, and sighed.
"I have had time to think on what Gordon said. It is very
possible that George's death was an accident. There was
never any evidence that his saddle was damaged. George had
been blue-deviled for a long time, and that jump was a bad
one even when he had all his faculties about him. I'll accept
that it was an accident, but there is no such explanation of
the incidents toward the twins afterward. Evan could have
been killed when his horse went off the bridge. You can see
the river from here. If Gregory shot at a man on that bridge,
he intended murder."

Robert's aristocratically narrow face deepened into gray
lines of anxiety as his eyes sought his sons in the melee. They
were younger than the twins, but not by enough to make a
physical difference. He flinched perceptibly as the younger
went sprawling backward under Evan's forceful blow. "The
shooting incident must have happened shortly after word that
Gregory was to resign his commission. With the war over,
they had no need of the excess of officers. He was devastated
and petitioned for relief, but he received no promises. I think
it festered inside him. We have never been close, so I can't
speak in certainties, but today's episode reveals much of his
state of mind. If I had only known . . ."

Both men grew silent over this sad commentary on the lost
years between them. The argument over Robert's marriage
to an actress had been violent and irrevocable, but at this
distance, it could also be seen as the folly of youth and not
worth a score of years from their lives. The brawl before
them now was as much a result of their separation as it was
of the marriage. It could easily have been averted.

"Never mind that. What should we do now?"

Robert looked startled as his father consulted his advice
for what surely must have been the first time in his life. His
lips quirked oddly in the corners as the earl refused to meet
his eye but continued staring at the brawl in the road. It was
as much of a truce as he would ever be offered, and he
accepted it. Age had a way of mellowing even the most
virulent of emotions.

Robert's glance went to the scruffy scoundrels on the

hillside and the two horrified women being held back by two
husky young men. He had been the villain for so long, he
wasn't certain anyone would consider his change of heart
now, but he had to begin somewhere.

"I'd suggest recruiting those young brutes to pull apart
the melee. They're already filthy. There is no sense in our
emulating them."

The earl's lips turned upward wryly at his son's bored
drawl. He had forgotten Robert's tendency to distance
himself from any form of disagreement. How he had ended
up with that fractious harridan of a wife was beyond the earl's
ability to comprehend, but Robert's coolness in the midst
of fury was always welcome. He nodded his head in
agreement and signaled the wooden-legged groom currently
preventing Melanie from running to join her brothers. If Rhys
Llewellyn were a groom, he'd eat his whole damned
carriage. But that was another story.

Rhys reluctantly surrendered Melanie's arm to Michael's
care and bounded down the hillside. At the earl's command,
he put his fingers between his teeth and gave a whistle that
caused the horses to whinny and jump in their traces. The
ragtag band of ex-soldiers swarmed down the hill to the lane.

Daphne breathed a sigh of relief as Rhys ordered the men
into a circle around the combatants and sent them into the
brawl. She actually leaned on Michael's arm for a moment
when Rhys caught the back of Evan's coat and Evan came
up swinging. Rhys went down, but another man was there
to jump on Evan's back, and in a few brief moments, it was
over.

She wanted to run to them, but seeing Gordon emerge from
the fight, she wasn't certain it would be appropriate. She
wasn't even certain how she knew which twin was which
since all she could recognize of them were torn coats and
mud. But she knew. Her gaze lingered a moment longer
while the earl and his son marched forward to give their
verdicts, and then she squeezed Michael's arm and looked
up to him.

"Let us go now," she urged softly.

Michael looked to the two women on his arm, down at

his father berating the coachman's attempts to right the barouche, and nodded. "Miss Templeton, would you care to accompany us to my aunt's? I can't think this is the healthiest place to linger at the moment."

Melanie looked questioningly to Daphne, and at her friend's resolute gaze, reluctantly agreed. The women gave a last backward glance to the shouting argument and mud-covered figures in the road, then silently returned to the only upright carriage remaining.

Agatha had apparently been returned home by one of the viscount's vehicles and was waiting in anxiety when the weary trio showed up on her doorstep. She immediately sent the servants into a frenzy of activity fetching hot water and tubs and clean clothing and relieving all concerned of any thought but of making themselves respectable.

Not that she would ever be respectable again, Daphne thought wryly as she resisted her aunt's suggestion that she retire to bed. The bed looked exceptionally inviting, and she thought she must ache in every bone in her body, but she could go nowhere until she knew what had happened. Sooner or later, Evan would come for her. She had to be ready when he did.

She wasn't ready for the whole lot of them, however. Daphne stared in disbelief and sank down into the nearest chair when a few hours later two carriages and two mounted horsemen rode up the drive. The twins together would be sufficient to wreck what remained of her sanity. Did she truly have to endure the earl and her father, too?

She ought to give thanks that Robert Griffin and his sons did not join the parade. She supposed someone would explain sometime why Captain Rollings wasn't called Griffin, but she really did not need to know right now. She clenched her hands in her lap and waited for the butler to show them in. When she heard Melanie tripping eagerly down the stairs followed by the sturdy tread of her brother, Daphne gave a silent moan of dismay and considered fleeing out the back door like the coward she was.

"For the last time, I tell you, this is most impolite! A

delicate lady like Daphne must be given time to recover
before you descend on her like locusts.''

The insistent tones carried from the foyer, and for once,
Daphne almost agreed with Gordon's verdict, but she had
no intention of letting him know. She might be exhausted.
Her knee might ache worse than after the accident. Her
emotions might be thrumming in terrifying beats through her
center. But she intended to be as regal and composed as her
aunt. She would give no one the opportunity to see her
weakness.

The men burst into the room still arguing, growing quiet
only when they found Daphne patiently waiting for them.
Freshly washed and groomed but sporting the vivid reminders
of their fray, the twins bowed correctly and stepped aside
to allow their elders to take seats. Melanie rushed in to
hug them both and burst into tears, which she hastily dried
upon Michael's appearance. Daphne merely signaled the
servant to fetch a tray.

''We regret the intrusion, Miss Templeton,'' the earl began
quite formally, almost giving the appearance of embarrassment as he glanced at his grandsons.

''But I want this settled once and for all, daughter,'' Lord
Thomas finished the sentence for him. ''I never saw such
a ramshackle lot in all my life. Actresses and highwaymen
and murderin' thieves! It's a frippery lot for all their toplofty
ways. My advice is that you come home with me. See what
happens when there is no one to look after you.'' He sent
a murderous look toward the twins.

Tears sparkled in Daphne's eyes at these words, but she
was given no time to reply. Gordon stepped forward and
made a formal bow before her.

''I realize you have not been given sufficient time to
consider my suit, but events have made it necessary that some
decision be made. If you will agree to be my wife, I will
give you all the time that is necessary to grow accustomed
to the idea.''

Leaning against the mantel, Evan watched this display with
cynical disinterest. It was patently obvious that his brother
had thrown his cap over the windmill to behave in such a

manner. It was equally obvious that Gordon was the better choice for a delicate lady. At the moment, he felt considerable sympathy for his Uncle Robert. A younger brother had little to offer a lady of station. If he did not wish to sell himself, he was better off looking among the petticoat line for companionship. But Evan's expression of disinterest dissolved with Daphne's reply.

She did not look at the man slouching against the mantel. Overriding Melanie's cry of joy, she met Gordon's gaze with equanimity. "I am no wife for you, Gordon, for all I know the honor you do me. I cannot know how much you know of me or my history, but suffice it to say that we would not suit. Your wife will be a countess someday, prepared to meet society on the highest levels. I would not let my past and temperament ruin your happiness."

Before she could add any more such faradiddle, Evan interrupted with a vile curse. Striding forward, he glared at Daphne and his brother. "I never heard such drivel in my life, Miss Templeton. If you don't want to marry him, just tell him so. What your mother did or did not do has no bearing on anything."

Daphne returned his glare. "And who asked your opinion, Mr. Griffin? It seems to me you have been wrong more than once in these last weeks. Leave me to make my own decisions, if you please."

Lord Thomas stepped in with a nervous plea. "Daphne, do not become overset. Perhaps I have rushed things precipitously . . ."

Evan spoke as if there had been no interruption. "Your own decisions! It was your own hare-brained scheme that landed us in the suds last night. Anyone who would ride out like that hasn't the wit to decide what to put on in the morning. The only fault with your past is that you're an impudent hoyden with more temper than sense. You need a keeper, my dear. If Gordon isn't strong enough, then it shall have to be me."

"Now wait one minute—" Gordon protested, but Daphne gave him no time for reply.

"I wouldn't have you if you were the last man on earth,

Evan Griffin! You think I need a keeper? You are the
madman who lived in the woods for no good reason at all.
And they question *my* sanity!''

Several voices rang out in protest at this, but the couple
looking daggers at each other had no heed for any interference. The earl and Lord Thomas exchanged glances, and
interpreting that exchange, Michael offered his arm to
Melanie, who accepted it with a worried look to her brothers
over her shoulder as he escorted her toward the door.

"There is nothing wrong with your sanity, Miss Templeton. It is your wits that are lacking. Gordon is a damned
viscount, for pity's sake! And don't give me that clanker
about not being suitable as a countess. There are more
harebrained countesses out there than I can count.'' When
Daphne opened her mouth to interrupt, Evan rode roughshod
over her words. "And I don't want to hear about your
damned leg or your mother again. If you love him, then
marry him and be done with it! Noble martyrs give me a
pain.''

"Martyrs! Of all the insensitive, idiotic . . . Were I a man,
I would call you out, Evan Griffin! If you think for one
minute that I don't know my own mind . . . Never! Never
in my whole life have I been so insulted.'' Daphne rose with
shaking rage and shook a fist in the face of the broad-
shouldered man leaning over her.

Gordon's shoulders visibly slumped as Agatha gently
touched his arm and nodded toward the exit. He appeared
ready to protest, but the old lady held an admonishing finger
to her lips. Ahead of them, Melanie and Michael had already
disappeared from the room. The two older gentlemen shook
their heads as the argument escalated into a shouting match
that could be heard by the servants in the attic. It was more
than evident, however, that no one would be able to come
between these two. With a slight smile as the "delicate" lady
rammed her fist into his grandson's broad shoulder,
producing a distinctive moan and wince, the earl took Lord
Thomas's arm and steered him toward the door. The north
country lord turned and gave his "invalid" daughter one last

questioning look, then reluctantly followed. Even he could see that Daphne had made her choice. His last look showed the younger twin retaliating by lifting Daphne from her feet, but Lord Thomas didn't think fisticuffs were the young man's intention.

TWENTY-ONE

"They say her mother was quite mad, you know," the elderly lady with her hair in a turban whispered to the stout woman on her right as the bridal couple weaved their way through the crowd.

"His uncle is here!" The stout lady replied with rapture at the *on-dit* she would have to relate later. "They say he is married to a common actress. That's his son over there, the one with the black eye. They say there was some sort of trouble—"

"And look at the groom!" A third lady interrupted in hushed tones. "He looks as if he's just been in a fight. Such a fractious family!"

"He *has* just been in a fight," the turbaned lady sniffed. "He and his cousin were threatening each other to a duel, but unfortunately, no one would provide them weapons. I believe the bride poured cold water over them to break them up. See, his jacket is still dripping. Mad as her mother, I daresay."

"Just in love, I'd say," Lady Agatha sniffed, coming up in time to hear this last. "Lord Shelce means to put Evan up for parliament, so you shall have plenty of opportunity to observe their madness. It's about time the stodgy government heard some youthful voices."

"Well, if fighting in the streets is the manner in which the young man makes his point, I daresay we will hear much of him." The lady in the turban nodded stiffly to her acquaintance before whispering aside to her companion, "Madness runs in the family, you know. Parliament, indeed!"

At that moment, the subject under discussion was carefully manipulating his bride through the crowd toward the

door. She sent him a nervous look as she recognized Evan's
direction, but his hold remained firm as he guided her through
the shoals of gossiping relations and into the freedom of the
hall.

"We cannot leave so early," Daphne protested, throwing
a last look to the crowd before facing the emptiness of the
stairway ahead.

"We cannot leave soon enough for me." Without a word
of warning, Evan swung her up in his very wet arms and
made his way toward the upper floor.

Daphne shrieked as the damp seeped through the fragile
silk of her gown. "Put me down, Evan Griffin! You are
ruining my gown."

"Fair enough," he replied with equanimity. "You have
ruined my best coat. We shall have to shop in London for
new clothes."

He had looked so absurdly handsome standing there at the
altar garbed all in brown and gold; Daphne's heart pounded
just at the remembrance, and she clung a little tighter to
Evan's broad shoulders. "I want to go to Italy first," she
murmured against his wilting cravat.

"We have to go through London to get to Italy. And if
I am going to be the breadwinner of this family, I must
present my credentials to the proper people before we go.
Grandfather's given me introductions to the ministers most
influential in the interests of our ex-soldiers. Do you think
you can behave yourself long enough for me to make a place
for myself in their cabinets?"

That was a considerably appropriate question since now
that they had reached the privacy of a spacious bed chamber,
Daphne was busily decimating the knot of his linen. "Oh,
I shall be all that is proper. You, I fear, are the one who
will make a cake of the entire process. Imagine inviting Rhys
to be your best man instead of your brother! They will have
naught else to talk about for weeks. And you never have told
me his story."

Grinning, Evan eagerly abetted his bride's attempts to
remove him from his sodden clothes. "Rhys will tell his tale
in all due time, my love. And I think the biddies might think

of one or two other things to cluck about. The bride's pouring a pitcher of water over the groom is not a wedding custom that I can remember, but no doubt everyone else will for a long time to come.''

"You were the one who gave in to the urge for fisticuffs,'' Daphne said stiffly, starting to pull away from the eagerness of Evan's fingers as they strayed from his shirt to her bodice.

"Young Hugh needed to be set to rights somehow. I wasn't the one who sent his bloodthirsty brother to India. Grandfather did. If he wouldn't listen to reason, he would have to listen to the point of a sword.''

"A sword? You would have fought with swords? How very quaint. And here I thought it was my honor you were defending.'' Daphne gave a happy sigh as her fingers at last found the warmth of Evan's hard chest through the linen of his shirt.

"Everybody knows that was already lost,'' Evan whispered maliciously as he began to work on the row of tiny seed pearl buttons down her bodice front. "Which reminds me, I owe your brother Michael a good thrashing when I see him next for reporting that little incident to the earl. He knew I had every intention of marrying you. It wasn't as if we were doing anything we hadn't done before.''

Daphne laughed against her husband's coat, then quivered a little as his hand eased into the openings of her bodice. "He didn't know that you made a habit of visiting ladies in their chambers in the middle of the night. I fear Michael has grown quite stodgy with age. He was most thoroughly shocked to find you there.''

"He would have been even more thoroughly shocked had he waited a few minutes longer. You have been driving me out of my mind since the first night I met you. I love you beyond all reason, Daphne Elaine. It is about time I had some satisfaction.''

"I thought we were going to London,'' Daphne protested faintly as Evan's hand successfully breeched the second barrier of her clothing.

"And so we will,'' he murmured indistinctly as he took

advantage of the now open neckline of her gown to press his ardent kisses there. "When I have taught you how the proper wife of a government official behaves."

Daphne's hands crept over the warm skin of Evan's shoulders to the strength of his neck as his embrace tightened. "I've changed my mind. I wish to be the wife of a country squire," she whispered maddeningly against his jaw as he carried his kisses closer to her lips.

"And you shall be that, also, my willful wife." As Evan's hand finally took control of the firm flesh beneath Daphne's beaded bodice, he silenced her cries with his mouth. As the kiss deepened and promised a passionate future, Evan tore himself away long enough to gaze down into his bride's rapturous eyes. "Gordon and Grandfather have given this to be our home when we are not in London. Do you think you can lead the life of Devon's splendid isolation?"

"Only if you are by my side every night. I am afraid of the dark, you know," Daphne whispered with a wicked glint in her eyes.

"Oh, no doubt you are quaking in your shoes at the thought of the night to come. Let me put an end to your fears right now, Mrs. Griffin. I know the best way of curing night terrors. . . ."

And murmuring idiotic reassurances mixed with all the words of love there hadn't been time enough to say, Evan carried his bride to the turned-down bed and began to divest her of any hindrance to his cure, while Daphne did her wifely best to prevent his catching cold from the damp humors of his own clothing.

And the only fears evidenced anywhere were of the guests below when they discovered the bridal couple had disappeared. The ladies shivered quite giddily at the thought of the kind of children such an outrageous couple could produce, and the men lifted their glasses and their gazes to the ceiling in toast to the same idea.